I0671231

The Beginning

The Quest

Todd LeRoux

Published by Todd LeRoux, 2024.

THE BEGINNING

First edition. February 27, 2024.

ISBN: 978-1738317547

Written by Todd LeRoux.

Also by Todd LeRoux

The Quest
The Beginning

Standalone
The Jinn
The Wanderer
The Quest
The Island

Watch for more at https://www.toddleroux.com/.

Table of Contents

I wish to dedicate this to my Grandmother. A great woman who taught me the grace of love and compassion. Ella Cellini was a woman who loved family above all else. She took a very angry young man and calmed him with her grace. It is because of her I am what I am today. Thank you Gran, you are so missed and loved.

THE BEGINNING
A NOVEL
BY
Todd LeRoux

My life has been one of servitude. This is the story of my life and the life of another I called brother. At the start of my very long life, this was the only life one such as myself could hope for. The life I was given was not a bad life; challenging at times, yes. As I look back on the life I was given, I realize it was a good life. I knew a man who was not my father, though he loved and raised me as a son. I was a young man when I met one of the most remarkable men I would ever know. This man would become my greatest friend, my brother, the one I could never forget. This is the story of my life, of my time in this world. I welcome you to read it, to see what I have seen, to go where I have gone.

I was born a bastard, the son of a young woman. A young woman who suffered rape by a powerful man. When this man found out the girl he forced himself on was with child, he sent men to kill her and her unborn child. My poor mother had no choice; she ran for her life as well as mine. As my young mother ran, she was forced to leave her homeland. The man who hunted her was very powerful and would stop at nothing to protect his family from dishonor. My mother found herself in the holy land. While she was there, hire killers of the rich man found her then, from out of nowhere, she was saved.

A kindly old man took my mother in. He hid her from the assassins. The rapist never stopped looking for either of us. He demanded the life of my mother. His reason for wanting my mother and me dead was all to do with his family's honor. This is what he told himself to justify our murders. In reality, it was to do with money. If his father was to find out, his son had raped a girl, fathering a child. The rapist would have been cast out of his father's house and will. I can't remember my mother; the assassins found her at the market one day. There they collected their silver. The man who took her in when she needed a safe place raised me as his son. He never let a day go by where he didn't tell me how much my mother loved me. As I grew, he trained me to fight as he was trained. I learned the sword and shield, and he taught me the art of fighting with my hands and feet. I would sit after our evening meal and listen to the stories Joseph would tell.

The stories Joseph told me were of a time when angels came to earth from heaven and took the daughters of man for their wives. Joseph would tell me stories of giants, angels, and demons. He kept the child in me entranced with the stories of great battles. Battles that took place in heaven and here on earth. I was taught how to work wood with my hands to make things people needed. Joseph told me it was an honest way to make money, and it was something my mother would be proud of.

I can still remember sitting in our small house at night, reading from the bible. This is what Joseph taught me to read with. I remember him saying no man should be left without the word of our God. I watched as Joseph grew older and older. I never noticed how he aged as I grew up. It seemed only a short while ago I was crying, telling him I missed my mother. Though I still missed her, there was a longing to see her face. I had forgotten what she looked like, her face lost to time. Joseph told me she would always be with me, no matter how far I traveled, then he smiled at me one day. I'll never forget the day he looked at me and, with his calloused hand, bade me come and sit.

"Come here, son. I need to tell you of the past, of how your life and mine came to be as they are. The day I met your frightened mother in the market was one of the luckiest days of my life." The man I thought of as my father started.

"You see, I was married once to a very beautiful girl. Though we were poor, we had love. My wife was a devout woman who loved our lord and would pray all the time, never for herself, mind you. She would ask for people to be safe or for others to have a good crop. Though we wanted a child, it seemed we would never be blessed with their grace." As Joseph told me the story of him and his wife, I watched as he grew weaker.

"Then one day my wife came to me, she told me of an angel of the lord, this angel came to her in the middle of the night. The angel told her she was to be with a child. My wife was distraught. She was afraid I would think her unfaithful. I should have told her the angel came to me also that same night. He told me why God had chosen my wife. However, I waited to see if it were true or if it had been a dream."

"Was she? Did the angel speak the truth?" I asked.

"Oh yes, what the angel spoke of came to pass. My wife gave birth to a boy. The night of his birth, I walked into the desert. I sank down on my knees to thank God for letting me raise his son. The angel came to me again in the desert with tears in his eyes. As the form of the angel came to me, I dropped my face to the hard sand. The angel bade me look at him. 'You will raise Jesus from this day forth and love him as he were yours. Know this, Joseph. He will die a young man; he will give his life over to serve his heavenly father.' The angel said.

"Why do this, I asked of the angel?" Joseph retold.

"I will take his place, take my life instead of Jesus. I give it freely; take it." As I said this, I reached for the angel's robes to beg for my son's life.

"The life you have is not yours to give Joseph. You know this." The angel said, his voice hollow with remorse. I watched as a tear fell from its chin and landed on my outstretched hand. When I looked down at the tear, the angel disappeared. I went to where my wife lay with Jesus knowing we would lose him." Joseph remember. I watched as a tear rolled down Joseph's weathered cheek.

"Let's stop for the night; I'll make us some food." I offered, hoping he would stop. I didn't like the strain I could see this remembrance of the past was putting on him.

"No, I can not stop now. We must finish this. You see, son, I took your mother in because she reminded me of my wife when Mary was young. Then when she gave birth to you, I knew there was a reason God placed me in the life of you and your mother. You see, Jesus was murdered by men who feared the loss of power and wealth." Joseph told me. I watched as a cough rattled the man I loved as my father. I sat at his side. I knew he was close to leaving me and going to be with his Mary.

"Once Jesus was killed, his body was taken, washed, and placed in a cave for three days. When he was to be removed, the guards rolled the stone back only to find Jesus's body had disappeared. It was then the greatest hunt for a person's remains began. The murderers wanted my son's body to prove he was just a man, nothing more. They hunted for his body. They hounded me for years. In the beginning, my wife didn't know anything about how Jesus's body disappeared. We fended off the leaders' questions for months until, one day, I broke down and told her the truth. It was on the second night after they murdered Jesus I rolled the stone back from the entrance to the cave, then in the dead of night, I made off with our son's body." Joseph told me. The look of shock on my face brought a rattling laugh from Joseph.

"That's the same look Mary had the night I told her it was I who had taken our son's body into the mountains. There I laid him to rest. She made me take her to his remains. I told her if we were to do this, we would have to move him for fear they would find his resting place and desecrate it. One morning, like so many others in the past. I hitched my small cart up to our faithful donkey and shut our gate after us when we left. Two days later, I watched as a man tried to find my tracks in the dust of the foothills. I prayed for forgiveness and then killed this man who followed Mary and me. I still remember how Mary wept when I showed her the stone altar I had built for Jesus and the cross I had carved. She told me I was going to have to build a chest for his bones so he could come with us. I did as she asked, and our travels brought us to this place." Joseph remembered. I could tell the recounting of his life and the tragedies he suffered were taking their toll on him. I dearly wanted Joseph to stop, to rest.

"One of the men who followed Jesus around the holy land came to me one night. He told me of how Christians were being tortured and killed for following the teachings of Jesus. He told me of a small group of men; these men started fighting back and were being hunted throughout the holy land. He then told me about others who believed in the teachings of Jesus. These men were Romans. They were men and officers in the roman military. For these men, it meant death if they were exposed, so they started a secret order called the knights of Sionis. It was these men who taught me what I have taught you. It was these men who brought me here to hide." Joseph said. As I listened to the man who raised me, who showed me love and kindness all my life, a horse whinny in the yard. Turning, I reached for my sword, wondering who would be skulking around our place in the dark.

"The man who comes to us this night is here by my wishes. I'm not going to be around, and I wish you go with this man." Joseph raised his hand to silence my building protest.

"He is going to finish your training. You were born a bastard; however, I am your father by love and time, and I love you. Now I need you to go with the man waiting by the door." Joseph told me. Turning, I looked at the door and saw a shadow under it. When I opened the door, a large man stood in the dim lamp light wrapped in a plain brown cloak. He didn't speak to me. He walked past and knelt in front of Joseph. I watched as the two men spoke for a brief moment.

"Son, you will go with this brother. He will take you to a place where your training can be finished. There is a church devout men have started; these men believe in the teachings of Jesus. They will welcome you, along with the treasures others hid many years ago. However, if at any time you and our brothers feel this church, along with the men who govern it, step away from my and God's path. Then you must remove the treasures from their care." Joseph said.

It was at that moment the man who raised me, who held me as I wept over my mother's body in the market the day she was murdered, the man I loved as my father nodded his head. The nod was so slight at the time I never caught it. I was wrapped up in the thought of going away with a stranger. The brother I let through the door that night saw the slight nod. All at once, I felt a sharp stab of pain at the base of my neck. Turning to the brother, I raised my fist to strike when I watched as a tear rolled through his beard. I watched the tear confused. How could this man stab me and be sad about it? Then the first waves of pain hit me, as the pain slammed into me. I felt the arms of the brother catch me as I fell, the pain driving me to the floor. I could hear him saying something to Joseph. I couldn't make out what this brother was saying. The pain I felt roared through me. My ears rang with the screams ripped from my agony. I can still remember how my brother sat down and placed my head on his lap.

"Oh, little brother, you are the first. We have no idea what is going to happen to you. All we know is it needed to be one as you are. One born of violence and loved like no other, one who has known the ridicule and the hatred of man. Also, the kindness of a stranger and the love of a mother and father. This thing I have done to you will purify your soul. To be purified, you must live through all the pain caused by man." The brother told me. Though I didn't know it, the brother sat with me for four days and nights as the pain of the world crashed over me. Then on the eve of the fifth day, I was lifted through a haze; once through the pain, I could see a hill.

Chapter 2

STANDING IN THE SHADOWS, I watched the three crosses as they were raised on the hill of Skulls. Tears blurred my vision; I watched as the soldiers of Rome stood two of the crosses. On these crosses were two thieves. One was defiant, and the other wept. The soldiers took their time with the third, for this one held Jesus Christ. The shadows held me as I watched the soldiers stand the cross and let it thump into the hole bored into the hill for it. Hours passed, and I watched as people taunted and ridiculed our savior nailed to the cross. Some hours later, I watched a roman soldier look at our savior and then run his spear into the side of gods mortal son. Turning, I watched the leader of the Hebrews smile as the blood of Jesus flowed out of his many wounds. The roman who had been ordered to stab Christ looked up into the face of Jesus once again, then he ran screaming into the desert.

Another woman came, and without being noticed, she collected the blood as it flowed out of the wound. I watched a woman I knew was Mary stand weeping silently; behind her, in the shadows, stood another woman. Mary turned and looked to see if the other woman stood in the shadows. Time seemed to speed up. I watched as roman soldiers lowered the cross. They pulled the hammered spikes from the hands and feet of Jesus. Then his body was washed and wrapped in linens. When Mary and the other woman finished, I watched as Joseph and another man lifted Jesus and carried him to a cave.

Time seemed to speed up again. I watched as the sun rose and set once. Smiling, I watched Joseph walk past the sleeping guard and roll the stone aside. A minute later, he gently lay the wrapped body of Jesus on the ground. He then rolled the stone back into place.

Then very early on the third day, I watched as Mary and the younger lady came to where the body of Christ lay. Joseph followed his wife, and straining, he rolled the stone away from the entrance. I watched as Mary came out of the cave, she was weeping, and Joseph held her.

Fast forward, I watched as Mary and the younger woman, who now held two babies in her arms, stood at the edge of a dock. Joseph was there talking to a man who nodded and waved to the two women. Joseph looked into Mary's eyes and gently kissed her. The young woman wept and hugged him. Joseph then took the babies and kissed each one on the forehead and smiled as the babies smiled. Somehow I was able to see the two women cross the waters to another place of safety. Men met the two Marys as they stepped off the boat. These men bowed to Mary and held the young children in reverence. Time seemed to flash forward; I could see Mary laid out she was dressed in simple clothes. A young man stood at her feet with a middle age woman who wept.

Joseph stood in the desert, the man I loved, as my father looked defeated. His heart broke. Joseph knew his love Mary had passed away. The young man stood with his mother, each mourning the loss of a loved one. They stood by a tower, which was built of dark stones. An island stood in the background, waves crashing on its armored stone shore. Pale birds with great broad wings sailed on the wind over the island. A man stood at the edge of a cliff, his face covered by a beard. A heavenly light seemed to shine down on him as he smiled at everyone. It was then the world seemed to crash in on me. Fists of hate and rage pounded down on me; through it all, I could feel the love of others.

I stood and watched as the sun rose over the desert. I listened to the steady rhythmic breathing of Joseph and the brother, who were still sleeping. Standing at the open door of the house where a stranger showed a young, frightened woman. One brutalized by a rich man, the only kindness her short life knew. I knew god had put me in this place for something greater than I could have ever known. Turning, I watched as the brother sat up from where he slept.

"How do you feel, little brother?" He asked as he stood and stretched.

"I feel...well, I feel everything. I could feel the sun coming up and the first rays warming the desert. I could smell the flowers as they opened up to gather in the first warming rays." I answered as I looked at Joseph.

"For the first time, I understand why he took my mother in. I understand why he raised me as his own when my mother had been murdered; it wasn't an obligation. It was a father's love." I told the brother as Joseph stirred in the next room. The following days were spent preparing for the journey, which would follow the route Mary followed with the young lady and the children. Joseph told us how they went from what port they had sailed from and where they had landed.

"You need to find a ship going to Gaul, though it's the Franks who rule there now." Standing, I looked at the brother and then at Joseph.

"What do you mean, I need to find a ship? Don't you mean we need to find a ship?" As I said, I turned and looked to the brother for help.

"No, son, I'll not be going with you on this trip. You see, my time on this earth is just about up. Unlike you, it wasn't the blood of my son that gave me this long life; it was the tear of the angel. It was Michael's grace that extended my years. I've been in this world far too long. Now I want to see my Mary and sit with Jesus." I looked at the man who had been my father and then at the brother who was nodding his head.

"Forgive this question, but how old are you...father?" Joseph would always smile when I would call him father.

"Well, I've been in this world for five hundred years. I've lived and watched for a prophecy an angel told me about the night I carried Jesus into the mountains."

"Five hundred years...I can't even imagine." I said, turning to the brother, who was nodding his head.

"This will be my last few days on earth. So I'll need to pass on what I know before you leave this place." Joseph told me.

"I don't know what to say...the thought of losing you, the only parent I can remember, causes my heart to hurt," I told him as I looked at the floor.

"Son, I know this will be hard. I want you to know having you in my life has made it so much easier. Now, this is information you will need to carry on with your mission." Joseph said.

The rest of that day was spent listening to what Joseph had to tell us before his time was over. Once Joseph finished, we broke bread for the last time, and I walked outside to watch the sunset. That night Joseph called me to his room. He told me he would be gone in the morning; I told him how I felt about him.

I thanked Joseph for saving my mother and giving what would have been another murdered child a chance. Then I kissed his wrinkled brow and sat by his bed while his life ended and another for myself began.

Tears ran down my face and fell onto the wrinkled hand I held until the end. Before he left me, my father told me I was to open a letter upon his death. The letter was on a small table by his bedside. The last thing I wanted to do was read a letter written by my father. As I stood, I folded Joseph's wrinkled hands across his chest. Then

I obeyed his last wish and opened the drawer holding the letter. Walking out of his room, I had the folded letter in both hands.

Josephus knew we had lost the man who had saved both of our lives. As I sat down, I looked up at the ceiling and unfolded the letter. Reading the letter, I was shocked at the words it held.

'Son, I know I have left you; this is what is meant to be. This is meant to help you move on to the next stage of your life. If you and Josephus can, I wish to be inturned in the cave where I hid Jesus's body. There is a map under my bed tucked into the weaving of the ropes; it will take you to the cave. Also and most important is Josephus. His life was stolen many years ago by the actions of his father. Watch over our brother, for he carries a terrible burden, a burden uttered in pain and despair.' When I finished the letter, I gently folded it and placed it in a small chest I used for other keepsakes. Going back into Joseph's room, I knelt beside his bed. Again I thanked him for everything and reached under his bed to find the map. Later that day, Josephus and I wrapped my father's body in linens, and in his folded hands, we placed a small cross. The rest of the day, Josephus and I studied the map Joseph had drawn to show us the way to his son's remains.

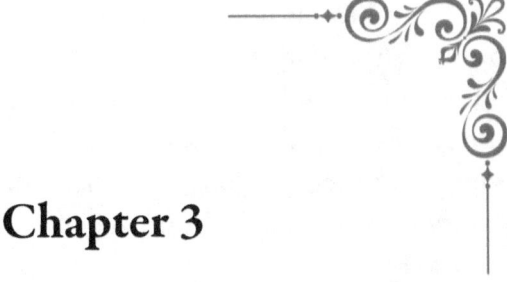

Chapter 3

WHEN THE SUN ROSE, it found me and my new friend and brother, leaving the home I loved. For the rest of the first day, I found myself on this earth without Joseph, my new companion, and I rode off into the desert. As the sun set, Josephus and I stopped at a cave. This cave was marked on the map my father had drawn for us. I knelt and put my hands on Joseph's chest for the last time; also, for the last time, I told the man who raised me how much I loved and was going to miss him. Josephus and I said a prayer over Joseph then we covered his face again and walked out of the cave back into the unrelenting sun. Turning, I looked back at the cave where we had placed Joseph. It was his last wish to be placed there, and the entrance be collapsed so he would never be found. Josephus turned and looked at me, then pointed to the horizon and smiled. Josephus had been an officer in the roman army when Joseph had found him dying, wounded in the desert. The man I came to think of as my father took in a man who was a member of the army that had overseen the torture and murder of his son. He had cleaned this man's wounds, nursing him back to health. Then when the time came, he had given his ward clothing and food enough to see him get back to his people.

"Out there is where you will learn, love, and live. Life is out there waiting, little brother." When Josephus spoke, I looked at him.

"You don't seem sad about losing Joseph?" I asked, anger building in me.

"I'm sad for us not to have him here; I loved him. He was the one who showed me the right path. However, I'm happy for him, his journey is over, and now he is with the only woman he ever loved. So instead of crying about our loss, I chose to be happy for his gain." I wanted to be angry at Josephus; when I thought about what he said, I knew he was right. So I turned and smiled back at the mountain and waved.

"Who is it you wave to, little brother?" Josephus asked me, looking back.

"Just waving to my father to let him know he has given me everything a bastard child could ever need, love," I answered, then looked at my new brother.

"You are no bastard, you had a father, and now you have more brothers waiting to meet you out there," Josephus said, waving his arm to the horizon.

The thought of others waiting for me to come to them gave me a warm feeling. I wondered what they would be like if they were all as big as Josephus. If they, like my new brother, they to had been darkened by the relentless sun and heat of the desert. We knew where we had to go; we even had the route Joseph gave us. So without a second thought, we headed out into the desert.

Days came and went as we traveled; in the cool of the mornings. Josephus and I would speak of things awaiting us around the next bend or over the next dune. On most occasions, it was nothing more than sand and dunes. However, every now and then, there would be a small town or settlement. Some towns we skirted, never stopping at them. While others, we would go in and buy what was needed, then leave, changing directions many times before stopping for the night. This started to bother me. I would start looking back, wondering what it was or who Josephus was trying to confuse.

"Brother, can I ask why we seem to change directions when we leave a town after we have gotten what is needed?" I asked.

"It's my nature to worry about security. When we buy things in a town, often it catches the attention of men who would think nothing of killing for what is in our purse. So I change directions, crossing our tracks. This way, I can see if others may be following." As we walked and rode our horses, I would catch myself turning back to see if I could spot anyone. The sun would find us in the saddles until it reached its highest point. Then we would stop in some shade so we could rest and water the horses. It was at this time we would practice with swords or spar.

"Joseph has taught you well; we will teach you so much more. It might not always seem so kind; however, it will be what you need to keep yourself and others from harm." Josephus said to me during one of our sparing matches, then hit me. I would like to tell you I fended off the punch and fought him back. This would be a lie considering he was kneeling beside me when I woke.

"Never let your enemy distract you from his hands and feet, for both can get you killed." He said to me, then helped me to my feet. I never knew a man who could be so tough in a fight and so kind a moment later. I watched the man Joseph had sent me out into the world with. I would often recall the letter my father had written. I often sat and watched Josephus and wondered about the burden he carries. Though the boy in me wanted to ask him about it, the young man in me thought it was best if Josephus told me when he was ready. If he never uttered a word about it, then my unslakeable curiosity would have to go unfulfilled.

I remember the day we stopped atop a hill and looked down into what looked like a fort. This fort was said to be owned by a cult.

"People around this part of the desert say the men and woman who worship there eat their victims as offering to some dark lord." Turning, I looked at Josephus and then back at the fort.

"If this is true, shouldn't we go and do something about it?" I asked, looking at the fort shimmering in the heat of the desert sun.

"If we were to do something, what would be your first-course little brother?" Josephus asked as he turned in the saddle.

"Well, Joseph would always tell me to look for myself, don't take any ones word when it comes to a man's name or his life. So, in this case, I would watch and learn." When I finished, Josephus turned and smiled.

"You would be right. The men who worship there don't worship a dark lord. They pray to the only God because they have a different way of doing so makes them strange. People fear what they don't understand. Remember, for in your future, there will be times when others will try to get you to do things against those who do not deserve your actions." Josephus told me. I followed my brother as he turned his horse. The rest of the day, we rode north until the sun was touching the horizon. In the years to come, Josephus's words will come back to me, and I will know the truth of them.

Days came and went the sun rose and set as it has from the moment God's will brought forth the light. The desert changed, as did the days when Josephus and I started our journey. I had started keeping track of the days, and it hadn't taken long before the tracking of days fell to the wayside. Days and nights began to meld together, as did the dunes when we first left Joseph. I was excited to be out in the world. Every sight and sound was something new. Now as we traveled, the heat pounded down on us during the day. Then at night, the cold of the desert sought to rob us of any heat built up during the day.

One day came to an end, and we stopped for the night. After we finished our evening prayers, we could hear a small flock of goats. Turning, I watched Josephus walk into the night. My brother wished to see if he could barter for one. I listened to the voices drifting out of the night. Then smiled when he walked back into our camp with a butchered goat. As the sun rose to greet us and another day, Josephus smiled.

"What has you in such a mood this morning, brother?" I asked, catching myself smiling also.

"I was just thinking about our brothers who wait for us. I know they will be happy to greet you, to show you things you have never seen before." Josephus told me.

"I am excited to meet them also. I just wish Joseph was here." I said. I knew it was better for the man who raised me to be with his wife and God. However, the greedy child in me still wanted him by my side.

"We all wish that could be so; you know as well as I do it was time for him to go," Josephus said as he placed his hand on my shoulder. I looked up into his face and nodded.

We were in the desert for months before we reached the coast. The breeze coming off the waters of the Mediterranean brought the smell of salt with it. The first morning we could see the sea, I stood beside my horse and watched the sunlight glint and sparkle off the small waves. One morning Josephus and I sat atop a dune looking to the east as the sun started its rise over the horizon. We watched as the first rays touched the sky. The water shimmered as the sun reflected off the water of the Mediterranean.

"Well, we have reached the water now to find the ancient port city of Leptis Magna. It was said to be a four-day ride west of Tripoli. We'll head that way and see if we can find a ship to take us to the land of the Franks." Josephus said.

Four days later, we arrived at a small town on the coast. Most of the people living and working there were fishing. It was nice to eat something other than goat and cheese for the first time in more than a fortnight. I held our horses while Josephus went from stall to stall in the market, talking to men. I watched as he bought supplies he thought we would need. When Josephus made his way back to where I stood, he was smiling.

"There is a ship we could take over the water to the north. The men I talked to all said the captain of this ship stopped at this port to load fresh water and food. When he does, we'll pay for our passage though they didn't know if he would take our horses."

Josephus and I spent the next week waiting for the ship to come. While we waited, we spared and prayed three times a day. I mostly prayed I wouldn't fail in my future. Then one day, while I sat on a hill overlooking the town, I could see the faint outline of a ship. I felt excited, wondering if this faint ship with its white sails would be the one to take me to my destiny. Gathering what I had brought with me, I met Josephus at the foot of the hill; he was coming to get me.

"The locals just told me the ship making its way in now belongs to a slaver. They said this captain and his crew have taken young men and girls from this place and smaller villages along the coast." I watched the ship as it lowered its sails.

"I think we should meet this so-called captain. I have heard of men who make their money by selling their brothers and sisters." As I said this, we watched a smaller boat being lowered into the water. A small group of men climbed down to the row boat. When the small boat reached the dock, Josephus and I were slowly making our way through a gathering crowd. We could hear what sounded like a heated discussion coming from where the boat had tied up. I reached the front of the crowd in time to see a man pull his sword and then threaten a man who stood unarmed facing him.

Before I realized what I was doing, I had pulled my sword and knocked the captain of the slave ship aside. Then with my left, I threw a punch catching the captain under his right eye. My punch opened the flesh, and blood flowed, staining his shirt. The men with the captain of the ship attempted to pull their swords. This was when Josephus and some other men laid their blades on their hands. I stepped back and offered the captain the room to stand.

"You can go back to your ship and leave, never coming back. Or you can pick up your sword and take the chance you'll kill me." I said to the slaver.

"I don't understand why you would trouble yourself in what is none of your affair?" The captain of the slave ship asked, glaring at me.

"It is my affair when you come and steal children for your own profit. These people have been kind to us, even after you and others have stolen their most precious gifts." I told the captain.

"If they can not protect what they call their gifts, then I have the right to do with their gifts as I feel." The captain said as he looked at his sword. I could tell he was trying to decide whether to grab it or go back to his ship. His pride overwhelmed his common sense, and his hand grasped the sword as he stood. The fight was short, and his attack was sloppy and ill-timed. Within two moves, the captain lay dead at my feet. His crew turned and rowed back to the ship, leaving the captain's body to whatever fate the locals had in store for it. That night the locals took the captain's body out in the water and weighted it down. I talked to Josephus about the fight and the death of the hated man. I told my brother how I felt. Even though the man had caused so much pain, I grieved about killing him.

"You feel this way because you know there was a better way. It wasn't your decision to fight; he could have walked away. It was his decision that caused you to kill him." When Josephus finished, he looked at me and offered some cheese with a smile. I looked at my smiling brother, and I could feel the weight of killing the captain lifting from my shoulders. Three days later, the ship we were waiting for lowered its sails and tied up to the dock. Walking through the market, I was again amazed at the smells of the cooking spices and the baked goods. Turning, I watched as Josephus talked to whom I assumed was the ship's captain.

"We have passage to the land of the Franks. However, if we want our horses to come along, it will cost extra. I told the captain I would have to discuss this with you." Josephus said as he turned and looked out to the water.

"Well, is the price of bringing them along worth it, or would it be more costly to buy two more when we arrive?" I asked, trying to see what had gained my brother's attention.

"The captain said we would be able to get horses when we land, and it would be less expensive," Josephus told me.

"Well, I think we could try to sell ours here. What do you think?" I asked. It was then a man walked up to us, smiled, and looked at our horses.

"The man you need to see about selling your horses will be here shortly. He is a good man though he will try to get these fine animals as cheap as possible." Josephus smiled at the man and thanked him. Josephus nodded to another man who was walking towards us. After a brief look at our horses, the older man turned to Josephus and clucked his teeth as if he found something terribly wrong with them.

"These poor horses have been ridden a long distance." The trader said as he brushed a hand along the flank of my mount.

"True; however, they have been well cared for, and no expense has been spared on their care and feed. So they are as good today as the day we left our home. I stood and watched as the trader and Josephus sat by their fire and smoked from a hookah. The smoke wreathed their heads while the two of them drank strong coffee. Soon a price on the two horses was reached, and with a handshake, the deal was signed, and both parties were happy.

Two days later, my brother and I were standing on the dock next to the ship, watching the last of the cargo being loaded into the hold. I remember standing on that dock, feeling strange about calling Josephus my brother. I was eighteen years old, and up to that point in my life, it had only been Joseph and myself for thirteen years. The captain walked down the gangplank and smiled at Josephus.

"You and the young man can go aboard now. We will sail with the tide. My first mate will show you where your birth is." We thanked the captain and made our way onboard. The sailors eyed us suspiciously as the first mate stepped forward and introduced himself. The first mate turned and led us to our birth which was little more than a closet with two beds stacked on top of one another. Then I decided to tell Josephus I had been feeling something pulling me towards this spot. For some reason, we had to be here on this ship at this time. My brother, who was as big a man as any I had ever seen, looked at me.

"I wish I could tell you what it is pulling at you, little brother; however, this is all new to me as well. In the brotherhood, there is an old man who gives us counsel at times of indecision; it could be he will know why you feel this way." Josephus said.

I was wondering what the others would be like when we reached them. Would they all be like Josephus? I had hoped some would be younger like myself. I thought it would be nice to have a brother my own age. It took a moment for me to realize our ship was leaving the dock. Josephus and I made our way to the deck and watched as the town slipped further and further away until we could see nothing but water.

"If you wish to pray or whatever it is you do, I ask you to do it your cabin. I have men of other faiths, and they also keep it to themselves." The captain asked us; Josephus smiled and nodded as we stood at the railing, watching as the sun fell lower in the sky. As the day ended, the last rays of the sun turned the water red. It was then I felt the first grip of fear.

Chapter 4

ON THE SIXTH DAY AT sea, Josephus and I walked out onto the deck and found the men busy draping nets over crates. The first mate walked over to us, looking determined.

"Sir, if you and your ward could see your way to it, we could use the extra hands to get things lashed down." Josephus and I could see the man was uncomfortable asking for help.

"Of course, we would be happy to help; just tell us what needs to be done," Josephus answered, and I smiled. Soon both of us were helping others pull ropes through tie-down rings sunk into the ship's deck. Turning, I looked at the sailor who worked with me; when he had tied the rope off, he smiled and nodded.

"Why are we doing this? Won't we be at the dock tomorrow?" I asked.

"If we survive this night, then we will see." The sailor said as he pointed behind me at a blackening sky. The clouds rolled over one another, again and again. I watched as the sky seemed to get heavier and heavier, then the first flash of lighting. Following the flash came the rolling boom of thunder crashing over the water. Standing there with the lightning still burning in my eyes, I had a vision. It showed the ship we were on sinking, men and goods tangled in ropes. Others drowning their sightless eyes gazing into the eternal night. I looked to where Josephus helped another sailor. Walking over to my brother, I looked around to make sure no one could hear what I had to say.

"This ship will not survive this storm. We need to get our things ready to float." When I whispered this to my brother, he looked down at me and then at the tortured sky and nodded. The captain looked at us strangely when Josephus and I brought our belongings on deck, tying them to empty barrels. Once this was done, I turned and watched as the storm marched over the water. Some of the other men stopped and wondered what had my attention.

When the storm washed over us, the winds slammed into the sails as the men were trying to lower them. A great ripping sound was heard as the foresail was torn in half. A man climbing in the rigging attempted to tie it off before the sail, and the lines became fouled. One part of the heavy sail snapped back, hitting the man and causing him to fall to the deck killing him. I watched as the first mate struggled over to the rigging. He used an axe to cut the ropes holding the foresail free, letting it blow away into the storm.

The storm seemed to hold us in its grip. It battered the ship tossing us where the whims of fate wished. Time seemed to stop as the storm hammered our boat. Caught in the storm's fury, the crew and Josephus and I hung on, hoping and praying the storm would soon release our ship. Sometime in the dark night, a grinding sound could be heard. At first, it was felt in the deck, then with a marching series of great waves. The grinding became louder, then a loud crack came from below. Josephus and I watched as the first mate, along with some men, ran below.

"We are sinking," I said to Josephus.

"Let us be ready then," Josephus answered.

I watched as the first mate walked over to the captain and whispered in his ear. The older man lost what little color was left on his face. I walked over to the captain and the first mate; both men looked grave.

"Lad, the ship is going to the bottom. Nothing in this world can stop it. Tell your Roman the keel is broken, and water is pouring in. God help us; good luck, lad." The captain said as he shook his head and then shouted for his men to come to him. I walked back to Josephus had untied the barrels holding our things.

"The captain told you we are sinking?" My brother asked, seemingly unconcerned.

"Yes, and why is it you don't seem concerned about the fact we are about to be dumped into this storm and forced to swim through it?" I asked as the rain lashed our faces. Lighting flashed around us, thunder slamming our words into nothing before they could be heard by others.

"I can swim, and we have these to help save us," Josephus said, pointing to the barrels smiling and shrugging his big shoulders. Before I could stop Josephus, he pushed me over the railing of the sinking ship and then tossed my barrel to me. I was coughing the water out of my lungs when he splashed into the sea beside me.

"You could have warned me before you tossed me over!" I yelled over the sound of the storm.

"Yes, I could have." He said, smiling, then tied our barrels together. We lashed ourselves to them so the storm couldn't separate us in the night. Floating in the water with Josephus, we listened to the cries of the sailors. The flashes of lightning showed us the ship as it surrendered to the water. The ship that short minutes ago carried us over the water nosed its way under the waves. Some cried out to god to save him, and others called the name of men who had been friends. Some hours later, the captain's body bobbed past Josephus and me. I closed my eyes and lowered my head. I asked Jesus to please take care of the poor man. The winds howled and raged at the water, throwing it into a frothing beast intent on killing the men thrown into it. I would like to tell you I knew how long we were in the water before my feet touched the bottom and I could stand. If I said that, I would be lying. To me, it seemed we were floating around for days though I can't remember the sun rising or setting.

Standing on the shore, I was shocked at how much debris from the ship came to this tiny island with us. Josephus and I waded into the surf time and again, gathering it up. After the shattered timbers and cargo from the ship sinking slowed down. The bodies of the sailors started to find their way to our shore. Like the timbers and other flotsam, Josephus and I gathered them up from the surf. That was the way the rest of the day went into the evening. The last man we found was the first mate; I wished for the captain to find his way to our island. He never did.

The first night on our island was spent taking stock of everything we found in the surf. We had enough foodstuff to feed us for about a month. Josephus said we would have to eat the fresh food first, then the salted food. He hoped we would have the means to get off this island by then.

"Our first job here will be to bury the men. They can not be left out." I agreed with my brother.

The sun found us digging one long trench above the shore. In the afternoon, we started to gather the men and take them to their final resting place. The first mate was the last man we placed into the grave. I said a simple prayer. I knew not all the sailors followed the teachings of Jesus. I didn't think they would mind being with their friends. The second night a great piece of luck floated to our little island. It came in the form of the top part of the main mast. Its ropes trailed in the water behind it. Josephus and I discussed the best way to leave the island as we watched the sunset. The sunset blossomed into the deepest scarlet vista, causing the waters of the Mediterranean to look as if they had turned to blood.

We started our raft the next morning. It took seven days to complete it. During those days, more things came to us. When we finished, Josephus turned and looked out to sea and then back at our raft.

"I would have liked a bigger sail." He said to the wind.

"Do you think it will get us over the water?" I asked, looking back at our raft.

"Oh, have no fear. It will get us somewhere; that is a certainty." Josephus said.

The sun found the two of us struggling to get our raft to the water's edge. When we reached the water, I looked back and laughed. When Josephus turned to see what I was laughing at, he let out a booming laugh of his own. We had tied the barrels of salted foodstuff to the raft in the night. Then we forgot to untie them, so all our hard work consisted of dragging the raft and the barrels after loading what the sea brought to us over the days on the island. I looked inland back to the cross Josephus, and I made. It marked the grave of the men from the ship. I hoped we did the right thing for them.

The waters were calm when Josephus pushed the raft out into the current. Standing at the front of the raft, I was trying to get the sail to catch the never-ending breeze. Then with a faint popping sound, the sail filled and started to pull our raft further from the island. Josephus told me we could be on the water for days or weeks before we spotted land. So when on the fourth day, the two of us stood and watched a coast appear out of a fog, we both smiled.

"Well, this is a bit of good fortune," Josephus said as he pulled on the ropes of the sail, trying to turn us into the shore. I silently hoped this was not where we had left from.

Standing on the shore, I thought how strange it was to be someplace, to have no idea where it is your standing. We tied the raft to a tree and then looked inland. I hoped my brother and I had found the land of the Franks. Neither of us was looking forward to more time on our raft. I looked at Josephus when he told me one of us would have to leave the shore to see if a settlement was nearby. We discussed who would be the best scout ahead, and I knew Josephus was right when he said it had to be him. I watched as Josephus walked into the trees. He turned and drew his sword and made a mark on a tree, then waved and disappeared. Sitting in the sand as I watched the trees, it was one of the last things Josephus said before he left.

"Don't sit here and look at the water. Watch the trees; if there is danger here, it will come from the land. Don't have a fire; eat a cold meal and keep quiet." Doing as I was told, I sat my back resting against a large rock. It didn't take long for Josephus to return to the beach, where I sat watching the treeline for movement.

"We seem to have had the good fortune to land on a deserted beach. I found a trail leading further inland. It might lead us to a village where we can find out what this land is." He told me as we started to gather the supplies we could carry.

As the sunset and darkness started to find its way back over the land, my brother and I topped a small hill. We found we were looking down into a small village. Looking around, both Josephus and I thought it was a strange village. There were no barriers, no defensive walls of any sort, no gates, no hedges, nothing.

"I've never seen a place like this. They have no defense from the outside." I said as we walked down what looked to be the main street. I watched as a man opened his door looking at us; I raised my hand in greeting. To my surprise, the stranger copied me and smiled.

"We are strangers in this place. Can you tell us where we are?" I asked, stopping at the edge of the path.

"Strangers in this place, well, now that's something new. Well, as for where you are, it used to be called Massilia. This village is now called Marseas, at least this is what the people here call it now. There's a place down the road where you can buy food. The man who runs it will tell you all you need to know." We thanked the man, then headed to where he had pointed. As we walked down the road, people would hold the curtains aside, and they looked out their windows as my brother, and I passed.

Opening the door of the building, we could hear laughter. The smell of cooking bread and meat made our mouths water. The large room held tables and benches, and for the most part, all the people were gathered around a large central fireplace. The meat was roasting on a spit, and the grease dripped into a large pot. The room quieted as our presents was noticed, and a big man stood up behind a bar.

"Hello, strangers; what brings you here this night." He said as he placed his big hands on the bar.

"Well, what brings us here is a long story," I said as I smiled.

"Oh, we love long stories; they help pass the night." The owner said and invited us in. I recounted how Josephus and I survived the storm at sea and then were shipwrecked on the island. Eventually, making it to the beach when I finished my story. The owner and the others looked at us and then shouted welcome. This brought another braying laugh from Josephus. For the rest of the night, the owner and some others gave us the history of the area of southern Gaul. The place we were in now had been fought over a generation ago, they told us. There had been a cruel ruling family who thought nothing about starving their subjects. They told us of the Franks who came over the border from Gaul, taking the land and adding it to their country.

"There is a man who has lodging. He can tell you more about the area. He also has horses and other things he will sell you if needed." The tavern keeper told us, then pointed to the Inn.

I was shocked at the Inn. As Josephus and I pushed the door open, we were greeted by a heavily pregnant woman.

"Ma'am, we are looking for your husband, my brother and I have heard he has horses for sale," Josephus said as he gave a slight bow.

"Oh yes, the tavern keeper boy ran and told me about you brothers. He does. They are in the barn out behind the Inn. I'll go find my husband." I was amazed the poor woman could walk in her condition. I was about to say as much to Josephus when he turned and walked out the back of the Inn. Standing at the door to the barn, we could hear a person humming a song of some sort. The innkeeper walked out of the Inn and smiled when he saw us waiting.

"Go on in, good brothers. I keep the horses inside on nights; they seem to like it. My brother takes care of them, and any questions you may have, he can answer." The inside of the barn was clean; hay had been placed in each stable for a horse. The animals showed no fear of strangers when we approached them. Two of the larger ones went so far as to nuzzle our hands when we reached to rub their necks. It didn't take long for us to pick out the two we wanted.

"We'll take these two big boys," Josephus said to the innkeeper as a smaller man stepped out of the shadows.

"This is my brother; he looks after the horses and a small herd of milk cows we have. If you need to know anything, he can tell you about all these horses." The innkeeper seemed proud of his brother and what he could do. I wondered why the fact his brother could do this type of work would be a source of pride for the innkeeper. It wasn't until the smaller man spoke it became apparent. The brother's speech was heavily slurred, not from drink. The smaller man slurred his speech because of a condition he was born with.

"Those two you have picked are good boys. They are easy to groom and will stand still for you to look at their hooves. I have their saddles and some bags that goes behind the saddle for carrying things," The innkeeper smiled at his brother as he spoke to us. Josephus smiled at the brother and nodded.

"Well, you've done a great job with them. We will take everything you have for the two of them, and thank you." The brother smiled, his grin lighting up his whole face. The men watched as the little brother walked to the other end of the barn and started gathering everything he had for the horses.

"He does do a good job with the animals." The innkeeper stated.

"I had a sister who was like your brother. She was a good girl." Josephus said as he watched the special brother work.

"In the village I was from, the head family wanted to drown him. The priest said he was a sign the gods were displeased. So I grabbed him and ran before anything could happen. We found this place, and the people here accepted him as he was. This is where I met my wife."

Josephus looked at the floor of the barn and shook his head.

"I couldn't save my sister. I was a boy when some men came to the house one night. They took her and killed her by throwing her into the sea, saying that's where all monsters belong." When Josephus told the story of his sister, I stood shocked. How could people think a child was a monster? The innkeeper's little brother was a little shorter than most people, a monster; I just couldn't see it.

When the horses were ready, we paid for them and received a bill of sale. The innkeeper insisted we have this for our own protection.

"Once you leave this area, there are men out there who will tell you they uphold the law for the king. In reality, they are little more than thieves. If they see you have better horses than they, or nicer things, they will try to claim it all for taxes. If you try to keep your things, they will kill you and take it all." The innkeeper warned us. Again we thanked the man and his brother and resumed our journey to find the brothers who waited for us and the treasures we were to find along the way.

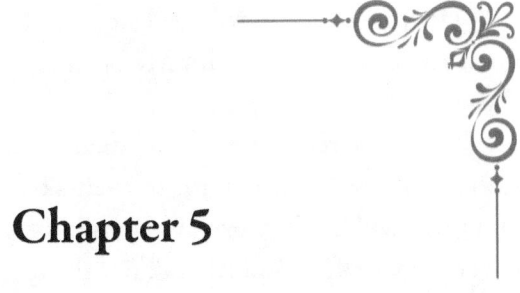

Chapter 5

I HAD NEVER SEEN MOUNTAINS before, for the entirety of my life up to that point had been spent in the sands of the holy land and Babylon. Now I found myself traveling with a brother through a strange, beautiful land called Massilia. As Josephus and I made our way into the mountains, we watched for the men the innkeeper warned us about. The sunset in the mountains stunned me into wondered silence. For the first time in my life, I slept with trees blocking the stars from my sight. So much of what I was seeing, I was seeing for the first time. I wondered what would be the next wonder to greet me.

Strange new birds sang, flitting from branch to branch in the trees. I remembered seeing my first deer. It was a doe, and I couldn't get over how beautiful this animal was. Until Josephus put an arrow through her heart. I must have looked strange sitting on my horse, jaw hanging open from the shock. Josephus turned and looked at me, then started to laugh.

"We now have meat unless you think you can breathe life back into it." He joked as he set to removing the gut and skinning out the deer. It didn't take long before we had the meat smoking over a small fire.

"Once we get the meat ready to travel, we'll head deeper into the mountains. I remember Joseph telling me about a stronghold the first of our order built." Josephus told me as he scraped the skin of the deer.

"Do you think it will still be out there?" I asked as I looked up at the nearby mountain. My brother looked into the forest and shrugged.

"I'm not sure. However, the men who built it were very skilled stone workers. So have faith in their skill, if we can find it. Joseph said there will be clues on how to find the greatest treasures man has never known of," Josephus said. For the rest of the night, my brother and I spoke of things to come. The next morning after a night of smoking meat and talking about a redoubt hidden in the mountains of this land, I was excited to be on the move. Days came and went as we traveled among the paths and roads winding their way through the mountains. Days turned to weeks, then to fortnights. Months passed with the grace of the mountain mists. Though we stopped many times to look at strange markings carved into rocks, we were forced to dismiss each. I was becoming discouraged, thinking our brothers hadn't left a mark to lead us to the first stronghold. I watched as Josephus stopped and looked into another crevice in a rock. He turned in his saddle and smiled at me.

"Come, little brother, look at our first sign," Josephus said as he pointed into the crack.

In the crevice was a carved hammer with a cross on the head of it. Below the hammer was three marks; each mark was offset to the west.

"What do the three marks below the hammer mean?" I asked as I looked into the crack. Trying to see if anything else was in there, to my amazement, I could see a jewel.

"I can see something else in there. I think I can reach it," I said when Josephus pulled me away from the crevice. Looking at my brother, I wondered why he wouldn't let me grab the jewel. As I turned to ask him why he had pulled me back, I saw his smile; he was pointing up. When I looked up, I was shocked to see a large stone balanced on another.

"I'm thinking if anyone had disturbed the jewel, then that mighty rock would be the last thing to pass through his head," Josephus said, and as I looked at the size of the rock, I couldn't help but agree with him.

We camped by the crevice that night, and as Josephus and I ate, we decided we should trip the trap. We worried that others might find it, so it had to be made safe. The deciding argument was when I asked what would happen if a young person found it and tried to pull the jewel out. The following day I notched an arrow and took aim at the gem. When I loosed my arrow, it flew true and struck the shining jewel.

What happened next caused the stone to fall and crash into the crevice. The jewel, on the other hand, snapped off the back of the crevice and flew out, hitting Josephus between the eyes. Much to my amusement, to tell the truth, I laughed so hard I couldn't breathe. Josephus sat on his horse, rubbing the spot where a bruise was forming.

"You know, little brother, I just don't see much humor in this situation," Josephus said as we started off in the direction the marks indicated.

"If it had hit me in the head instead?" I asked, looking at him.

"Then it would have been funny," Josephus returned as he tried to hide his merriment. Slowly we walked off deeper into the mountains. With this single sign, we knew the treasure was still waiting for us to find it. Days passed, and each morning Josephus and I would watch as the shadows shifted. As the morning gave way to the afternoon, the shadows would crawl up over the mountains we found ourselves in. I was held in awe of their beauty by the sheer power that created these great stone ramparts.

"This is how I know there is a higher power than us here," I said one day. Josephus turned and looked back at me with a question on his face.

"The mountains, their beauty, what power it must have taken to create them," I said as my brother turned and looked around us.

"These are only one of God's many creations we take for granted every day." When I realized Josephus had tried to make a pun of the situation, I rolled my eyes, shaking my head at him.

Three weeks after finding our first clue, I watched as a brother, in the order I only knew a little about, tried to squeeze his large body into another crack in a cliff.

"You know it might be easier if I was to try. After all, I'm smaller than you are," I offered. I tried not to smile when Josephus turned to look at me.

"What are you trying to say, brother?" Josephus asked as he looked down.

"What I'm trying to say is with your armor on, you make quite an imposing figure of a man," I said as I stepped out of my saddle. Then started to take off my armor to tell the truth. Right then, I wanted out of the heavy leather. As I turned, I found Josephus standing without his armor.

"If you think you are going in there alone, well, little brother, you had better think again," Josephus said as he squeezed his way into the crack; shaking my head, I followed.

It was only a short way until what was a mere crack opened into a wide path, looking ahead on this path. I didn't take long to see this hidden area had been forgotten for many years. The floor of the path was covered with moss and leaves. On the walls in different places, I could see faded paintings. Stopping, I studied one of the paintings, and what I could see forced me to step back. The look of shock on my face at what I saw caused Josephus to stop and come back to me. The painting I was looking at depicted a great war in the stars. I could see angels and another great being I took to be God in this war. They were fighting a great darkness. The painting showed many angles falling to a planet as the darkness was defeated.

"I don't understand what this painting is trying to tell us," I said as Josephus stood beside me and looked at the faded painting.

"It tells us about the war God and his first creations fought against. It was the first war; this came to be when God brought light to the vast darkness. This is when God and the arch angels first saw the greatest evil to have ever existed." Josephus told me. I looked at Josephus, confused, then back to the painting. I shook my head and moved on to the following image.

This painting showed a paradise. A beautiful city of gold and silver sat in the background. The city gates were closed, locked. In the background, God could be seen sitting on his throne. His angels surrounded him, their hands folded in prayer. As I looked closer at this painting, I could see God and the angels weeping. This painting shows some angels were injured. Each of these poor angels reached beseechingly to God to help them. While others were in chains, it was these poor creatures I looked at; each seemed to be cursed. The angels in chains were changing from the once beautiful creatures God created into grotesque, twisted things. Their once white wings of grace given by a loving father now turned to scorched flesh and blackened feathers. Their bodies were bent and twisted by the evil they fought against, their minds as twisted as their bodies. Looking at Josephus, he could see the question on my face before I could ask it.

"Most people believe God just thought this all up one day. Then set to work for the next six creating all we see here. Well, some of that is true. You see, when God and his angels were looking for a place to create his children. They roamed the ethereal plane for thousands of years before finding this area in the stars. However, this area wasn't empty. Other things were lurking in the darkness, in the nothingness. When God and the arch angels first saw these things, they knew they were looking at pure evil," Josephus told me. I stood looking at the painting as Josephus told about the story behind it.

"Joseph and I read the Bible many times. This was never in it." I said as I turned and pointed to the painting.

"No, this truth is not in the Bible. The men who wrote the Bible did so under the direction of others. The men who oversaw the writing of the Bible we have today left out many things. They thought themselves of higher intelligence than the lower classes." Josephus said. We stood looking at the painting. I knew a brother in the past had stood here and told gods story. He painstakingly painted this here for others to find and see the truth.

"I don't understand what's happening to the angels?" I said as I looked closer at the painting.

"The angles are changing. They were injured during the war to clear out the evil. Because of their injuries, they are changing. It is making them evil. It was these injuries that festered and grew until Lucifer and the others tried to revolt against God and their brothers." Josephus said. Again I looked at the painting as Josephus explained what it depicted. We walked further down the path until we came to another painting. This one I knew about showed the battle in heaven between Lucifer and the angels who follow him and the angels loyal to their father.

"This one is in the bible, and it is about the fall of Lucifer and the others," I said as we stood in front of another painting.

"Yes, it is, though unlike the bible story telling us hell is a place of damned souls. Its overseer is Lucifer, along with the others who do his bidding. However, that's not exactly correct. The ones who were sent to hell were sent there to heal. God thought if he could separate them from their brothers and sisters, he could heal them. Lucifer misunderstood his father's intention and thought he was being expelled along with the others. It was then that he gave in to his injuries. The pure evil Lucifer had been fighting up to that point took over, and he tried to attack his father." Josephus told me as I looked over the story painted on the wall of the passage.

"This is what started the fall. Michael and the other arch angels were forced to throw Lucifer and the others out of heaven?" I asked, looking at the point of the painting where it showed Michael standing over the twisted form of Lucifer.

"Yes, as you can see, the Bible isn't quite right, though. The Bible tells of how triumphant Michael was. The truth was he never wanted to fight his brother. Michael didn't stand victorious; instead, he sat and wept. As his brothers fell into hell, their wings burned off, leaving trails of black smoke showing their paths." Josephus said. I turned and looked at my brother and the only friend in the world. I knew he would never lie to me.

"So Lucifer was injured in a war; it was his injuries that caused the fall?" I asked, trying to get it all straight in my head.

"Yes, this is what happened; hell went from a place of healing to a place of evil. Torture, every kind of degradation known to man, souls are not sent there by God. They are captured by Lucifer and his demons. They can see if a soul has a stain on it. They can see this stain and will steal the soul while it rises," Josephus told me. I walked further down the path and then stopped.

"Where is the painting of the garden of Eden?" I asked, turning back, thinking I had missed something. Josephus laughed.

"There is another thing most people don't understand, God and the angels are forever. So the men who translated the Bible from Enochian to Hebrew came to the part of the texts where this was all explained. Well, they had never heard of everlasting, so they came up with a number they could grasp. If God is eternal and had eternity to do anything, would it be six of our days?" Josephus asked as he smiled.

"This is what we are led to believe, so your telling me this part of the bible is also wrong?" I asked.

"Not really wrong, just misinterpreted. God didn't do all this in six days. He took his time and did it over eons. He brought forth many creatures and plants. Everything we see, touch, smell, and even love was carefully planned and conceived. When God brought forth man, he did so, starting with two. Adam and Eve, by this time, Lucifer's wounds had overtaken him and the others completely. It was his first act to try and corrupt God's first man, and though it took many tries, he did finally convince the man to eat the forbidden fruit." Josephus said. I looked further down the path, wondering what other paintings still waited to be found.

"So it was Eve's weakness that caused us to be thrown out of the garden of Eden," I stated, knowing this story from the Bible.

"Well, that is what we are taught by men. There has to be someone to blame for them; it could never be the man. When God created man, he gave them the one thing he had never given any of his other creations. This gift was free will, and with this free will, the first humans chose not to follow the one rule god had set down. So they ate from the forbidden tree of knowledge. Now let me pose a question. If God is everywhere and all-knowing, it is said he knows the heart of man. Did he know his first would disobey him?" Josephus asked. When Josephus posed the question, I turned and looked at him.

"Well, I guess he would, seeing he is everything," I said as I looked at the painting.

"Of course he did. God knew when he started this wonderful world that would happen, so he made a world where we could flourish and love." Josephus said.

Turning, I started further down the path, hoping to find another painting. I stopped at a turn in the path. I couldn't see around the wall unless I exposed myself. Something was telling me to be careful, not to just walk around it; there was danger. I looked back to Josephus standing in a shaft of sunlight, watching me.

"You feel something is wrong ahead, don't you?" He asked, then smiled as I nodded, pointing up meaning from above.

"Whatever trap they set up comes from higher on the cliffs," I said as I looked up to see if there was a way we might be able to go around the danger.

"There is no reason to go looking for another route around the danger. The men who created this would have done so in a way only a brother could get through it." Josephus said as he sat down.

"OK, what is the way through, brother?" I asked and smiled as Josephus looked up at me and shrugged his big shoulders.

Chapter 6

FOR THE REST OF THE night, the two of us sat over a small fire. After our evening meal and prayers, we pondered what kind of trap could have been left by the ones who had painted these stories.

"I think the men who did all this wanted people to know the truth," I said, looking back to where the other paintings clung to the wall hidden in the darkness.

"Oh, I agree; the trouble is there were others in the past, and I hate to say it. Well, they would have killed these men for painting these." Joseph told me once his most significant anguish was watching the teachings of his son being twisted for profit.

Looking into the darkness, I caught a glint of firelight off something metal.

"Did you see that?" I asked Josephus, who looked up from running a stone over an arrowhead.

"No, see what?" Josephus asked, looking in the direction I was now staring at in the night.

"I just saw something flash in the light of our fire," I said. As I finished speaking, the firelight sparked in the night as Josephus, and I watched a flash appear in the darkness again. I stood up and was about to go and find out what it was when Josephus reached out and grasped my arm.

"Think about it, little brother, we are in a canyon with paintings depicting the truth about the creation of this world. Not to mention the truth about hell. Now we see something, who knows what, in the night by firelight, and you are ready to go into the darkness to find whatever, or whoever it might be.

I turned and watched the area where we had seen the flash, hoping it would come again. Sometime in the night, my eyes grew heavy, and finally, sleep claimed me. I felt something crawl across my hand in my sleep. The sensation of tiny claws on my flesh caused me to fly from my dreams.

To me, it seemed I went from sleeping to standing by the ashes of our night's fire. Turning, I looked to see what had woken me, and my eyes fell on a small stick. I looked at Josephus, who was trying his best to look as if I had awakened him with my cry and movement.

"Can you not wake up like the rest of the world, little brother?" He asked, trying to hide his smile.

"Oh, you are funny this morning, brother," I said as he laughed. He stood beside me, and we turned to look at the spot where we had seen the flash in the night.

Standing in a strange canyon, the two of us would have made an even stranger sight, standing there looking at a small hole someone took the time to bore into a large boulder. Whatever caused the flash came from inside the hole. I watched as Josephus took out an arrow shaft. He looked at the hole in the rock and then at the shaft.

"Do you think it a good idea? After all, we don't know if this is a trigger for a trap or an answer to our question?" I asked.

"We should be ready to move, you know, if something happens," Josephus answered, looking back to our camp.

I watched as Josephus carefully inserted the arrow shaft into the hole. He stopped and turned to look behind us again, then pushed on the shaft. I looked around, waiting for something.

We heard a faint click, then a rumble from within the face of the cliff, behind the boulder. Josephus and I looked at each other, then retreated back from the boulder, leaving the arrow shaft sticking out of the hole. I looked behind us, hoping to see nothing dangerous fly by the two of us.

I couldn't see anything; however, the sound grew and grew until we could feel whatever was on the move vibrating in our feet. I looked at Josephus. I was going to ask him what to do when part of the cliff opened like a door.

Josephus and I stood silently, letting the last of the rumbling echo around the walls surrounding us. Standing still, we looked beyond the door that hadn't been there until a few moments ago. Now the darkness from the other side of this new door seemed so foreboding.

I knew we needed to see what was in the darkness. The boy in me still wanted to run from it. The man I wanted to become needed to see what was beyond the door. The man won the argument. I decided to gather some tinder and fashion a torch. Along with what I thought we might need in the darkness, though, to speak the truth, I had no idea what we were walking into.

The darkness relented slowly. Josephus and I watched as shadows jumped, fleeing back. Like creatures of the night, the darkness sought the corners as the light from our torches forced it back into crevices. The room was round. In it, the wall had been painted, unlike the ones outside. These paintings had been protected from the weather. They were still as bright as day the artist finished them.

"I don't understand this; why would they go through the trouble of making this room and the hidden door to hide this?" I asked, holding my arms wide and turning so I could take in the whole room and its paintings.

"Well, look at it," Josephus said as he walked along the wall, his fingertips gently touching the painting.

"It looks like the story of who I think is Jesus. Most of this I've never heard of." I said as I looked at who I thought was Joseph. For a moment, my breath caught in my chest. When I looked up at the painting and saw what looked to be a younger Joseph, my heart seemed to stop beating. I could feel the heat of unshed tears floods my eyes.

"Most of his life has been left out because religious leaders find it too controversial for men and women. There was also a call about his travels in certain areas in the deserts of the holy lands."

"I understand all that, but this shows him direct contact with God and Satan. At the same time, they were sitting around a large table. Satan looks sickly as if he is dying," I said. I looked closer at the painting.

"It was at this point in Jesus's life that he found out the truth about Lucifer. About the injuries, he and the others suffered. The state you see Lucifer in is caused by his injuries; the evil is rotting him. At this point, he and the others have been infected for millions of years, and the evil is actually killing the angel," Josephus told me.

"How did the others find out about this meeting?" I asked, standing in awe at what I saw and being told.

"These truths were brought out of the holy land. They were told to the first brothers by a person who was always by Jesus's side even through his trials," Josephus told me. I looked at my brother; I thought Josephus was going to tell me it was one of his disciples.

"It had to be Peter; he was with Jesus through it all right," I said, looking at the painting for a clue.

"Not even close little brother. It would be the last person you would think of, the last person you would hear of," Josephus returned as he stood and walked over to me. I watched as my brother pointed to a spot in the painting. A streak of red could be partially seen behind a rock. It looked like someone was trying to hide.

"Someone is hiding in the painting," I stated.

"That person has been hidden for good reasons. She would have been killed if it were discovered who and what she was." My brother told me as he walked up beside me, reaching out with his fingertips to touch the streak of a red robe.

"She, I don't understand. Was Mary with him as he traveled?" I asked, trying to get a better look.

"It was a Mary; however, it wasn't his mother. Though Mary would have liked to have been with her son during this time of his life. It is the one woman people have been calling a whore throughout history." I turned and looked at him, knowing who he was talking about.

"Mary Magdalene? You're talking about Mary Magdalene. How does she fit into all this?" I wondered how it was the woman who prostituted herself to men, then came to follow Jesus throughout the holy land. How was it she was at a meeting such as this one?

"Come here; there is one thing you need to know to understand." I walked over to a stone bench Josephus was sitting on.

"Jesus was born and raised Jewish, which in itself brings certain laws and rules they lived by. At the time of Jesus, his father, Joseph, would have been responsible for finding him a suitable wife. This was done so Jesus could start a family of his own. Mary's family received Joseph, and before long, the two young people had been married in accordance with Jewish law. Now Jesus and his family knew what he was, so they sat Mary down, they explained it to her before they were wed. Mary loved Jesus and said it didn't matter to her. She would follow him anywhere he needed to go," Josephus told me. I sat stunned as Josephus explained the son of the man I called father had a wife.

"On the day Jesus was nailed to the cross, both his mother and his wife were there. His mother stood and watched her son die while his wife was forced to hide in the shadows, her belly full of his child." The room started to spin, and I felt sick to my stomach as I remembered the scene after I had been given his blood.

"She was there; she watched her husband murdered by so-called men of faith his father had gathered and taken out of bondage," I stated.

"No, it wasn't the Jewish faith that killed Jesus. It was a small group of men who were afraid of losing their power and standing. These men alone went to Pilot and begged for Jesus to be crucified. It was these men who bribed the guards to torture him. One of these men paid the roman soldier to run his spear into the side of Christ. When it looked like the people on the hill started to sympathize with the plight of Christ." When Josephus finished telling me about the last days of Christ, I wanted it to be quiet for a few moments. I just needed to sit and gather my thoughts. It seemed impossible to me Jesus would have been married and started a family.

"Why did his wife take the baby away?" I asked as I sat holding my head, fearing I was about to be sick to my stomach in this place.

"Joseph knew their grandchildren needed to be protected. So he told Mary she was going to have to take Mary Magdalene back to her homeland. Though Mary protested, Joseph was stern about it. It was this very night the angel came to them together for the last time. He told Mary she had to protect the babies, for the men who killed Jesus would stop at nothing to get the children. So as the sun rose, Mary and her son's wife looked back to Joseph as he waved goodbye to his love," As Josephus finished, I looked at the paintings again. I knew the toll this loss had on the man I called my father.

"So Joseph had no idea where they went after the port?" I asked.

"No, he had no idea; once we stepped foot on that boat, we were truly on our own." He told me as his fingers brushed over the image of Christ. Both of us sat in the room, looking up at the painting. We both knew no one had entered this room after it had been sealed.

I wanted to say something, anything to break the silence; I just could not find the words. Knowing the truth about our savior seemed to make the room brighter. Looking at the dying Lucifer, at the suffering he was brought to, I wonder if he still survived.

"I do have one question, did Lucifer survive his wounds?"

"Well, I wish I knew Rene, some say our lord ended his suffering in the cave that night. Others say God imprisoned what was left of Lucifer under a mountain somewhere though no one knows where." Josephus said as we stood and looked at the painting again.

The two of us would have made a funny painting ourselves. Both sat looking up at the images of this room. Standing up, I looked at the walls to see if any other key locks were hiding other treasures. Slowly I walked along the walls hoping to find something. It was when I reached the painting of the meeting I thought I had found what I was looking for.

"What do you make of these marks by gods right hand?" I asked Josephus, who by this time had taken an interest in what I was doing. Josephus came to where my interest held me. It was then he took a closer look at the marks.

"They're chisel marks, made by a very small fine chisel. The man who would use this kind of tool was a master of the highest order." He said as he brushed his fingers over the marks touching gods hand.

"Well, if the man who put these here is a master, then we can say these are not a mistake then," I said, leaning in for a closer looked.

"No, not a mistake; a distraction, yes, but no mistake," Josephus said as he tapped my shoulder and pointed to the opposite wall smiling. I looked to where my brother pointed. I found I was looking at another wall with a painting on it.

This painting showed a dark castle on a hill with a lake beside it. In the painting, there was a small group of men. These men were all on their knees in front of two women.

"Is this painting showing the point where both the mother and wife of Jesus went? Are these men part of the order?" I asked as I walked over to the painting.

"These men are the ones who, along with Joseph, started the order. They knew the two women were coming; you see, Joseph knew someday he would have to send them away. It was Joseph who started the stories of Mary Magdalene being a whore. It was something he agonized over when he told the first person this lie." Josephus said as he again reached up with the softest touch placing his fingers on the painting.

"Why does it look like Mary Magdalene isn't pregnant anymore?" I asked, looking closer at the image of the woman.

"She had the babies as they reached this land." When my brother said babies, I must have looked stunned.

"Yes, babies, twins, a boy, and a girl, they were healthy. The two women carried the twins to this place, wherever it is." He finished as we sat and stared at the walls. It was then I saw the tiny hole in one of the castle windows in the background.

"There is a hole in that window," I stated, pointing at it.

"What window?" Josephus asked as he stood. I reached up and tapped the window.

"Here it is; it looks to be the same as the one that let us in here," I told him as we both stood and examined the hole. Josephus reached into his quiver, pulling the arrow shaft out again. He looked at the spot before he inserted the arrow shaft into it.

Again we heard a click, then a grinding rumble. Stepping back from the painting, we watched as another door started to swing open then it stopped. Turning, I watched the other door. Shocked, I stood anchored to the spot as it finished swinging closed.

"I think we may have made a mistake," I said as the darkness enveloped the two of us. Josephus reached out and touched my shoulder. To which I am ashamed to say I cried out and jumped back. I smiled in the darkness when I heard my brother laughing at me.

"Tell me you brought our packs in with you?" He asked.

"Yes, I brought in both our packs. They are by the bench." I answered and then listened. I could hear him moving to where we first sat and looked at the paintings. All at once, there was a flash, then a spark and one of our torches flashed to life.

"Look at the door and see if you can find another hole." He told me as Josephus dug out another torch and lit it. Going toward the door, I looked for a keyhole, to no avail. I looked at my brother and shook my head. I watched as Josephus nodded. He knew there was no keyhole in this door. So as most explorers do when they find themselves at a point like this, we pushed on. Both of us hoped there would be a way out further in the next room.

Our torches showed a raised dais and more paintings adorned the walls of this chamber. Though with the dancing shadows caused by the flames of the torches, these paintings were harder to discern. I watched as Josephus walked over to a bowl being held by chains anchored to the ceiling by a heavy chain.

I did the same and looked into the bowl. I could smell oil when I touched my torch to the wick. Josephus did the same in total; we found five oil lamps and lit each. The oil lamps flooded the chamber with golden light.

Chapter 7

THE PAINTINGS SEEMED to gain a life of their own; Josephus and I turned in a circle, trying to take everything in. These paintings were strictly about the voyage the mother and the wife of Jesus were forced to take to save his children.

The first painting showed a man crafting a chest of wood. It wasn't decorated with gold or jewels. It was a simple chest well built and covered with hides. Then treated to make it waterproof, it was small enough to carry on one's back. The man who crafted it had attached straps for this purpose.

As the painting went on, it showed two women sitting in a cart with two babies. In the back of the cart sat a chest. It could be seen despite being covered. The man who had built it waved to one of the women who had a tear on her cheek.

"These are the stories of the voyage they took," I said, touching the painting. I looked at the small chest sitting on a raised dais and then back to the image. I looked at Josephus. He was looking at the chest, beads of sweat dotting his brow. Again I looked at the chest. It was the same as the one in the painting, precisely the same.

"Do I see things, brother? Is the chest in the cart now here in this place? If it is the same, what do you think is in it?" I asked, afraid of the answer.

"Well, these chests were built by families to hold any number of things. Usually, what they put in them had the greatest value to the family." Josephus told me as he walked around the dais.

"Ok, we know what was of the greatest value to Joseph and Mary." As I finished my sentence, we stopped and looked at each other, then back to the chest. I couldn't find my voice; every time I tried to speak, the only sound to come forth was a horsed croak.

"You don't think these are his remains, do you?" I asked, and again I felt weak and was going to be sick. Then without thinking, I stepped to the dais and started to brush dust away from the front of the chest.

As I cleaned, I could begin to make out the writing, so I blew the rest of the dust away. For a moment, the shock of what I was reading forced me to hold onto the dais. It seemed all the strength my legs had just mere moments ago had deserted me.

When I felt I could, I let go of the dais and stepped back. Tears ran down my face, leaving dirt trails as they cut the dust on my skin. Josephus rushed to my side as I sank to my knees, covering my face with my hands.

"Little brother, what is it? Tell me?" He asked as he held me.

"That is our savior, it says; the chest holds the mortal remains of Jesus. This is the chest Mary had Joseph build to keep him. Until others, as devout, came to take him to another hiding place. Mary's last wish was to be reunited with her son after death. When I told Josephus what the writing said, he let me go, and the two of us knelt in front of the dais weeping.

I still don't know how long we were there before I could stand. When I did, I walked to the chest and placed my hand upon it. I don't know why I did it; the urge came over me; I stood and then spoke an oath.

"From this day forth, I will devote all of my life, all of my strength, to bringing you to your mother." I had almost forgotten Josephus was behind me. I started when his hand gently laid over mine as he took the oath I just spoke.

"We, little brother, we will do this." He said as he smiled.

"However, first, we need to find our way out of this place." He said as we both turned in a circle again. Searching the paintings for anything looking like a keyhole. After hours of staring at the smallest detail of the images, I realized these two caves took time to create. Then it could have taken as long to paint the walls with as much detail as these paintings held.

Again I found myself at the dais looking around the floor and then up each side. As I looked at the second side of the dais, I found what we were looking for.

This time there were two keyholes. I sat down on the floor and just looked at the two holes. I wondered if one was the key that would let us out of here. Or if they both would seal us in the tomb of our savior until the end of time.

"Well, we should try something," Josephus said as he sat beside me.

"Yes, we should; however, is it the right thing, or could we make our situation worse?" I asked, not really wanting an answer. Sitting in the dust on the floor, looking at the side of the dais where the two holes were, we would have made a funny sight. Soon, Josephus and I decided it was becoming tedious, and we should try something.

I watched as Josephus took the arrow shaft and placed it in the first hole. He looked at me with a small smile touching the corners of his lips, then pushed the shaft further. We both heard a click from the other side of the dais. I looked around to the opposite side of the platform and found another door had opened.

Standing aside, I used my foot to push the door open all the way. I crouched down to see what was inside the hidden compartment. I looked up at Josephus when I saw what was sitting under the chest holding Jesus.

"What is it you see, little brother?" Josephus asked me as I looked over the chest at him.

"A small booklet," I answered.

"The writing on it is Enochian, the language of the angels," I added as Josephus stood and walked over to me.

"What does it say?" My brother asked, barely able to contain his curiosity.

"This is the lineage of Christ, God's mortal son," I whispered as we knelt in the dust, neither of us reaching for the small booklet.

"We need to protect this; it is as important as our saviors remain's," Josephus stated. I knew he was right, of course, if the truth ever became public knowledge. The men who started our order knew there were certain groups. These groups would hunt down the children born of the holy family. The men of these groups would pass their zealous nature onto their sons. Because of this, the bloodline of Christ would forever be hunted, and their lives forfeited if ever found.

When I reached in and took the book, a golden cross was hidden behind it. With the cross, there were four vials of what looked like blood in them. Josephus took the cross and the vile setting them aside, I opened the book and started reading the language of the angels.

I had only managed to read the first page when a case of lite headedness came over me again, and I had to stop. I looked up when a grinding rumble started again; I turned to see what Josephus had done. He was standing behind the dais, smiling.

"There was a third hole. It was behind the cross," Josephus stated as the door holding us in there opened. The two of us knelt in front of the dais and prayed to be forgiven for disturbing his remains. Then we stood together and lifted the chest holding Jesus's earthly remains off its resting place.

To our surprise, there was a recess under the chest. We found a note elegantly written; it asks the brother who found her son to care for him. To bring mother and son together when it was possible.

Josephus and I were forced to put the chest down when we realized I was holding a note written by Mary. A letter written by a loving devoted mother, one hoping to be with her son in the life after this one. Holding the note my thoughts flashed back to my own mother and the day she died. Murdered in a market and left to die in a filthy street. Looking at the note, I smiled, knowing my mother would have loved me this much.

"Come, little brother, let us be out into the light again," Josephus said as he started to lead the way out. He stopped so suddenly that I almost walked into him. I was about to ask why he had stopped when I saw the map. The map had been chiseled into the stone of the wall. It was beside the door.

Josephus turned and looked at me, then at the chest in his hands. I smiled when he returned it to the dais. Neither of us wanted to place it on the dirt of the floor. I was busy digging out a scroll and something to trace the map from the wall. Once I had copied the map in every detail from the wall to our scroll, Josephus pointed to some writing on one side of the map.

"If I'm not wrong, this tells the brother who has found this crypt, to destroy this map for it shows the route taken by the ones who came before us." I turned and nodded to him, then back to the map. Neither one of us wanted to destroy the map. We also knew we couldn't leave it behind for others to follow. So without a second thought, Josephus and I destroyed the map.

Emerging into the bright sunlight of the mountains. Josephus and I found the horses contently eating; they looked at us and then blew dust from their noses, looking quite bored with the day.

"We should make sure the rooms are safe. Later, we can tell the brothers where we found this treasure and the paintings there," I said.

"I agree; I would like to come back here and just sit to study all of them." He told me, and I knew what he meant.

"They are wonderful; I wish we could take them along," I said as Josephus turned and inserted the arrow shaft into the keyhole and pushed again. The grinding rumble again was heard, and we stood back, watching the hidden door close. We both looked at each other, knowing we would be back in this place someday.

Chapter 8

SITTING BY OUR FIRE the first night after finding the rooms, I read the booklet. I needed to commit the names of the two children to my memory, so they would never be lost again. I was shocked when I came to a part where Mary told of the plan to separate the twins. The boy would go with his mother and grandmother.

"The girl they would leave with the Magdalene family to be raised as theirs. The family had wealth and standing with the crown, it would afford the child protection." I read out loud to Josephus.

"Mary was smart. I know it would have broken the hearts of the two women to leave either one behind. It was done for their safety; hard as it would have been to let one go, it was for the best." Josephus said as he started to cook our evening meal.

"Leaving either was not a good choice," I said, becoming upset.

"No, I agree; however, think about it, little brother. You are being chased by agents of a group who wants to erase any evidence your son ever existed. You have two babies and a handful of men for protection; what do you do as a woman." As he spoke, I could start to see the logic in his argument, though I still didn't like it.

"They didn't have a choice," I stated.

"Exactly. If Mary had left the boy because he was a boy, and the family had standing with the crown, he would have been put into service as a knight. He most likely would have lost his life in some skirmish out there someplace. Another unknown body being picked over by the crows." Josephus said as he waved his arm towards the mountains.

"So they chose the girl because of what she was?" I asked.

"Yes, as a girl, she would be given an education, taught the finer points of life. When she was of age, she might even marry into the royal family; who knows." When Josephus said the daughter of our savior could marry into a royal family, I became enraged.

The thought of some inbred, pompous slobbering idiot pawing over the girl brought me to the point of murderous rage. Seeing my state, Josephus smiled and shook his head.

"I know how you feel, my brother; however, this is the life we have; all either of us can do is find and protect the children of the twins. That little book can never find its way out of our control, ever." He stated as he pointed to what I was holding.

"What about the girl, her children out there somewhere," I said, then realized like their mother, the daughter of Christ, they would be long passed away. We had to protect the great-grandchildren of our savior and their bloodline.

"We will not; when we find the others, it will be the first order of business. The others will agree. We need to set something up to protect the whole family."

The night before, we left the hidden rooms covered in paintings showing the times of Jesus in the holy lands. I decided to start a map of our journey, so we could recall all the places Josephus, and I went after we left Joseph in his resting place. Josephus remembered all the villages we had been to. The most difficult was during the shipwreck. Josephus told me it would be allowed if I added a bit of the writer's imagination.

I had wanted to leave out the two rooms we now sat outside of. Josephus told me I couldn't. He wanted me to put them exactly where we had found them.

"We want to save those wonderful things in there. I know the brotherhood would, and the only way we can do it is by turning this place into a monastery." I looked at him and knew he was right.

"Your right. It will be added." I told him, then started to write again. I found as I wrote about the rooms, the remembrance of the past came easy.

"I know it will be you who comes back to start this order of the brotherhood," I told Josephus. I knew it would be him to start it; he smiled and looked up at the peaks of the mountains.

We sat and rested outside the rooms where we had found our savior and the paintings for the rest of the day. I wrote down all I could remember. After I put down my scroll and quill, Josephus and I sat waiting for the beautiful day to end.

The colors at the end of each day held Josephus and me in amazement. We would watch as the mountains surrendered the last light of their day to the night. The most vivid oranges and reds painted themselves over a canvas god laid down untellable eons before. Then to mark the beginning of another day, the pallet was brought forth. With all the colors intended for our eyes, the stars winked one last time before the sun took over the sky.

The shadows of the night crawled down the mountains as the sun came over the edge of the world. It found Josephus and me sitting by our fire, praying for all those waiting for us in lands we haven't traveled in thus far. We also prayed for those we left behind in lands past.

We spent two nights in the canyon. The two of us would stop and marvel at faded paintings of people, hands, and strange animals. These paintings were made by people thousands of years long past. These faded paintings told of great beasts, and some showed other people. Some small who we took to be children. Josephus and I looked at them with wonder as I added them to the map I was making of our route through the mountains.

The first fortnight after, Josephus and I left the rooms where we found our savior. We set up camp under a great overhang. By the light of our small fire, we found more paintings and what looked like a crude carving. The next day we spent more time looking this carving over. We speculated about the man who tried to carve the rock.

What kind of tools he would have had if he was alone if he was moving around with his family. We had so many questions and no real answers. So with no answers, Josephus and I decided it was time to move on. I added this place to my map; I knew this little mystery would give us something to discuss. We would speculate about the people from the past; it was a great way to pass the time.

During our ride through the mountains, we looked at many things on the fourth day after we left the overhang. I was looking up at a small peak of some unknown mountain when a shape caught my eye.

"Now, what do you think caused that?" I asked aloud, pointing to the shape.

"Caused what?" Josephus asked, following my outstretched finger. I could tell by the look on his face we had found something significant. Before I knew what was going on, Josephus turned his horse and started to ride up a game trail leading off the path onto the mountain.

I wanted to ask what we were doing. I knew Josephus would tell me what I needed to know when we reached the object.

The narrow game trail we followed grew steeper and steeper until it came to a small plateau. It was on this plateau the object I had seen sitting. Because of the mountain's steepness, I could only see the top of the thing. Now we stood in front of it, both of us again speechless. I looked at Josephus to be sure what I was seeing was real.

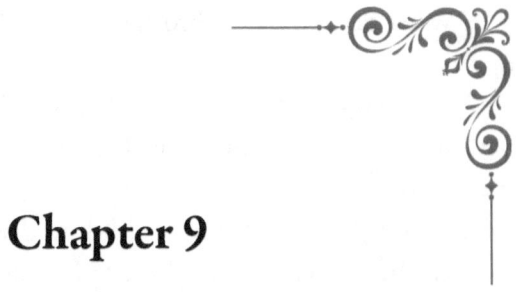

Chapter 9

"WHAT IS THIS DOING here of all places?" I asked, walking closer to the object.

"It's a marker. Who built this wonderful statue is a question I can not answer." Josephus said as we marveled at the craftsmanship it had taken to carve the fifteen-foot knight. The knight was holding a shield with the brotherhood insignia on it. On the pedestal in Latin, the words' **Donum deorum esse thesaurum**'. It translated to 'gods gift is our treasure.'

"They were telling the world they are the protectors of the bloodline. Even back then, they knew the line of Christ needed to be protected," Josephus said as we looked the statue over.

"How old is this, though? It looks hardly weathered," I added.

"Well, Joseph was five hundred years old when we left him. He and Pilot himself started the brotherhood. Pilot faked his death shortly after the creation of the brotherhood within the Roman officer's ranks stationed in the holy land. Now it would have been about fifty years after the murder of Jesus. So I'm going to say this here is between two to four hundred years old." As Josephus was speculating about the statue's age, I walked around it for the third time. It was then I recognized a small indentation. It had the shape of the cross I always wore around my neck.

Without saying a word, I took my cross and gently sized it with the indentation. To my surprise, it fit perfectly. Looking around to see where Josephus was, I beckoned him over.

"What do you think, brother?" I asked when he saw what I was up to.

"Well, go ahead. Let us see what wonders our big brother holds within." He said, smiling, as I pushed my cross into the place seemingly carved for it.

Nothing happened, and I can admit disappointment was starting to rise. Then Josephus asked me if I could turn it. To my surprise, I could turn the cross to the left. It only went a fraction of an inch before it stopped.

To our shock, the shield opened, revealing a small chest. Looking at the chest, Josephus and I hesitated to reach in and pick it up. After a few moments, we both smiled at each other than I gently removed the chest. Again like the first one we found holding our savior, there was a note under this one as well. This note asked the unknown brother who found the chest to bring it back to the order.

"It tells of how it will not be safe for the church to know the bloodline. It begs us to hide all the information about his bloodline. It also says the brotherhood might have to go as far as taking it over the great water to the west. I think it's signed by Joseph and Mary. Both Joseph and Mary knew before his death their son's bloodline would be hunted." I said, holding the note and looking at my brother holding the small chest.

"What do you think is in it?" I asked Josephus as I sat it down.

"I don't know. To be truthful, I'm a little nervous about opening it." He said as we both stood looking at it.

Josephus and I got down on our knees, and I was surprised to find myself saying a small prayer. When I was done, I looked at my brother, then tried to lift the lid of the chest. I say tried because the top wouldn't budge. It seemed to be fastened down somehow.

"What is the matter, little brother?" Josephus asked, watching me struggle with the lid.

"Well, it seems Joseph, if it was he who built this chest, has fastened the lid somehow," I said as I looked the chest over.

The sun had started to set when we closed the statue of the brother, then returned to the canyon floor below. The stars found Josephus and me studying the small chest by the light of our fire. We both puzzled over the chest as the stars turned overhead. It was Josephus who tried to twist the top of the chest, and it moved the tiniest fraction; it was enough.

A faint click was heard, and a small round piece of the chest popped out. Sitting beside our fire, we looked at each other as I reached out and gently pulled the round shaft of wood out of the chest. As I pulled out the small shaft of wood, I felt it start to resist and then stop. I didn't want to pull it further for fear of breaking something.

"It has stopped," I said

"I can see that," Josephus returned.

"Just try and turn it again," He told me. Taking his advice, I tried to first turn the shaft to the right and then to the left. To both our surprise, it turned to the left, then another click was heard, and a small drawer popped open. We were so unprepared for this that Josephus almost dropped the small chest. Sitting there shocked, I looked at him and then at the drawer.

"Well?" Josephus asked. I knew he meant, 'well are you going to look to see what is in it.' I just wasn't ready to see what Joseph had left all those years ago.

"I'm going to," I said, smiling at Josephus. I knew he was just as nervous as I was. I looked up to the sky and smiled, knowing my adopted father was looking down and smiling at us. Then I gently pulled the drawer open.

To both of our shock, in the drawer were three small rolled-up scrolls and a key. I took the key out first and looked it over. Then

Josephus turned the small chest over to see if we had missed a keyhole, and we didn't.

The three small scrolls held something entirely different, though. It held the name of the family the daughter of Jesus had wed into when she came of age. They are the family that rules Great Britain. Her children have married into most of the royal families. To our surprise, her scroll gave the names of her twelve children.

The three scrolls held the three names of the most powerful families. They also had the names of the children and a short family tree of sorts. Again Josephus and I looked at the small chest over and over, trying to see if there was another drawer. While I turned it over, we both heard something rattle inside it.

"There is something else in there," Josephus said as he reached for the scrolls and set them aside. What I found was two small locks of hair banded by small beads. One lock had blue beads around it the other had light purple beads around it; I looked at Josephus, confused.

"What a strange thing to put in this chest and then to leave it here," I said as I put the locks back in the chest.

"I think they may be the hair of the twins." Josephus speculated as we both looked at the small twists of hair.

Grasping the shaft, which still protruded from the end of the chest, I tried to pull it out further. It wouldn't move, so in frustration, I pushed it, and to my surprise, it slid back into the chest, and the lid popped open. I looked at Josephus and then at the chest. Without thinking, I handed him the chest and smiled.

"It's your turn to see what it holds," I told my brother

"I would prefer you do it, little brother," He said, holding the chest away from himself.

"No, it's your turn," I insisted. Josephus smiled and nodded.

I stepped back to let Josephus open the chest to see what wonders they had left behind in times past. Again we looked at the chest. I watched as Josephus reached for the lid and started to lift it. We sat in wonder at the two small keys sitting in spots for them. Looking at the keys, we both could tell one was for a boy, and the other was for a girl.

"What do you make of these?" Josephus asked as we stared at the keys.

"I think we will know when we find the twins or where their last resting places are," I answered and watched as Josephus nodded.

The sun had long since past the high point of its travel for the day, leaving the canyon in darkness. We removed the saddles, then placed the two chests on a small ledge of the stone provided by the canyon wall. Once the fire was going, Josephus and I prayed for the twins who had long passed away and for our brothers who we hadn't found yet.

The night passed quickly, and before I knew it, Josephus was waking me with his usual grin. I still don't understand people who wake up in a great mood. To tell the truth, it was the only mildly odd thing about my brother, though, at times, it was truly infuriating.

That wonderful day in the canyon where we made the greatest discoveries. A path through the mountains where so much was revealed to us came to an end. We sat upon our horses and looked out over a beautiful green valley. I watched as a bee flew from flower to flower, its hard work spreading the seed to make them strong.

We must have made a strange sight to behold. The farmer working his land stopped and shaded his eyes to see us clearly. We sat on our horses and watched as the man turned, looking back to a small house. I raised my hand in greeting, hoping to put the farmer at ease. Josephus sat on his horse as we reached the man; I could tell he was afraid of us.

"Hello, sir. Can you tell us what the nearest town is and if there is a market there?" I asked the man as he tried to put his mule and plow between him and us. I looked at the man then a movement at the house caught both Josephus's and my attention.

A woman rushed out of the house. Even at this distance, we both could tell she was terrified for her husband's life. I looked at my brother, then smiled and waved to her as I got down from my horse.

"We are monks and mean you no harm, sir," I said to the farmer.

"Most men who come out of that place are touched in the head, spouting about ghosts and evil," The farmer said as he turned so he could see the house and his wife. To me, it was as if he wanted to see his wife one last time before we struck him down. He was surprised when I took off my sword and hung it on my horse.

"Well, we haven't seen any ghosts, though my brother loves to scare me as I wake up from a night's sleep," I told the farmer, who smiled up at Josephus, who was now standing beside me.

"One must enjoy the little things," Josephus said as he shrugged his big shoulders. Still, the farmer looked uneasy as the woman held her skirts off the ground and ran towards us.

"If you brothers need food, I have put down pork and lamb as well as vegetables. We can discuss prices if you wish, and truth be told, I can use the coin." As the farmer talked about payment for supplies, I could see it made him nervous.

"That would be nice, and we could avoid the trappings of a town," Josephus told the farmer as his wife slowed, then walked slowly to her husband. As she reached her husband, I watched as she reached out and took his arm, clutching him out of fear and love.

I watched as Josephus smiled at the loving gesture. Behind my brother's smile, a familiar trace of heartbreak chased across his face again.

"These brothers want to buy supplies from us. They have coin." The farmer told his wife, whose eyes grew dark.

"Are they like the last men who called themselves brothers, men of the cloth?" I could tell when she talked of the others they had been less than devout. Josephus turned and looked at the woman.

"Others, brothers? Tell me about these others, good lady." When Josephus asked about the others, the woman stiffened.

"They came out of the mountains as you did. They even came out of the same pass. My brother and father were here working the field as my husband does. These brothers came to my father. One of their men was ranting about the ghosts protecting a knight on the mountain. They demanded my father give them what they wanted. When my father refused, they killed him right where you stand now. Then they came after my brother and wounded him. They came to the house looking for food and wine. One of them looked at me, and I knew what he was thinking. That is when my husband came home and fought with one of the monks. He killed him, and the rest of the bastards ran like cowards," The woman told us. The farmer looked at the ground as his wife told us about the others. I looked at Josephus and then back to the farmer.

"I'm glad you were not hurt, sir. Did you keep anything of the monk you killed?" I asked.

"Yes, I have it in the barn, buried." He answered.

"May I go and get it. If there are any insignia on it, we will know what order the men belonged to and will bring them to justice," Josephus said as he looked to the barn.

"Well, I mean no offense. The others were like you, burnt dark by a hard sun." The wife told Josephus, who turned and looked at her and then pointed to his arm.

"Dark like this or lighter?" He asked.

"Like you, just like you," She answered then we all walked back to the barn. It didn't take too long before Josephus was holding the belongings of the dead man who called himself a monk. I watched as my brother unfolded a dirty tunic. Josephus looked at me, shock written all over his face. My brother looked at the farmer and his wife, then at me. I could see a deep rage building on the face of my brother.

"You say you killed the man who wore this. I need to know how you did this," He asked the farmer.

"I had a sling. When the man who wore that saw me coming, he pulled his sword. I knew I could never match him at hand to hand, so I used my sling." The man told Josephus.

"Good, I'm glad you had the sense not to test your skill against him. He was no monk; this man was a soldier though he and the men he traveled with deserted years before they came here," Josephus said, then explained to me.

"I was charged with hunting them down and bringing them back for trial. When I didn't return, my officers thought I had joined them," Turning, Josephus handed the things back to the farmer.

"You should use this and make something to use on your farm. It has been used to kill. Now let it be used to grow and bring life," Josephus said. The farmer and his wife smiled, the man nodding; they set aside the dead man's things and took us to the modest house. The smell of freshly baked bread stopped both of us at the door.

"Come in! You are welcome here," The farmer said as he realized we had stopped at the threshold of his house.

"Oh, my, what a wonderful aroma," I said as the smell of baked bread enveloped us. Josephus looked at the interior of the house, and again, I could see his heart breaking at a memory long passed. I wanted to ask him what hurt him, so I knew he would smile and say it was nothing.

After washing our hands and faces, Josephus and I were invited to sit at the table while the lady of the house served us lamb stew and loaves of bread. After the meal, she brought apple pie to the table. I had never had an apple pie before. Josephus told me it would seem like a slice of heaven. My brother was not wrong; at the first bite of that wonderful pie, I had to stop and put my fork down. A slice of heaven, he was right. I took my time with the pie wanting to enjoy every bite.

That night we gathered the supplies the farmer could give us. When I pulled out a gold piece, the farmer and his wife became nervous again.

"What is it? I wish to pay for our wonderful meal and these things." I said as Josephus walked back to us.

"It's gold, brother. If caught with the gold, they will be accused of stealing from the crown, and he will be jailed or killed." Josephus told me. The look of surprise on my face made him laugh.

"It is not like the holy land here. Not everyone has a gold coin in their purse." I nodded, then got out three silver coins.

"That is too much, brother." The farmer told me then was shocked when I took his hand and pushed the coins into his palm.

"For you and your wife, I may want to come back for another apple pie in the future," I said and smiled at his wife. I never knew what came over me. As I turned, I placed my hand on the woman's head and blessed her. I climbed onto my horse and followed Josephus past the barn through the field, into the forest.

Riding in the forest between the Languedoc and the Midi-Pyrenees regions of southern France, I could tell something was bothering Josephus.

"Brother, when you decide you need to talk about the past, I'll be here," I told Josephus. He turned in the saddle and nodded his thanks, then, for the rest of the day, we rode in silence.

I was enjoying the sounds of the forest, the birds flitting through the trees. Some little rodents with strips on their back would chirp and chatter at us as we passed under their trees. Deer stopped and watched us as we passed by.

The day went on as the shadows grew longer and longer until we stopped. Sitting by our fire, I was in awe at the trees of the area between the mountains. After our meal and prayers, I laid out my bedroll, getting ready to sleep.

"You know I was married once." Josephus started as he stared into the fire.

"No, I never knew that," I said, turning around to look at him.

"Yes, I married young; she was the love of my life. I was given to a unit of the imperial roman army. This unit was wholly comprised of bastards. Men who were the sons of generals who had slept with native women. These generals could not claim their offspring, so we went into this special unit." I lay on my back, silent as Josephus told of his past.

"The whole of my life, I was treated like an animal, so that's what I became. After my training, I was sent to the edges of the empire and told to fight and kill for the glory of Rome. I did; I killed all those who stood in my path. Then after one hard-won battle, I stood among the bodies of the men I had killed. Standing among the carnage, covered in the blood of others, I saw her at the edge of the forest. She watched me as I started towards her, but she never ran. I was shocked by her beauty, awed by her courage as she stood watching me walk up to her. She asked me if I was proud of what I had done in the battle. I told her the truth; I told her it's what I do because it is what I am," I watched Josephus as he took a drink of water, hoping he wouldn't stop.

"She shook her head, turned, and walked away. I don't know why, but when she turned away, I followed her. I found out she was the house girl to a general's wife. So I had myself attached to his protection guard, and for the next year, I courted my wife. Then with the general's permission, we were married and moved into our own house on the general's estate," Josephus said. I watched my friend and brother recount a part of his past, then it seemed too much for him. At this point in his retelling, Josephus just rolled onto his bedding, turned his back to me, and went to sleep.

The next morning I woke to Josephus looking at me while eating some meat. He nodded and pointed to a trail of smoke rising into the morning sky.

"That is a small fire, like a campfire." He stated, pointing to the smoke.

"Well, shall we see if they need any help?" I asked him as I stood and started to pack my things.

"Yes, let us see if they require anything." For some reason, the way Josephus spoke, I could tell his mood was still dark from the night before. After we ate and packed our things, we ensured our fire was cold. Taking one last look around, we started towards the thin trail of smoke.

Stopping just inside the treeline of a small clearing, Josephus and I watched as two men sat at the fire. There were two large wagons, each covered by heavy cloth. I was about to say everything looked fine when a young woman's scream floated to our ears on the breeze.

Without speaking, I moved out of the tree line so the men could see me. I didn't wait for Josephus; I just moved out into the light of the morning. I could hear my brother moving beside me, the leather of his saddle creaking. The two men saw us and stood up. One turned and called a name, and a third man crawled out of one of the wagons. As he threw the flap open to get out, I saw frightened faces holding onto each other.

I knew Josephus had seen the faces as he kicked his horse into a gallop. The three men stood at the fire and watched as we came closer.

"What do you want here?" The one who had climbed out of the wagon asked.

"We heard a scream as we were going by, we thought someone might need help," I answered, looking at the man.

"No, no one needs your help; now, leave our camp." He ordered us. I smiled when the man tried to act with authority over us.

"Well, we heard a scream. We are duty bound to help any who need it." I told the man as Josephus slowly walked his horse around the camp. I watched the three standing in front of me. The youngest looked nervous. His eyes would dart from me to Josephus, then to the sword, he left leaning against one of the wagons.

"So if everything is as you say, there shouldn't have any issues with bringing everyone out of the wagons so we can see for ourselves, then we'll be on our way," I told the man as he turned to look back at the wagons.

"No, and you will leave now, or things will get bad for you, now leave." He ordered again while he was trying to watch Josephus and me simultaneously.

"That will not be happening, you grubby little worm," Josephus said as he cut one of the covers on a wagon revealing eight girls tied in the back.

"You peddle in the flesh of the young, so you see there are people here who do need help," I said as the young started to move.

"Son, if you lay hands on that blade, you will die here in this meadow," I warned him as the older man who was the leader started to sweat.

"We are just taking these unwanted girls to the markets in Espagne. We don't grab them; we are paid to transport them. We are only doing what we are paid for." The leader said.

"Do you get paid to rape them, pig!" Josephus asked as he cut open the second wagon.

"It is, as I said, no one cares for these girls, so if we do manly things, it's not so bad." The sweating leader said, trying to smile through his black rotting teeth.

I watched as Josephus got off his horse and then started to help the girls out of the wagon. The second oldest man, who had been quiet to this point, turned and began to walk towards him.

"I would stay here with us if I were you," I called to him as a warning to Josephus one of the men was coming.

"Those are not your concern; get away from them!" He shouted at Josephus, who turned and faced the man.

"You would be better off going and talking to my brother. If you come closer, I will be forced to kill you," When Josephus spoke, I could tell he was done with talking, so I got off my horse. As I touched the ground, the youngest of the three again looked at his sword against the nearest wagon.

"Son, I will kill you if you go for that blade. I will not hesitate." I warned him, and the oldest reached out and tried to stop him. As he touched the arm of the young man, he took off running for his sword. The oldest pulled a belt knife and tried to charge me, aiming low for my gut.

I didn't have time to pull my sword, so I grabbed the man's arm and turned my hips into him. This flipped the man onto his back, and when he hit the ground, I kicked him in the back of the head, dropping him into unconsciousness.

I turned, knowing the youngest was coming at me with his sword. I knew I had told the young man I would kill him. Then I realized killing this boy would be cruel. So as his very unskilled attack came to me, I pulled my sword. I stepped aside and slapped him in the back of the head with the flat side of my blade. I watched as he plowed face-first into the dirt beside the campfire.

When I turned around, I watched as my brother and the other man squared off. It was over in seconds as the man threw a punch intended to knock Josephus out. The punch never landed. Josephus grabbed the man's arm and twisted; I heard the bone in the arm break. He then grabbed the man by the head and twisted hard. The neck was the second thing to break on the slaver.

Looking around the camp, I was dismayed at the sight greeting me as I looked into the wagon closest to me. It was full of girls, I mean girls. Not one of them was over the age of twelve. All going to a slave market, where they would be sold to only god knew what kind of monsters.

"Who speaks for you?" Josephus asked as he helped the young women out of the wagon he had walked over to.

"I do." The oldest woman said as she climbed out of the wagon.

"These girls, do they have homes to go back to?" He asked her.

"Most do; we can get them back home. There are two; the youngest, the bastards raped and killed their mother two days ago when she refused to willingly sell them her girls."

I stood shocked; I couldn't believe what I was hearing.

"These men tried to buy her daughters, and when she refused to sell them, they raped and killed her?" I asked to be sure I understood her.

"Yes, it's the two little ones; they were excited, saying they would fetch the best price at the market." As the oldest of the young women finished speaking. I turned and walked over to the young man I had knocked out and, grabbed him by the hair, then dragged him over to the red-headed woman.

"This one also?" Holding him so she could see his face.

"In some ways, he is the worst; those two pigs would come in and paw at us, but they would never rape us, saying it devalued our price. This thing was more interested in the little ones. His father would have to be around him all the time."

I looked down at my gloved hand as it was twisted in the greasy black hair of the young man. A feeling of disgust crawled through me, I dropped the thing on his face again. I looked at Josephus as I used my boot to roll the molester onto his back. I was standing looking down at the young man trying to think of the best way to deal with him. Then Josephus walked over, placed his boot on the throat, and stepped down, crushing the airway.

It was then the women took turns spitting on the corps of the youngest salver.

"These two were pigs; the young one was a real monster." The redhead explained.

"Now, about the girls, they need to get home to their families. You say you'll be able to do this." Josephus said as he turned and looked at the group standing by the fire, holding each other.

"Yes, all except for the two little ones. They have no one to care for them. I'm afraid they will become victims on the streets." She said as the two youngest came to her.

"Can you not take them?" I asked her.

"No, I have to get home to my family and my children." As she said she had her own family, the look of shock on my face made her laugh.

"I'm in my thirties." She stated, then laughed at Josephus, and I gawked at her.

"Us Benoit women age gracefully." She added.

"A bit more than gracefully, I'd say," Josephus stated as I knelt down so I could look at the two little girls. They tried to hide behind the pleated skirt of Mrs. Benoit. I smiled at the two sets of blue eyes as they peeked out from behind the dress.

"What about the farmer and his wife?" I asked Josephus.

"I was just thinking about them, they have no children, and we know how kind they are. Surely they would love and cherish these little ones." Josephus said as he crouched down for the girls to see him better.

"This farm, is it far. I would like to meet the man and his wife; I need to know the girls will be safe." The Benoit woman said as she touched the girls.

"It's not far. I'll go and tell the farmer and his wife about the girls, and Josephus will bring you all there." I offered. Josephus nodded, and the girls started to gather back at the wagons. Gathering the reins of my horse, I looked at Josephus.

"Be safe, brother. I will see you soon."

"You as well, ride safe, keep god in your heart." He returned. The Benoit woman looked at us and then at our armor and weapons.

"I assumed you two were knights." She said. I laughed as I turned my horse and started out as a fast gallop shouting to Josephus.

"You explain it to her brother," Then I was gone heading back to the farm.

I caught myself hoping the wife of the farmer had baked another apple pie. I knew my horse liked to run; however, I was surprised to find out how much he wanted to stretch out the miles. It took the rest of the day to reach the farm. The sun was setting on the day we found the girls. For them, it was the end of the nightmare. A nightmare that would have carried on until their lives ended in the future.

The farmer was coming out of the barn when I thundered into his yard. I reigned my horse to a stop. Then tried to ease him as he pranced around, agitated. Climbing down from the saddle, the farmer walked over, took the reigns, and spoke softly to my horse to calm him.

"I do apologize for coming back like this; I need to discuss something of great importance with you and your wife," I told the farmer. He nodded as he tied my horse to a ring set in the fence, then led the way to the house. Like the first time, the smell of freshly baked bread and supper cooking greeted me at the door. Once the loving couple were seated at their table, they looked at me. I was still in my full armor and carrying my weapons.

"I do apologize for coming back like this," I said as I held out my arms.

"I would not have come back if I knew what else to do," I said, looking at them.

"Under this roof, you are always welcome, brother." The farmer said as his wife nodded.

"It is not for my brother or me that I return for. I can not tell you everything, for there are things not needed to be said under this roof." I said as I looked around the home of friends.

"Josephus and I came upon some slavers. They will not be slaving any longer. We have freed their victims, all girls, and most are old enough to go home and live happily. Saved for two, there are these two little ones. Their mother was killed by the slavers so they could get the girls. They have no one in this world. They are so young it breaks a heart to think of them alone out in the world." I watched as the farmer and his wife clung to each other.

"So Josephus and I thought of you. We were hoping you would take the girls in." As I told the farmer and his wife about the girls. His wife spoke, and for the first time, I could see the mother in her.

"You go tell brother Josephus to bring those babies to me." Standing before me, I realized how small a lady she was. At that moment, I wouldn't have tried to argue with her.

"He is on his way with all the girls, two wagons full. The woman who spoke for them wanted to meet you before she would leave the girls." I said.

"How long before they get here?" The farmer asked.

"Maybe in the morning," I said as his wife started serving their meal; seeing this, I turned to leave.

"Where is it you think you are going, brother?" His wife asked me.

"I was going to wait outside while you have your meal," I told her.

"Go take that armor off and wash up; you will sit at this table and eat with us." She said. I looked at her husband, who was smiling then he nodded his head. Once we had finished our meal, she turned to me, smiling.

"I told my husband having you and your brother come to us was a sign of good fortune. Now I want you to go to your brother and bring those girls here, so we can get them back to their families." The farmer stood beside his wife and put his arm around her. I walked out of the house to the sight of my horse eating hay with the two dairy cows the farm had. I smiled at the peaceful scene as I strapped on my armor and picked up my weapons.

I was turning back to take another look at the house of the farmer and his wife when I caught movement. A man came around the corner of the house on a horse. He kicked his mount into a run as he spotted me. I knew he had to be another slaver; I turned as his horse rushed at me. As he raced past, I reached up and grabbed his reigns and a hand full of his hair. This dragged the horse and the slaver to the ground. He came off the ground swearing as he pulled his sword free.

"You killed my family to free what is mine." The slaver hissed in the farmer's yard.

"When I kill you, I am going to kill him and burn this place to the ground.

"I pray god has mercy on your soul, for you are about to be judged," I answered as I slid my sword free.

He slowly circled me and then attacked. As we came together, our swords rang with the force of his attack. My movement shocked him. I reached up, took hold of his head, then slammed my forehead into his nose, crushing it. Blood flowed from his ruined nose as tears flooded his eyes.

Blinded, the slaver swung his sword wildly, fearing an attack, while he wiped at his eyes. Watching his wild swings, I timed my movement. Then for a split second, he left himself open, and I stepped inside one of his swings. The pommel of my sword slammed into the slaver's shoulder, breaking the bone, then I spun around the slaver. With one final thrust, my sword entered the body of the slaver. I felt my sword quiver as his heart clenched on it with its last beat.

Looking at the farmer and his wife, I could see the fear in their eyes. Then I looked at my armor, at the blood dripping from it.

"I am so sorry for this coming to your home. I will leave and never return." I said, grief gripping me for what had found its way to a peaceful, loving home.

"You will come here, brother, and wash that filthy man's blood off. When you're ready, go get your brother and the girls.

"I will take that thing and bury it out past our fields." The farmer said as his wife led me to the wash basins. Moments later, I was leaving the yard and heading back to find Josephus.

The sun was down and the moon high in the night sky when I came upon the wagons rattling their way through the forest. Josephus held the reigns of the lead wagon, his horse tied to the back, being fed hand fulls of green grass by a pair of young girls. Mrs. Benoit was driving the second wagon, the two little ones sitting beside her.

Josephus nodded his greeting as I turned, so I rode beside him. The first thing I did was to tell my brother of the last slaver. I explained how the bastard had watched us from the trees, then followed me to the farmer's home. Josephus looked me over and nodded.

"You did the right thing. Killing men like that is a kindness for the rest of the world." Josephus said as he smiled.

"I spoke to the farmer and his wife. They are excited to have the girls. They want all of them to come to the house to get cleaned up and have a good meal before they start back to their families." I reported, then, as if forgetting about the slavers. Josephus changed the subject of our conversation to food.

"I knew they would jump at the chance to have a family, so what was for dinner. I know you ate dinner. She wouldn't let you leave without feeding you first, so what was it?" He insisted.

"I shouldn't tell you, however, because you asked it was roasted pheasant she raises with vegetables," I told him.

"Um, huh, any bread or pie?" Josephus asked with a rye smile.

"Yes, however, I refrained, it took all my willpower, but I managed," I told him with a smile, knowing if he had been with me, I would have eaten a whole pie myself.

"Well I'm proud of you, if it had been me there I would have eaten the bread and a pie." Josephus laughed as he told me he wouldn't have refrained.

I took over for Mrs. Benoit as we rattled through the night; the two small girls laid down and slept next to her. I would look back to see if all was well every so often, only to find one of the little ones awake looking up at me. I would wink and smile at them, and to my delight, one of the girls tried to wink back.

Before I knew it, one of the little girls was sitting beside me. I looked at her and then patted her little blond head. I had never been around a little girl before, and I didn't know what to do. I could see her shivering in the night air, so I took my cloak off and wrapped it around her. A few minutes later, her sister joined her under the cloak. A while later, I could feel their weight on me as they fell asleep.

The sun was brightening the eastern sky when Josephus and I drove the wagons out of the forest. This was the first time the girls, who were bound for a life of god knows what saw their new home. The farmer and his wife were standing in the middle of the yard, the two dairy cows in the corral beside the barn. Chickens, geese, ducks, and pheasants were all pecking at the ground.

They came to us as we brought the wagons to a stop in the yard. The two little ones beside me watched as the farmer and his wife walked over to the wagon.

"You made it. Have you pushed through all night?" He asked as we shook hands.

"Yes, we want to get these girls here so they can get cleaned up," I said as Josephus walked over and greeted the farmer and his wife.

"Most of them want to get cleaned up and get home to their families. Some are from towns around here." He told the couple.

"Well, if that is the case, we could get word to their families. They could come here and get them rather than all these poor things traipsing all over the land." He told us. Mrs. Benoit walked over to us and smiled, knowing how she must have looked.

"The girls need a good home. They have no one in this world." She stated as a tear rolled down her cheek.

"They do now, dear; they will have a home and all the love we can give them." The farmer said as his wife hugged her and then took her into the house so she could wash.

"I'll get word to a family down the valley to send their boys here. We will get all the girls' names and then send the boys to find their families." The farmer said.

Josephus and I looked at each other and nodded; this was the best idea they had so far. It was better than going from town to town, returning the girls one at a time. When we explained the plan for getting all the girls back to their families. Mrs. Benoit and the farmer's wife agreed it was for the best.

That night, after all the girls had been fed and a place set aside for them to sleep, Josephus and I went out to the field to do our evening prayers. As we knelt down, I heard the sound of tiny feet in the grass. I looked at my brother and found him smiling. Looking over our shoulders, we found the two small sisters watching us. I nodded to them to show it was ok to come over.

They knelt with us in the dirt and copied us as we prayed for forgiveness for the killing of the slavers, along with other sins we may have committed during the day. We also prayed for the families of the girls who were at this moment thinking their family was probably out of reach. Then we looked at the two little blond heads knelt down between us and prayed they would be happy for the rest of their lives.

When we finished, the two girls jumped up and ran back to the house. When we stood up, I looked at Josephus and put my hand on his shoulder, smiling.

"This day I think Joseph would be proud of us," I said as we turned and found the others watching us.

"Of that, I have no doubt, little brother," He said as we started back towards the house. As we walked back into the yard, still smiling, the farmer walked out to meet us.

"Brothers, we have set aside a place for you in the house." He said to us as Josephus, and I reached our horses and started to remove our bed rolls.

"God has given us our bed," Josephus said as he tapped the ground under one of the wagons.

"Along with the greatest blanket to ever be woven." He finished as he pointed to the stares. The farmer looked up into the night sky and nodded.

"I couldn't agree with you more; some nights when worry has me, and sleep eludes me. I come out here and look up. The stars seem to lift strife off me," The farmer told us as I stood beside him, looking into the heavens.

"Sir, do you ever just feel like talking to someone when you are out here looking up to the stars?" I asked him.

"Every time I come out here." The farmer answered.

"Well, when you do, you are speaking to god. If you ask him for advice, you will get it. You will not hear it with your ears. However, you will find you have the answer." Josephus told him. The farmer nodded, then turned and walked back to the house.

That night I could not sleep as the hours passed. The tiny creatures of the night found me wandering around the farm. I was walking by the house for the third time when I heard a sound I knew. It was the sound of someone trying to sneak up on me. The person doing the sneaking was good at it, what gave him away was mother nature.

As the person moves through the crops behind the house, the night creatures would go quiet, trying to hide their presents. Knowing there was at least one hiding in the tall stalks of corn. I walked on, trying to act like he was not there. As I walked past the west corner of the house, I caught movement out of the corner of my eye. Whoever was hiding in the corn had exposed himself. As I passed the corner of the house, I broke out into a fast run, trying to get to the other side before he could.

As I ran past where Josephus was sleeping, the sound of my pounding feet woke him. I never saw my brother wake up; however, I knew he was on his feet, armed and ready for anything.

One of the older girls was at the well getting a drink of water. When she saw me running fast, fear grabbed her, and I knew she had run back to the house. Running past the corner, I caught sight of the person as he headed toward the barn.

The stranger heard me as I ran towards him. I watched him turn and start pulling at his waist. Whatever he was trying to get out of his belt had gotten caught up, and he couldn't get it free. I watched as the young man held up his two fists. I slowed down and then walked up to him.

"Young man, if you do not put your hands down, I will hit you on the nose," I told him.

"You bastard, return my mother, or I will give you a beating." He hissed back. It was then his red hair caught my attention.

"Boy, are you a Benoit?" I asked him. He lowered his hands for a second.

"I am, and I will not be leaving without my mother. Now you make up your mind how bad a beating you want?" He asked again. I knew from the way he was standing he had no training, and it wouldn't be a fair fight, though I did admire his courage.

Josephus stepped out of the night to my side; the young man's face paled at his size of him.

"What have you found, little brother?" He asked as he eyed the young man over.

"Well, it seems this is a young Benoit. He's offered me a beating or give his mother back." I told him just then, we heard the door of the house open and the rustling of skirts as Mrs. Benoit ran across the yard.

"No, no, please don't hurt him." She cried as she ran to protect her son.

"I wasn't going to hurt him," I answered.

"He said he was going to beat me up, or I could turn you over," I told her as she ran her hands over him checking to see if I had hit him. She turned and looked at me to see if I was being serious, then back at her son.

"You told these two you would beat them up?" Mrs. Benoit asked her son.

"Well, only him. I was sleeping when all this happened; in truth, he could use a good beating." Josephus said and winked at the young Benoit. Who was now trying to get his mother behind him so he could place himself between any danger and her.

"These two are monks. They are trained warriors; they dispatched the men who took me and the others with no effort." She told him as he tried to step in front of her. I smiled at him again, then stepped back.

"Come over to the fire, son." I offered as his mother took his hand and nodded. I could see him relax a bit. He nodded and walked with her to our fire.

"Are you hungry?" She asked him. He looked at the ground, then at his mother then smiled.

"Look at you. I come to rescue you, and you are worried if I've eaten." He said as he kissed the top of her head.

"Your brothers, are they safe?" she asked.

"Yes, they are close by but safe." He said as she stopped.

"You brought them here?" She questioned.

"I'll go get them." He said as he looked at his mother.

"Are they close by?" Josephus asked as he added more wood to the fire.

"They are not too far." He said again as I moved my armor and sword. I looked up and watched a young boy duck his head down behind a stack of hay.

"Your little brothers wouldn't have hair like us?" I asked as I pointed to my own short red hair.

"All my boys have red hair. It gives them their fire and a willingness not to listen to their mother; why do you ask." She turned and looked at me.

"Well, they don't listen to their older brother either; one is behind the hay stacks," I told her, then watched as Mrs. Benoit and her oldest son ran out to the stacks.

Watching a mother run to her sons, scooping them into her arms, hurt my heart. I will be forever ashamed to say I felt envy at how the boys in the field had a mother to run to them. To reach for them, to love them. Before we knew it, the farmer and his wife, along with the two little ones, came out of the house; behind them came a trail of girls.

I looked over my shoulder at my brother Josephus. There was the pain of heartbreak on his face again. Though he smiled, I could see it. I'm sure he could see my pain for my lost mother. Though I was just four years old when she was murdered, I still missed her love.

I lifted my sword and armor into the back of a wagon as Mrs. Benoit returned holding her boys. She introduced them to us, and the oldest boy, now smiling, apologized to me for threatening to beat me up. I smiled at him and offered him a seat by the fire with Josephus and myself.

"The way you carry your knife, while it's good for keeping it out of sight. It will get caught when you need it." Josephus said as he handed the lad some bread.

"It did when I was trying to get it out when he caught me by the barn." He told Josephus.

"I'm sure glad it did get caught," I said as I ate.

"Me too. To tell you the truth, I've never been in a fight before." He told us as he looked at the dirt between his feet.

"That is the best way to have it; we try to avoid a fight whenever possible. Though many times men never give others a chance to live a peaceful life." I said to young Benoit as Josephus nodded in agreement. It started in the morning, and families started getting word their daughters were safe. They were at the farm waiting for them to come and get them.

Mothers and fathers started rushing to the farm as soon as that afternoon. Josephus and I had packed our things and were on our mounts when the farmer and his wife came out of the house. We said our goodbyes, then rode out of their lives and back to the all-consuming quest in ours.

Chapter 10

THE RIDE THROUGH THE forests of the midi-Pyrenees was one I longed to do again. The beauty and the splendor of the forests between those peaks. We had to find our brothers, to bring the treasure to them. So through the mountains, we rode, the trees of the valleys hiding our passing. Until the day we came to a pass in the mountains leading into a valley.

Sitting on our horses, Josephus and I looked out over the valley. Without saying a word, I started my horse down a faint trail. The faint trail we followed had been left by whatever wildlife calls this high alpine valley home. That night as we set up camp, I looked over at my brother.

"How long are you willing to look for the others?" I asked Josephus as he rolled out his bedding.

"For as long as it takes to find them, to get the things we have found to their safety," He answered.

"It could take years for that to happen." I reminded him.

"We are young and have many years ahead of us yet," Josephus answered.

I was trying to get him to admit our quest could take the rest of his life. No matter how subtle I tried to be, Josephus wouldn't take the bait. So I decided the best approach would be straightforward.

"We have found the vials with the blood of Christ in them. It may come a time when you have to take his blood." When I told

Josephus he may need to be purified by the blood of Christ, he turned with tears in his eyes.

"No, that can never happen; I can never be purified. Not until I kneel at his feet. Joseph knew what I am and what was done before me. He knew about a curse placed upon me. You don't ever have to worry about my leaving you. I will live as long as you do. I will reunite Mary with her son and keep them safe," Josephus told me.

"I don't understand. I can see this is hard for you; we will not talk about it now. You can tell me about it when you feel you are ready," I told Josephus. He nodded, then went back to setting up our camp.

I lay on my back, watching as the stars came out one by one; their brightness took my breath away. The following day we studied the map I copied from the cave wall. It showed a trail in these mountains. This trail led to another cave where we would be given another clue.

I was hoping it would be another map; I wasn't going to get my hopes up. The days came for my brother, and I then fell behind. The mountains gave way to the rich fertile valleys guarding the foothills. Josephus refrained from talking about what had happened to him; I knew he would speak of his past someday. I was content to wait until that day. We did talk about Joseph and the good times he and I had together. I told Josephus about the first time I had called him father. Of how he got down on one knee and wrapped his arms around me.

We followed the map copied from the wall of the first set of caves, and it led us out of the mountains. We walked our horses down a trail into a valley ringed by a verdant forest. The smell of the trees kept me enchanted; everything smelled so clean and inviting. I was surprised to see how tall the grasses grew in these valleys. Looking around, I watched as a stag, and then a deer lifted their heads.

They watched us as we passed by, then went back to eating; they didn't fear us. It was as if they had never seen man and horse before. Looking at the map, I pointed to the valley we were now in.

It showed a small river running through it. Josephus and I rode on until we came to a dried river bed; I sat struck by sudden worry.

"A rock slide higher in the mountains must have blocked the source of the river," Josephus said as he turned and started to follow the river bed. As the light of the day was beginning to fade, we came to the dam; it was a slide. The river backed up behind the natural dam creating a large pool. Then as water always does when a path is blocked, it will inevitably find a way around the obstruction. The water now ran in a new direction, needing to find its way to the ocean unrelenting.

Before I knew what was going on, Josephus had dismounted and had started to splash water over himself. We stayed at the pool for the rest of the night. Rolling over in my bedding, I found a large stag looking at me from the other side of the pool.

"He's been watching you for a while now. He can tell there is something different about you." Josephus said, watching the stag.

"Do you think they can tell I went through the cleansing?" I asked, hoping the stage would stay until I could draw him.

"I think so; I'm not sure. However, I have never seen one act as this." Josephus answered.

I was surprised as the wild stag stood almost posing for me as I drew him. Josephus stood and slowly walked over to me, then sat and watched as I put my charcoal to the back of a scroll. When I was done sketching the stag, I looked at him and thanked the wild creature. We watched as it turned and leaped into the forest.

Josephus reached out and put his hand on my shoulder, then he went back to his bedding. He sat watching the stars come out for the night. I could tell he wanted to speak of something. Whatever it was, Josephus had kept it to himself for so long that it seemed to be part of him now.

"There are bad things I have done in this life, some worst than others. I have killed many men, and I can say most have been in wars. Some are in defense of the weak and young such as the girls. However, there is one man whose death was not at my hands. There is one death where the punishment was thrust upon me as a child, a death I can never repay. A death I can never be forgiven for though I never held the weapon." Josephus said. I sat and watched the stars as my brother spoke of his past. Then he stopped and laid down, silence falling over us like a blanket.

The following day I turned and looked at the small lake the river now flowed out of.

"Do you think the brothers would have followed the river as it was, or do you think it was here when they had passed by?" I asked Josephus.

"I think they would have followed the river. As for your second question. What if they caused the slide to change the direction of the river intentionally, to hide something." When Josephus had answered, I stood and looked around the area. Walking to the other side of the lake, I looked back to where Josephus and I had camped the night before.

From where I stood, I could see a large boulder at the bottom of the lake. Looking at the boulder, I wondered if it was holding our next clue or if it was just a victim of the rock slide. I walked into the cold lake, its waters fed by the mountains.

As the water reached my shoulders, I looked at my brother, concern on his face. Then smiled at him and dove under the surface; the boulder blurred as my eyes went under the surface. As I swam to the front of the boulder, I could see marks on its face.

I traced the markings on the face of the boulder with my fingers. Swimming to the surface, I looked at Josephus and smiled, then pointed to the boulder I was now standing on.

"There are markings on the face of the boulder," I announced. Josephus looked at me, confused, then he smiled.

"Well, how are we going to bring those markings back to the light of day?" He asked as we looked around the lake. I looked down at the boulder and then at the water of the small lake. It was then I knew the first brothers to come here caused the rock slide creating the lake.

"We are going to have to drain the lake," I said as I looked at the water again.

"You don't say how many buckets you think we will need, brother?" Josephus asked sarcastically, hands on his hips. I don't think he wanted an answer. I pointed to part of the rock slide; it was the only portion of the pile of rocks that did not look entirely natural.

"I think our brothers built this part of the slide to cover the map on the boulder," I pointed out to Josephus and watched as he went to where I pointed. I dove off the boulder back into the cold water of the lake. I swam to the point of the slide I had pointed at and stood dripping as Josephus searched for a way to drain the lake.

We puzzled over how to get the map above water for what seemed hours when all of a sudden, Josephus cried out.

"There it is!" I jumped and almost fell back into the lake from the shock of his yelling out.

"There what is?" I asked, trying to see what he was talking about.

"It's that stone; if we remove this stone, it will let the water out. When we are done, we can replace the stone, and the lake will fill back up, hiding the map once again." Josephus said as he pointed to a squared stone. I did not want to dive into the lake's cold water again, so we climbed off the slide. It didn't take too long before we realized the stone had to be removed; it could only come out one way. It had to be pulled out from under the lake.

I climbed back up the slide and dove back into the lake, swimming down to the stone holding the water in. Looking at the stone, I soon discovered a borehole through it. I looked and could see the distorted image of Josephus looking into the water.

"It is a strange thing; there is a hole bored right through the stone," I told my brother.

"Not so strange, our brothers place the stone knowing someday, in the future other brothers would have to see the map. So they made it possible for us to get the stone out, not easy but possible." Josephus said as he looked to the forest.

We worked for the rest of the day before the night started to steal the light. Sitting at our campfire that night, I looked at the only person in the world I knew I could count on to help me no matter what I fell into.

"Where do you think the map will lead us next?" I asked as he looked up at the stars.

"I would not dare to say, little brother; however, where it is, I would wager it's going to be an adventure," Josephus said as he smiled.

The night passed with the stars overhead and the night creatures singing their songs. The sun found us standing on the rocks used to keep the lake's water from escaping. I stood holding a shaft of wood Josephus had made from my description of the borehole.

"If it looks like it will fit, pound it in place with another rock. I'll have the rope ready for you. Then we'll use the horses to pull the stone out." Josephus said.

It was midday before the rope was attached to a horse. I stood at the edge of the lake to watch and see if the stone was moving. Josephus urged his mount to pull, and I watched as the horse leaned into the rope harness. It didn't take much for the stone to slip out of its home. My brother and I watched as the lake thundered out of the hole left behind. I waved to Josephus came over and stood with me to watch as the boulder was exposed to the sun.

Slowly the map to our next destination came into view as the water ran out of the lake, filling the riverbed once again. The water of what was the lake again winded its way to the ocean.

We soon discovered the problem with hiding a map at the bottom of the lake our brothers had created. When Josephus and I started to walk out to the boulder, the mud tried to pull our boots off our feet. So we turned back to shore and removed our boots and leggings. Again we walked out into the muck left behind by the water.

This time we made it to the map, and with reverence, both of us reached out and touched what was created by a brother so long ago. Josephus watched as I pulled out a parchment and a piece of charcoal. I lost all track of time as I started to copy the map as it dried in the afternoon sun. The stars had started showing when I finished the last detail of the map.

"This map shows a route through the mountains, then along a coast. This coast runs north. It shows towns, large and small, marked on the map with a cross. The thing I don't understand is how the brothers made this map. How did they know what they would find? The men who drew these maps, well, they had never been here before; how could they know where they were going?" I asked as I studied the map I had drawn.

"Who says they were not from the area, like so many before. You are working under the assumption these men were from the holy land. When the truth is, these brothers are from the Magdalene family, when Pilot and Joseph started the brotherhood centuries ago." Josephus reminded me as we sat by our fire.

"So the men we follow are from this land; they had a better working knowledge of it," Josephus told me. Again I was astounded to hear another secret from the history of our order.

"In the morning, go over the map rock one more time, then we will put the rock back so the water will again fill the lake. We will have to stay here until the boulder is covered, keeping the map a secret again." Josephus said as we started to eat.

I looked up to the stars and nodded, then gave a silent thank you to my father, Joseph, for this life he saved. The next morning found me standing in the muck of the lake. I was going over the boulder again, trying to see if I had missed anything the day before. Once we were both satisfied, the recreation of the map was perfect on the scrolls. Josephus and I set to work replacing the stone.

The lake filled faster than either one of us thought. Once the stone was replaced, the waters dammed up again. Josephus and I sat on the shore with our fire, listening to the waters complain through the night. The lake was filled, the boulder with the map once again hidden from the eyes of man as the sun climbed over the mountains.

Stopping at the edge of the forest, my brother and I stopped and looked back at the lake. My breath caught when the stag that let me draw him stood at the water's edge, watching us. I gave a silent goodbye to the stag and then moved into the shadows of the trees.

The forest gave way to the rocky foothills of the mountains. I looked back at the verdant forest we climbed through. Then I looked at the mountain range standing in our path. Smiling, I found myself hoping there were other clues left long before I came into this world.

Chapter 11

ON OUR FIRST NIGHT, we set camp in a small valley between what Josephus called glaciers. He told me they were giant ice sheets made of fresh water. During the long hours of the night, a loud popping sound woke me. Laying still, I strained to hear what could have made the sound.

"It's the ice shifting. A piece could have broken off." Josephus said as he looked over our fire at me, then went back to sleep. I lay awake for a while, listening to the sounds of the mountains while looking up into the blanket of stars. The moon and stars made the night incredibly bright. I could've walked through those mountains without a torch. Again the thought of my mother came to me, and for the first time, I smiled at the thought of her.

In the morning, I came flying out of my slumber, much to the amusement of Josephus. Josephus had decided to see if he could toss small pebbles into my ear while I slept.

"You do really hate to see others sleeping," I stated as I stood shaking the pebbles out of my hair and smiling. I knew my brother meant no harm with his little jokes. It was his way of saying he wanted me around with him. I laughed when I wondered what trick he would play if he didn't want me near?

"The day has started, we don't have time to waste, and we have to cross that," Josephus said as he pointed to the glacier. After we ate and finished our prayers, we walked our horses out onto the ice. I was surprised to find snow on top of the ice, and we had some traction for the horses. Still, we wouldn't ride them; it would have been too dangerous for them and us, so we walked.

Looking around, I could hardly believe where we were. I, a bastard who started life being hunted with his mother by a rich man. Like so many others in a position of wealth and power in those days. This rich man thought he had the right to rape girls. If one of the poor girls he forced himself on became pregnant? This rich man would send his assassins to kill the girl and the child before she could give birth.

My mother was a young mother with a baby, and we were found by a kind older man who took us in. A kind man who then raised me when my mother was murdered. I am a bastard, one born with no father; I am now a brother. To my amazement, this bastard was with another, and we walked over a glacier in the Pyrenees mountains. We are two brothers looking for clues left behind centuries before. Strange are the paths life travels down.

The glacier gave way to the rocks of the mountains, and our days were spent in rugged beauty. Our nights were spent discussing the next day and studying the map from the boulder under the lake. Josephus and I knew we would have to find a lake high on a mountain ahead of us. As we led our horses through the mountains, we often stopped to look for landmarks.

As we found the landmarks shown on the map, we would try and go to them just in case something was left behind. Some we could get to, while others were out of reach; however, they were there. As we found each one, hope and excitement built.

I lost track of the days again as our quest followed its own time. I laughed at Josephus one day when he told me we should keep track of the days by when I needed to shave.

"That's a good idea, brother. God blessed me with brains, not facial hair." I returned with a wink and laughed, our laughter echoing off four peaks surrounding us. As we looked at the four peaks,

Josephus climbed off his horse and turned in a circle. Knowing what he was looking at, I climbed down with the map.

"I know there is something on the map about the four peaks," Josephus said as he looked at them; he watched me unroll the scrolls.

"There is. It shows a cave and talks about the brother who was placed there. Why would a brother stay behind?" I asked more of myself than of Josephus.

"Why indeed," Josephus answered as he placed his finger on the map and then pointed to a peak.

"That's the peak." He said as I turned and nodded. We never said a word. We just gathered our reigns and started to hike up the mountain towards the peak. Our horses seemed to be breathing harder as we climbed then I realized so were Josephus and I.

"The air gets thin up here; the horses will become used to it. We have to go slow for them and us." Josephus said as we rounded another outcrop the mountain had placed in our path. The sun had fallen behind the mountains when we reached the peak, and we found the cave on the map.

Our horses were happy to be stopped and in the cave. It didn't take too long to get a fire going. We welcomed the heat of the small fire as the winds were never-ending high up on the mountain, though not a breeze could be felt inside the cave. The discussion of the evening was what we would find further in the recesses of the cave. I wanted to go exploring as soon as we had finished our meal.

For the first time on our quest, I woke before Josephus. I sat looking at the man who I called brother as he slept. I wished I could take the pain haunting him away. There were times while I was with him I could see his anguish as it lay on him. It was an anguish that would have crippled another man. Eventually, he told me about his life before he met Joseph. I knew how true heartbreak looked. This is part of the story I will save for later.

The following day I was up first gathering food for our morning meal. I know Josephus was as excited to explore the cave as I was. So we ate a light meal, fed the horse, and started deeper into the cave with torches. It didn't take long before Josephus, and I knew we had found the right cave. A small cross marked the wall above a painting. This one painting showed a trail in the mountains.

"That trail is on the map from the boulder; however, something is different on this map," I said as we stood studying the painting.

"I'll go and get the map Josephus said as he turned to walk back out to our camp. In mere moments he returned with the map. Unrolling our map, we found the difference right away. The difference was a small building on another mountain. To Josephus and me, the building on the map looked to be built at the very edge of a cliff. A tiny cross sat over the building, and what looked to be a man lay in front of the door.

Without a word, I took out a piece of charcoal and copied what we found on the back side of the map. Then we moved deeper into the cave again; Josephus and I only went a little way when we saw another painting. This one showed a group of brothers, each standing with their heads lowered. Behind the brothers stood another. This lone brother was adorned with jewels and gold; his head held a crown. As I stood looking at the painting, I was about to ask Josephus what he thought it meant when he spoke.

"They know one of their brothers betrayed them. The traitor did this for land or a title, for the wealth bestowed with either." Josephus told said as we looked over the painting. Standing beside my brother, a brother I could never think of betraying for any reason.

"How do you think they found out?" I asked, not really caring so long as they knew. I watched as Josephus shook his head, indicating he didn't know or couldn't care how the brothers knew.

"What do you think happened to the brother who betrayed them?" I asked. Trying to memorize the painting so I could draw it later with my charcoal and a nice scroll.

"I think these paintings are a chronicle of their run from the people who would wish harm on the holy family," Josephus answered as we looked deeper into the cave. We found the cave had two tunnels at the back of it. There was a painting where the two tunnels started. On one side, the image showed a group in the mountains. They had pack horses with two women.

A heavenly light shone on the group as they trekked through the mountains. I looked at this painting, trying to see if anything was hidden in it. On the other side of the painting, it showed a lone man sitting in a cave weeping. A group of men stood in a semi-circle in front of the sitting man. The men were brothers of our order, and each of the brothers held a sword. Standing to one side were two women and a small child.

"I think this is about the brother who betrayed the order as well as the holy family," I said as we both leaned in so we could see better in the torchlight.

"Yes, it is; he has been caught, and now the brothers are deciding his fate," Josephus said. We both wondered why whoever the artist was would show the brothers' trial on one side, then the brothers with the holy family riding away.

"Well, which do you think we should go first?" I asked as we each looked down a different tunnel.

"Well, that's a good question; let's go to the right first," Josephus said.

Turning to the right, we started down the tunnel. The first thing to catch our attention was the fact there were no chisel marks on the tunnel walls.

The second thing to cause Josephus and me to stop and wonder was the painting of a man. This lone man stood beside a seated brother who was bound hand and foot.

The bound brother and the other man watched the others ride off over the mountains. The man standing held a sword, the hilt of the sword held a cross on it with the brotherhood's insignia. In the painting, the man had tears running down his face. A heavenly light shone down upon the travelers.

I turned and looked at my brother, the man who would eventually have to leave me. Josephus leaned in closer to the painting, and my brother studied the face of the man holding the sword with the brotherhood's crest on it.

"This is going to sound as if I've lost my senses." Josephus started to say when I finished his thought for him.

"It's Joseph holding the sword; he was in this cave." When I finished, Josephus turned to look at me. We stood staring at the painting for the longest time before we started to move deeper into the tunnel.

"Sometime in the future, I am going to come back to these places. I would like to see if I can get all these paintings off the walls and keep them safe." I told Josephus as we slowly made our way through the tunnel's darkness.

At the end of the first tunnel, we found a door of sorts. It was made of stones. Someone had piled squared stones, effectively blocking the tunnel.

Sometime in the past, Joseph stood where Josephus and I stood. The man I loved as my father had painted on the stones a cross. A man stood at the foot of the cross with his head lowered. I looked closer at the cross, and on it was a name.

"Guiscard seems to be a name; do you think it the name of the brother who betrayed them?" I asked Josephus, who was looking at the stones.

"Yes, it could be. I think I remember that name from something Joseph might have said years ago." Josephus told me. When he had finished looking at the stones, Josephus turned and smiled at me. I watched as he reached out and stuck his finger into a hole, then pulled.

I was amazed again on our trip when the stones opened just like a door. On the back side of the door, Josephus and I looked at the same cross as the painting on the outside. Now instead of standing at the foot of the cross, the man was lying at its base. In this painting, the sun was setting in the background, and a raven looked down on the man from one arm of the cross. Its beak opened, showing the blood-red interior of its maw. On the raven's head was a crown.

We turned and looked into a room hidden by the stone door. Walking around the wall of the room, Josephus and I found a small trench. We found the channel ran around the whole room. When I knelt down, I could smell oil. Smiling, I looked to where Josephus held his torch. I silently hoped the oil would still lite. I laughed when the oil ignited. As flames raced around the room, I watched Josephus jump back from the shock.

"I don't see the humor in trying to set fire to your brother." He said as I chuckled.

"Oh, you didn't see the look on your face, though." I returned.

"Shock and horror was the look." Josephus returned as a smile broke out on his face. His smile fell when we looked around and found a skeleton sitting on a stone throne. The sword he would have carried throughout his life in the brotherhood was jammed into a crack in the throne. The hilt of the sword was under the brother's chin holding his head up so he was effectively looking at the back wall for all eternity.

"Why would they place him facing this part of the room?" I asked, wondering out loud. Josephus and I walked to the wall trying to find something to explain the position the traitor was left in.

Our question was answered when after searching the wall and finding it. What Joseph left the traitor looking at until the second coming was a tiny cross. It was at his eye level and would have been the last thing he would have seen. On the cross was a scarlet sash on one side and a dove on the other.

Turning, I looked at the former brother, and though I tried to, I could not find any words for him. I just shook my head as I looked over what was a man hundreds of years before. He was left with his armor and weapons, and the cloak with the crest of the brotherhood was draped over the back of the throne. The crest was cut in half from top to bottom. As I walked over to it, I saw something else.

"Brother, come and look at this," I called out as I bent over to have a better look.

"It is a Damascus dagger, it would have been his in life, so our brothers used it to carry out his sentence of death," Josephus told me as we looked at the hilt of the dagger sticking out of the back of the former brother's neck.

"This is a very compassionate way to kill someone; whoever did this was very well trained. You see, there is a bump at the base of your skull. Whoever executed this traitor slid the dagger in through the neck at that bump. It kills right away with no pain; not even beheading is faster." Josephus explained to me if they wanted to, they could have chained this person up and left him to starve, or they could have bled him.

"They wanted to be merciful in carrying out their sentence. Even though this brother betrayed the holy family and his brothers. They loved him enough to give him a merciful death." Josephus explained.

I looked at Josephus, wondering how he came to know how to kill this way. I wanted to ask him, then thought about it. There are some things better left untold. Then I lifted the cloak from the back of the throne. This was when things became a little disturbing. As I lifted the cloak, something shifted, and the bones of the traitor rattled. Then the bones started, the most disturbing dance I have ever seen. The ribs turned slightly then his arms fell off, followed by the rest of his bones.

The only part of the former brother not to hit the floor with a rattle was his skull. It was still perched on the pommel of the sword. I stood behind the stone throne, holding the cloak of the traitor in my hands. I was shocked and disturbed when Josephus let go with one of his braying laughs.

"Now that is funny. You should see the look on your face." Josephus laughed as he made a face of shock, then fell back into his braying laughter.

"That is truly disturbing; he fell apart," I stated as I still held the cloak. Looking down at my hands, I realized what I was holding. I dropped the cloak wiping my hands against my leggings.

Josephus went around to the front of the throne and bent down to look into the traitor's skull. Then he looked at the sword; I watched my brother start to reach for the sword and then stop. Standing behind the throne, I watched Josephus, his hand hovering just in front of the hilt of the traitor's sword.

"Little brother, let us be out of this place now," Josephus said as he stood up and ushered me back to the tunnel.

"What is it?" I asked as we walked out of the room holding the traitor.

"The sword is a trigger for something." He stated as we turned and looked at the back of the throne. The back of the skull is still being held on the sword hilt.

Then out of nowhere, Josephus threw a bone at the back of the traitor's skull, who was still wearing the crown. The crown placed on his head by others centuries past was a statement of his punishment. It was what he had betrayed his brothers and the holy family for. Now he could wear it for all eternity.

When the leg bone of the former brother hit the skull, it was knocked forward, taking the sword with it. The reaction of the trap was immediate. The first thing to happen was the stone door to the room with the traitor slammed shut. We stood looking at the door, but we didn't try to open it again. Josephus and I knew it would never move again, not until the end of time.

Then a rumbling sound started in the room. Though we couldn't know for sure, we thought the ceiling was falling into the room, burying everything. My last thought of the traitor was he still had his crown. The land and title he craved came in the end. The land was the rock of the mountain now covering him. The title he earned, in the end, was traitor.

Josephus and I walked back down the tunnel passing the paintings. Both of us seemed to breathe a sigh of relief when we rounded the corner of the tunnel and could see our horses and small camp. Silently we walked to our bedding and sat down. It wasn't until I reached for a water skin a word was spoken.

"You had to throw one of his own legs at the bastard's head?" I asked as a laugh started.

"When I knelt down to look at the sword, I put my hand on it; that's when I saw the trigger for the trap," Josephus explained.

"So you threw it?" I asked, chuckling, as I took a drink of water; Josephus nodded.

"Do you want to go and see what wonders the second tunnel has for us, or shall we save that for tomorrow?" Josephus asked.

"I think we have had enough for today. Those wonders have waited for centuries; I don't think one more day will make a difference." I said lightly, mocking him. That night we sat and talked about the fact we both thought Joseph was in this cave, and if he was, was he the one who executed the traitor?

"Joseph told us he did not know which port the two Marys had sailed to after leaving home. If he did not know, how was it he found this place?" I asked, wondering.

"I think Joseph knew people were after Mary and the children. I think he would have waited until they were gone, then followed his love knowing about the traitor. Joseph would have had to wait to see who the traitor was dealing with to show themselves. Once Joseph knew who they were, then he could act. When Joseph found out this group had followed his family to Gal, he chased the group keeping them near. Joseph knew catching them would put the children in more danger." As Josephus explained how he thought things would have happened. I could see Joseph leaving his home chasing the men who were a threat to his beloved wife and grandchildren.

"When Joseph caught the men who were hunting his family, he would have killed all but one. The one man he kept alive, Joseph, would have used to get the name of the brother who betrayed them. After getting the information he needed, Joseph would have ridden hard to catch his wife and expose the brother." Josephus finished.

"Which brings you and me here to this cave in the mountains," I added as we watched the stars poke through the darkening sky. For the rest of the evening, we debated who the men who would want the children of Christ dead were. We agreed it would have to be men who stood to lose everything. Up to this point in time, I would have put everything I owned on it being men of the Jewish faith. Then Josephus said something that shocked me.

"Well, think about this, Rome is now following the Christian faith. When Joseph and Pilot started the brotherhood, it had to be kept secret. Now men in the army of Rome openly pray; the church is now called the Holy roman church." Josephus told me it was then we looked at each other.

"It would have to be someone or a group if it became known Christ had fathered two children. These men would stand to be wrong and, in being wrong, would lose their standing. Who or what kind of group could justify killing a whole bloodline?" I asked, looking at the stars.

"Rene, believe me, many bloodlines have gone under the sword throughout history. It is usually done for a kingdom, kill every last heir to the throne, then set in a king you want." Josephus said as he looked to the north.

"So these men who claim to be of Christ's faith, they profess to follow his ways, think nothing of killing his mother, his children, and wife," I said as I could feel anger building in me again.

"I think we will find the answer in the days, months, and years to come, little brother," Josephus answered as he stood and walked over to his bedding.

I sat watching the stars shine in the firmament of gods creation. Over the years, I have lost count of how many times I have looked up and wondered if my mother was up there looking down upon me. As I looked up to the stars that night, I hoped she approved of the man I was becoming.

The morning came, and we were both excited to explore the second tunnel. Morning found Josephus and I packing our things and getting ready to leave the caves.

Then we walked to the back of the main cave where the two tunnels started. We had taken the right-hand tunnel the day before and found the traitor. Who was now buried under only god knows how much rock. Now we stood looking down the left tunnel.

"Well, shall we, brother?" I asked Josephus, who looked at me and smiled.

"Oh, we shall." He said as we both started to walk into the darkness, our torches held out in front of us.

I was shocked when we found the first painting. It showed a lone man standing in the mouth of a cave. This lone man watched as a group of people and horses rode over a mountain.

"He stood at the mouth of the cave and watched as they rode over the mountains, never knowing he was so close," I said as I reached out to touch the image of Joseph.

"They could not know he was protecting them. If Mary had found out her beloved husband was so close, she would not have let him go a second time. So Joseph hid the fact he had followed her and their grandchildren. He kept them safe, never revealing that he was so close." Josephus told me as we studied the painting.

I looked further down the tunnel. I waited until Josephus was finished looking at the image of who we thought to be Joseph. The next painting was of two men, one bigger than the other. The men stood at the grave of another. Each man stood looking at the tomb, tears running down their cheeks.

I looked at the painting, then at my brother. I could see the shock on his face, then I looked back at the image.

"This reminds me of us when Joseph passed away," I said as we both turned and looked at each other.

"This isn't just a painting of what had taken place in the past. This is a painting of Joseph's death." Josephus said as we both touched the painting.

"How could this be of his death? We think he painted these hundreds of years ago." I stated as I took my fingers off the painting.

"I don't know how he could have known about us, being here at this time. However, here we are, and here this painting is, so...."

All I could do was stand in front of the painting and nod my head, truly at a loss for words. Josephus and I both turned and looked further down the tunnel.

"Well, let us see what is next," Josephus said as we started into the darkness. For a moment, I thought this was the last painting when out of the gloom, the end of the tunnel appeared. We could see another painting on the stone of the mountain.

The painting showed a lone man standing on a Beach. On rough water, a ship sailed into the distance, its sails filled with a stiff wind. The man on the shore waved as tears rolled down his face. On the ship, you could just make out the image of another waving back.

We both stood studying this painting. Again without knowing it, I reached out and touched the image. For a split second, I thought I had found a trap or had been bitten by a snake.

A tremendous jolt of power coursed through me, starting where my fingers touched the painting. I saw a great sea, and on that sea was a ship. On the ship was my friend and brother Josephus. He was sailing to the west. We were forced to take different paths by fate.

Josephus was forced to look for a new land, a place where he could protect the blood and the bloodline of our savior. I was myself racing through a field below a great black fortress. I felt death close behind. I could see others waiting for me. I felt my death by poison, an evil used to wound me, to kill me.

Then I saw something else; I saw a young man coming to a great black fortress on top of a mount. Then everything stopped, and I collapsed onto the tunnel floor. I could feel Josephus grasp my shoulders, trying to help me.

"Little brother!" Josephus was calling me. I could hear him though it was faint with the ringing in my ears. I lifted my head and nodded to him.

I raised my hand, touched his face, and smiled, showing him I was fine. It was then he grasped my collar in his big fists and lifted me off the floor. I knew my brother was strong; it wasn't until then I realized how strong he truly was. His fear for my health and the safety of our quest scared him when he thought I was hurt.

"You need to be more careful. I have no one in this world, only you, and we need to find everything left by the family. I can not do this alone." As he spoke to me, I could see the fear in his eyes. He was not afraid of failing; his greatest fear was being alone. I wanted to tell him of the vision given to me when I was overcome with the power. I looked again into my brother's eyes and could see the fear and despair written in his eyes.

Chapter 12

"I AM HERE NOW, BROTHER," I said as he looked at me and then nodded.

"Do you think that is us, me standing on the shore and you sailing away?" I asked.

"No." That was all my brother would say. Then I watched him as he shook his head. I knew it was far into both our futures. I also knew every day, every passing year brought the truth of the painting closer. I started back to our camp, desperately wanting out of the tunnels and into the fresh air of the mountains.

As I stood, I leaned against the wall; the surge of power that had coursed through me made my head swim as I stood up. When I could, I opened my eyes and found I was looking directly at a small hole. If I had been taller or shorter, I would have missed it. I looked at the spot and somehow knew it was another keyhole.

"Brother, look at this. I think it is a keyhole to open something," I called to Josephus without taking my eyes off the hole.

"Stand aside. I do not want you getting hurt," Josephus said as he gently moved me to the side. I watched as my brother took out the arrow shaft and inserted it into the hole. The way he had at the first cave of paintings we had discovered in the canyon. We both heard a faint click, then a rumbling, and we stood still, looking for a doorway. A new tunnel, anything. We were both at a loss when, as far as we could tell, nothing happened.

"Well, that was a bit disappointing if you ask me," Josephus said as we started to turn around.

"It was. I was hoping to find a room with more paintings." I told him wanting to sketch more of what we thought was Joseph's paintings. Walking out to the central part of the cave where our camp was. My brother and I found the rumbling sound was another door opening, showing us another room.

Standing at the threshold of this room, Josephus and I looked in as far as our torchlight could penetrate. Remembering the room with the traitor in it, I looked at the floor and found another trench with oil in it. Holding my torch to the channel, I breathed a sigh of relief when the oil caught and flames raced around the room. Once the oil was lit, a golden light was given off from the fire illuminating the room. The light cast the shadows back into the rock of the mountain.

In the middle of the room, there were two stone pillars. At some time in the past, someone cut the pillars so each was flat on top. Then a large log was split along its length and placed across the pillars.

On this rough table were four objects, two of them were suits of chain mail and armor. Each of the chain mail and armor had been covered in some sort of oil. Over the long years, the oil had stained the rough split log. This equipment looked like it was placed on the rough table days before our arrival. Josephus and I turned our attention to the other object on the table.

In the middle of the table was the head of an old roman spear. When Josephus saw the head of the spear, he stopped, and his eyes grew wide with shock. I glanced over to my friend and brother, then to the spear. Walking over to the table, I avoided the spear and picked up one of the suits of chain mail.

"This looks like it will fit you," I said as I held up the armor, then looked back to Josephus, who had gotten to his feet.

"I think you are right, though I am at a loss how this could be for me here," Josephus said as we looked around the room.

"Try the chain mail to see if it fits you," Josephus said as we walked around the room, each of us trying to avoid the spear.

I wondered if the spear was used by the cursed roman soldier who stabbed Christ on the cross.

Standing in this room, in the mountains where we had found so much. I looked at the spear and thought about everything else we had seen to this point. It would only be one more on the list of holy objects we needed to find.

Once Josephus and I had tried the chain mail and the armor, we placed those items outside the door of the room, in the central part of the cave. Then taking deep breaths, my brother and I walked back to the table and stood looking at the spear.

"What a strange thing to find in a cave up here in the mountains," I said as I bent closer to have a better look at the spear.

"Well, over the centuries, many tens of thousands of these pilums have been lost and found. I can imagine they can be found almost anywhere if one knew where to look." Josephus said as he watched me.

"Pilum? Is that what this spear is called?" I asked as I looked at Josephus.

"Pilum is what a full spear is when the blade and shaft are one," Josephus said.

"So it was called a pilum at one time. Now we just call it a spear. What I would like to know is what it is doing here, in this room, just sitting there." I said as I reached for the spear.

"Don't touch that thing!" Josephus cried as he grasped my arm to stop me. Shocked, I stopped and looked around, thinking I had set off another trap.

"What is it, brother?" I asked, turning to make sure everything was ok.

"I don't think we should touch it; if it is what I think it is, that thing is one of the most cursed objects in the world," Josephus said as I turned and looked at the spear again.

"Let us think about this for a moment. We know Joseph was here. He was the one who carried out the sentence on the traitor back there. We also think he was the artist who painted the paintings." I said as Josephus nodded his head, confirming everything I was saying.

"If Joseph has done all these other things for us, somehow knowing we would be here at this time. Then it only makes sense we should take this thing with us; somehow, it must be important." I finished, just to make sure I wouldn't trip anything which would bury us under a pile of rocks. I walked around the table, checking for traps. On the other side of the table, I found a note carved into the wood.

"Brother, come here, look at this," I said as I read the note. Josephus slowly came around to where I stood. As he moved closer to me, I could see the pain written on his face.

"This thing is called the spear of destiny. This note says it was the spear used by a poor roman soldier to stab Christ while he was on the cross.

"Does the note give the name of the cursed soldier?" Josephus asked, standing behind me.

"No, not directly about the soldier. However, it does reference what Christ whispered to the soldier as he hung on the cross." As I spoke, I felt Josephus move up beside me. When I turned to look at him, I could see he had started shaking.

"I know the curse Christ spoke on that horrid day, word for word." He told me as he reached out to touch the spear with his fingertips. I watched as his fingers traced the edge of the spear, blood trailing behind.

"It is still sharp after all these centuries," Josephus muttered almost to himself. I watched as he turned and walked around the table and then back to me, his eyes never leaving the spear.

"This cursed object has killed many men, including Christ. The man who held this on the day of the crucifixion was cursed, he must walk the earth until Christ comes back to us. The soldier lost everything his family murdered, his wife and children butchered in front of him by the officers of his own unit." Josephus started as he bent down, looking the spear over.

I knew he was looking for a trigger that would trip a trap designed to keep whoever found the room from leaving with the spear. A trap designed to bury the person who found this room and the spear forever.

"The soldier fled from the top of the hill, out of his mind with grief. When he stabbed Christ, our savior's blood ran down a channel cut in the shaft of the spear in a battle months before." My brother recounted the life of the spear.

"The soldier saw a terrible light in Jesus's eyes, a light he had never seen in any man he had killed before Jesus. Terror grasped the soldier, and in his terror, the soldier put his blood-soaked hand to his lips. When the blood of the redeemer touched his lips, the roman soldier saw the truth of what he had taken out of the world. As Jesus hung from the cross, he looked down on the soldier and then cursed the soldier.

'This thing you have done, this pride you feel for what you are, for the feel of a gold piece will see you walk this earth until I come again and make my family whole." As Josephus recalled the words uttered to a roman soldier so many centuries before we found this room and the spear, I could feel his grief.

I was surprised when Josephus reached out and lifted the spear out of its cradle. My brother and I looked around the room expecting the walls to fall in or the ceiling, something. Deciding we had pushed our luck far enough, we decided to rush back to our horses.

"I think we have found all we can here in this place, don't you?" I asked Josephus.

"Oh, I do believe it is time for us to carry on with our quest, little brother." He said as I watched him wrap the spear in an extra blanket we had. Then he grabbed rawhide and tied the blanket tightly, trapping the spear inside.

"You can't stand to even look at it, can you?" I asked him as he finished knotting the rawhide.

"No, a poor, uneducated bastard was given a gold coin, then he was told to let a man on a cross suffer for a time and then to end it. Up to that point, the only people who had been crucified were thieves, murderers, you know, criminals. So when a chance came to make a gold coin for his family, the soldier took the coin," Josephus told me.

"I always wondered what had happened to the soldier after he had fled the top of Golgotha?" I asked, looking at the man who I called brother. The man Joseph found and rescued took the time to heal his wounds. The man I was starting to suspect was on top of a hill where three crosses held three condemned men. Josephus stood up and looked out to the bright afternoon sky.

"Well, after the soldier touched the blood of Christ to his lips, he went mad for a short time. He then remembered what he had done and raced home to save his wife. It was then when he found his unit had been there looking for the gold coin." Josephus told me, then sighed deeply and carried on.

"You see, the man who paid the soldier told criminals in his unit he had paid a gold coin for his service. The others in his unit raped and murdered his wife and daughter. These men thought they had killed the son, but they didn't. The boy was injured terribly and was dying. Another man who was walking by as his own son was being taken off a cross. Joseph found the son of the soldier dying and took him home. With his wife, they nursed the son of the cursed soldier, for so long the boy never improved, he just lingered near death. The soldier buried his wife and daughter, his heartbreaking, the gold coin weighing heavy as he placed it with his daughter in the ground." Josephus took a drink of water and then continued.

"The soldier thought the others from his unit had sold his son into slavery, as he had done it many times before. So he decided he would kill every man in the unit. Then he would find his son and save him. A week later, the group of men who had killed his wife and daughter was dead. The soldier knew he would never be able to find his lost son. Instead of looking, the madman found a holy man, and he tortured this holy man for weeks. All so he could have the curse removed and placed on another." I sat quietly, not wanting to disturb my brother.

"As the holy man tried to explain, he could not place the curse on another of his choosing. The soldier would not listen, so the holy man carried out the spell. Once complete, the soldier was beheaded, his body buried facing east. It was then the boy Joseph had found the day of his son's crucifixion, started to come back from death's door." I had to sit down as Josephus recounted the past.

When Josephus uttered the word '*son*,' he looked around, his head hung and tears rolling down his cheeks.

"You are the son of the cursed soldier," I stated as I stood and walked up to him, wrapping my arms around my brother.

"We will reunite the family and lift this off, you brother," I told him as he nodded.

"I need to tell you the rest of it," Josephus said.

I stepped back and nodded, then decided we would need a glass of tea, so I started making a fire. For the rest of the afternoon, I sat and listened to the story of Josephus' life. The part of his life was how Joseph and Pilot came up with the story of him being the bastard son of Pilot. Pilot then placed him in the particular unit for the bastard offspring of the generals.

Josephus was always in the center of the fighting when his unit went into battle. He showed no fear and often would be the first on the field and the last off. This hadn't gone unnoticed by others in his unit.

The other men became jealous when Josephus found love. Josephus had asked to be attached to house security for a general and friend of Pilot. These others in the unit went to Josephus's home and killed his new wife, then ran. Josephus begged his general to be allowed to hunt these men down, and he was given permission to go and find the men. He was told not to bring them back, just proof of their deaths.

"I hunted these men for months, years. When I finally found them, they had others to help them. They wouldn't fight me, man to man. They waited in the mountains while the others took turns attacking me. When they thought I was weakened enough by the attacks, they came at me.

I fought as hard as I could and managed to kill their leader. Then I was hit with a stone from on top of a hill, and all went black. When I woke up, I was in agonizing pain, and Joseph was by my side dribbling water on my lips." The man I called brother told me his story, and I believed every word of it.

"It was during this time Joseph told me who I was, who I really was. Explained about my father and how he came to be on the hill that day. Joseph also explained the curse and how it works. How they kept my real father dead, they had cut off his head. They buried his body, and the holy man kept his head and wandered off into the mountains with it." I looked at Josephus as he told me how the holy man had killed his father.

"It is the only way for me to die. My head must be separated from my body. You see, little brother, I do die then because of the curse.

Well, because of the curse, the death process is reversed; with the reversal comes all the pain. The mending of bones and tissue is truly agonizing. When I finished healing, Joseph told me to go and find the men and finish it." I sat and listened as Josephus took a drink and then continued.

"He told me when I was done to come to him, he was going to a friend to have me listed as killed by the men I was hunting. So I did, and that is what has brought us to this point, and finding my father's spear." When Josephus finished, I looked back further into the cave.

"Do you believe, I mean truly believe, god knows all and is all, is everywhere and because of this is everything?" I asked, still looking at the back of the cave.

"Yes, with all my heart; why?" Josephus asked.

"So if you believe this, you must believe he knew this was going to happen. You must believe he set into motion the actions of others. Yes, we have free will. However, he knows the heart of man. These men you hunted, he knew they would do something. I can not believe he would turn them on your wife with intent. He knew your heart, and God knew you would have to have retribution. So your actions brought you back to Joseph and to this point in time." When I finished explaining my thoughts on the subject, I turned and looked at him, wondering why he was so quiet.

"I always wondered why Joseph stopped what he was doing the day he saw your mother running from some men. He gently led her into his tool shed. Tears of fear leaving trails on her dirty face. I stood in the shadows watching the men who were after her and you. I would have killed them if they had come near the shed. However, Joseph sat outside, carving a piece of wood. When the men came to him, Joseph looked up at them and lied. He told the men he never saw any young girl with a child come by his home. We watched as the men turned and started back the way they came. That night Joseph told your mother she could stay with him to raise her baby in peace.

I watched you grow, the pain in my heart growing with you. My wife had been with a child when she was murdered. My son dying with him, never knowing the warmth of his mother's love or my hand holding his." Josephus told me. I was shocked at the depth of his pain. I was forced to watch my brother's shoulders shake with profound grief over the loss of his wife and child.

Chapter 13

"JOSEPH CAME TO ME ONE day, and he told me of the plan to gather everything holy left behind by his and gods son. That I would be taking you when you were old enough to be purified. Together you and I would gather Jesus' remains along with Marys and the bloodline, then go with all we found to our brothers. Even then, Joseph was having doubts about the men who started to run the church." Josephus told me. Sitting, holding my cup of tea, I was trying to come to grips with the fact Josephus knew my mother.

"I can hardly remember my mother; I catch glimpses of her in my mind. Mostly her smile. I wish I could remember her face, smell, or voice," I said as I looked out at the darkening sky.

"Your mother reminded me greatly of my wife. She was a woman of exceptional beauty. Her skin was as white as the snow that cling to the top of these mountains. You have her hair, fiery red. Joseph said it gives you your temper and your will. She would sing a song to you when you would start to cry. You cried a lot when you were young. Joseph said it was in her language. He called it french and said it was what they spoke in Gal. He told me this is where your mother was from. A lot of the time, your mother smelled of spices; she cooked all the meals. After a few years, she hoped her raper had given up looking for you both. She went to the market to buy vegetables for our evening meal. This is when the men found her. Joseph and I had taken you to see elephants. On our way home, we found your mother; you know the rest." Josephus told me of that terrible day.

I could feel the rage building in me at the memory of my mother dying, murdered.

"I wish I could have found the man who ordered her murdered and told him who I am." I wanted to say more however couldn't bring myself to utter the words.

"The man who had your mother murdered lived here in Gal. He was part of the royal family and will never know you. He traveled to the deserts for trade." Josephus said, then sipped his tea.

"I loved your mother as I would have loved my sister. The loss of your mother threw me into such a rage that I traveled to Carthage. I found this man, and before I took his life, I told him about you. About your red hair and how good a boy you were. I told him how fine a lady your mother was. I told him I was going to erase any trace of his existence in this world. I watched as the raper and murderer wept for his life, begging, pleading, trying to buy my mercy. Just as he thought he was going to let him live, I drove the dagger you now carry through his heart. I watched him as he realized death had placed a hand on his shoulder and was about to take him to his final judgment." Josephus said. When Josephus finished, I sat there stunned into silence. For the longest time, I just sat, then I had to get out of the cave. I felt lightheaded, needing fresh air.

I heard Josephus stand up and walk out into the night air with me. He put a large hand on my shoulder and smiled at me. He knew what I was thinking.

"Your rage and hatred are a waste of energy. The man who thought he could get away with anything is dead. The instrument of his death hangs on your waist." When Josephus reminded me, my dagger had once had the blood of the vile beast who would rape then hunt down a young lady, my mother. I could no longer stand to have it around me. I took out the dagger and looked at it, then without thinking, threw it as far off the side of the mountain as I could manage.

I took one last look at the stars of the night and then walked back into the cave. I still do not know where the feeling came over me. When I entered the cave, a complete sense of peace washed over me. I looked over at Josephus and smiled, and he smiled back.

The morning sun greeted the two of us as we walked our horses out of the cave. They seemed happy to be on the move again. If truth be told, so were the two of us. We didn't ride our horses down from the cave. We feared they would falter and fall with our weight on them.

We reached the bottom of the mountain just as the sun dropped behind them. On the first night out of the cave, Josephus and I talked about the past. I spoke of the time I lived with Joseph and how he would tell me of my mother. Josephus said he would sit and watch as my mother would play with me when I was a baby.

"It is up to us to make sure the family remains safe from all who think they have rights over them," Josephus said as we drank the last of our tea. It was nice to go to sleep with the stars overhead once again.

The morning greeted us as god intended when he created this world and all in it. I watched as the sun rose over the mountains, lighting a new day. Showing us all the possibilities ahead of us on this day, all we had to do was start. My brother and I started by finding a well-worn path weaving through the granite ramparts guarding the green valleys.

"I think we should try to find the small church depicted in the cave," I said to Josephus as we rode along the path.

"I was thinking the same thing. I wonder if anything was left behind we should look at?" Josephus asked, wondering out loud.

After the cave and the revelations spoken in that secret place, I knew we had grown closer as friends and as brothers in the order. Now the air was turning colder, and frost lay on the ground longer into each new day. Josephus and I knew we would have to find shelter for the coming winter or take a chance of getting caught in the mountains. Josephus and I talked about how late the year was becoming. It was decided we would have to get out of the mountains for safety.

We had been out of the cave, where we had found the spear of destiny, for a fortnight. When one morning, I woke to the sound of weeping. Looking around our camp, I feared for Josephus. I worried the remembrance of the past was too much for my brother. As I listened to the weeping, I knew it wasn't my friend weeping; to me, it sounded like a woman crying. Following the sound, I walked out to a clearing. Standing among the tall grasses of the small valley was Josephus. My brother also heard the sound and followed it to this small valley. The sound we were hearing was the calls from a strange-looking bird with long legs.

The odd-looking birds would poke their heads above the tall grass, call then their heads would duck down again. We stood at the edge of the valley listening and watching as heads rose above the grass, then ducked down again. Some hours later, we watched as others came back, gracefully landing and sinking below the grass.

"This must be their mates coming back from gathering food for the females." Josephus speculated as we watched more of the birds fly back.

"Do you think they been out over the water?" I asked, thinking we might be close to the ocean.

"No, not an ocean; however, we could be near a large lake," Josephus returned as we walked back into the forest, leaving the valley of birds to themselves. When we arrived back at our camp, I watched our horses. To me, they seemed nervous and seemed overly interested in the hill behind them.

I looked up the hill, trying to see what had our normally quiet horses so skittish. Josephus watched as I started up the hill. We did not like that our horses were afraid of something they couldn't see or hear. As I climbed, I could listen to Josephus coming up behind me. My brother and I became closer as the days passed after the cave.

When I reached the top of the hill, I stopped. The sight below was something I will never forget. The hill Josephus and I climbed was one of four. If you were to draw a line from the one we were standing on to the others, it would be a square. In the center of the square sat a stone building. Around the building stood dozens of stone monoliths.

"By all, that's holy; what is this place?" I asked, looking down at a small building with stones around it.

"I have never seen anything like this before, little brother." Josephus returned as he looked back to our camp.

"We need to see this; however, I don't want to leave everything we have and the horses alone." He added, looking at me.

"If the horses come, I say we bring them, and if not." I shrugged my shoulders. Nodding, I turned to look at the horses and then back to the building.

"I think I see a path coming through the forest over there. The horses might be more willing if we do not try dragging them up this hill." Josephus said as he pointed to a gap in the trees.

Josephus and I started on the path we had seen from the top of the hill. Looking at the track, Josephus and I slowly walked our horses down it. We could tell it had not been in use for many, many years. Whoever had made the path, we thought, must be the same people who stood the stones.

As we walked the path, our horses twitched. To Josephus and I, it seemed as if they could smell a predator in the trees. They tried to turn back when we wouldn't let them retreat. The horses tried to run to the clearing with the stones ahead of us. Their behavior worsened when we came upon the first monolithic stone.

This stone had been stationed at the edge of the forest. I thought it was a strange spot to place the stone. It was standing right in the middle of the path as if whoever had placed it was trying to block the way to the building. Josephus and I had a hard time controlling our mounts. Looking at the stone, Josephus tried to calm his horse, then he tried to get the poor animal to walk around the stone.

The frightened horse would not get any closer to the stone than four or five paces. So we took the horses back to the trees and tied them so they could see us. We could watch them and the treasures they carried for us.

Walking around the large stone, someone stood long years before we came along. Josephus and I stopped and stared at a five-pointed star with a circle around it. This symbol had been carved into the stone long ago. The stone had darkened with age, and moss and lichen had found a home on the stone over time. However, the symbol was free of any growth. It seemed darker than the stone around it. To me, it looked as if even the light of day somehow avoided the symbol.

I looked over the stone at Josephus and shrugged my shoulders, then went to retrieve the horses. I knew the poor animals would not enter the clearing with the stones. I took them to the hillside and picketed them so they could eat the green grass and watch Josephus and me.

As we moved deeper into the circle of stones, from the path, we could see the stone building, along with four of the five stones. The fifth was hidden by the building itself, going to the first stone. Josephus and I found strange symbols on the ancient monoliths. What we found were straight lines with shorter lines coming off of them.

There were many of them as if it were some kind of written language. Again my brother and I walked around this stone we found, unlike the first one. The moss and lichen had covered the entire stone. It was even covering the writing. We assumed that was what the lines were. I stood in the sunlight, looking at the lines on the stone. I caught myself wondering about the people who made the marks. Were they the ones who built this place, or did they come to destroy it?

"Look here; you can see something was carved before the lines. Whoever made the lines in the rock took the time to chisel off whatever was on the stone before." Josephus said as he ran a hand over the stone.

"I think people came here before us. I think they came to bolster whatever the builders of this place did." I said as we walked around the stone, looking at the lines and how they were carved.

"I remember Joseph telling me there were people who worshipped everything god created. They worshipped nature, not the creator. They were called druids, and they believed in the magic of the world around us. The trees and plants, the rivers and oceans, he told me they fought against anything. Or anyone who would threaten the balance of the world. I wonder if they thought whatever was going on here threatened that balance?" I asked as we walked around the first stone again.

Looking around, we walked to the second stone and looked it over. This stone had suffered a crack running across its face from the top right corner to the bottom left. This stone also had lines carved on it.

Unlike the first stone, which held two angels summoning sigils, the sigils were carved in pure enochian on its front and rear face. I looked at Josephus. He was looking at the stone, then he turned and shook his head.

"Whoever was here, they were definitely trying to fight an evil spirit or demon of some kind. These markings are angel summoning sigils." Josephus said as we stood looking at the markings.

"Which angles would they be trying to summon for help?" I asked as I reached out to touch one of the marks.

"We would have to copy the marks and then find an ancient bible, one of the first ever written. In some of these bibles, the men who were given the information were also given the sigils of some of the arch angels." He told me as we looked at the sigils on the stone.

I traced my finger along one of the sigils, wondering which of gods first children it would call. Turning, we both looked at the door of the stone building. Without saying a word Josephus and I started toward the building. As we stood at the door, Josephus and I could see someone had stood there before. Whoever last stood on this spot had carved angel sigils into the door.

On the door, we could see what was left of the carvings they tried to cover up. I was shocked at what we could still make out. It looked to be what was called a demonic summoning sigil. I looked at Josephus and then back at the door. If this was on the only portal into the building. I had strong reservations about going into the building.

I was about the tell my brother of my misgivings over going into the temple when he spoke about his.

"A time long past, a group of men or women came through here and discovered what people had found on this spot. The first people here discovered a spot. One of many that scar the earth, these sacred places hold power. The power these places hold is evil. They are a stain on the world, a stain nothing can ever remove, no matter what man does." Joseph said as he looked at the symbols on the door.

"So the first people came here, found this spot, and built this building. What were they trying to do? Was it to contain whatever is here, or were they trying to gain from its power?" I asked, wondering out loud.

"I think the first people to come across this place would have been caught off guard by what had happened here. I think it was the first people to place the stones here. On these stones, they would have carved simple spells to hold in evil. Later others would have come and taken the time to build this." As Joseph said the word this, he slapped his hand on the side of the stone building. I started when Josephus yelped and jumped back.

"What is it? What happened?" I asked as he looked at me.

"I'm alright; the whole building is vibrating from a very powerful evil trapped within," Josephus said.

"So the others came and built this to house whatever is here," I stated.

"Then some others came and thought they could benefit from the evil here?" I asked.

"Yes, then, after Satan's minions, I think the last group to come here did so to strengthen what the others did before it would have been them who chiseled off the demonic summoning sigils," Josephus said, looking at the door again.

"However, I'm not entirely convinced their magic would have worked against whatever evil lurking in this place," Josephus said. Just as he finished speaking, something heavy fell on the other side of the door. We backed away from the building, never taking our eyes off the door. As our feet reached the path winding through the stones, we could hear a low growl from inside the building.

We both stood locked in place as the door groaned. It was as if some unseen force pushed on it. Then the sigils on the doors glowed, and whatever evil was being held inside the stone building cried out. The cry shocked Josephus and me; it was a sound of pure rage and pain.

There was a rage in the cry then the door creaked and groaned again before everything became quiet again. Looking at my brother, we slowly returned to where we had left the horses on the hillside, looking at the stones. All seemed quiet, save for a light breeze blowing off the hills.

It was then a soft voice floated to our ears on the breeze. I looked back to the stones and then at my brother. As we stood on the hillside, mere steps away from the last monolithic stones placed long eons past, a child-like voice floated to us.

"Help me, please; they hurt me." The voice cried softly. I was about to ask who hurt the child and where she was when Josephus reached over; he grasped my arm to keep me quiet. I was so invested in trying to find the one speaking when Josephus reached out and took hold of my arm. I cursed out loud while my feet left the ground.

"Do not answer this thing. Come, let us get to the top of the hill," Josephus said; I agreed and started to lead the horses to the top of the hill away from the building.

"Some men hurt me; they locked me in here. I have no food or drink. Please don't leave me; I miss my mother and my family." The thing inside cried through the door in a small child-like voice. The fact it was using the voice of a small girl angered me.

I looked at Josephus and then back to the stone building. When we finally reached the top of the hill, the voice seemed to fade away.

"Just as I thought, the thing inside the building has the strength to speak through the walls of its prison. It does not, however, have the strength to be heard past the stones." Josephus said to me.

"What is it you think is in there?" I asked as I looked back at the stone building. Before Josephus could answer, we both heard the actual voice of the creature trapped. Its real voice caught somewhere between a legion of voices, and growls came to us.

The cry issued from the small stone building sounded inhuman. Josephus and I looked at each other; the horses pulled at their reigns.

"Can we leave this place without knowing what sort of evil is in there?" I asked, pointing to the building surrounded by stones.

"No...we can not, also I'm not sure; however, I think the spell. Or whatever was employed to hold that thing in there is starting to weaken." Josephus said as we both turned to watch the building.

"It is times like this I wish Joseph was with us. He would know what is being housed in there and how to kill it." Josephus said as he tied our horses; they seemed happier to be at the top of the hill.

Chapter 14

SITTING, WE WATCHED our horses grazing. Josephus and I started to eat. As we sat and pondered the stones, a thought came to me.

"When we found the first room hidden in the crevice. The painting of the meeting between God, Christ, and Satan. Before that, I learned about the first war of how the injured angels changed," As I spoke, Josephus turned to look at me.

"What happened to the angels that fell? Did they really fall?" I asked my brother.

"Well, now that you ask, I always assumed the fall was more a fall from grace. I think this is something most people assumed," Josephus said as we now both looked at the building in the center of the stones.

"So maybe the fall was a real fall. That would mean the angels would have hit the earth." I was thinking out loud when my only friend and brother took up my thought.

"The place where a fallen angel hit would be tainted by the evil forced into the earth." Josephus finished. We both stood and walked down the hill and around the outside of the stones. While we remained on the outside of the stones, the voice from the building was little more than a whisper on the breeze. When we ventured into the stones again, the thing could be heard. Again it spoke in the voice of a child.

"You've come back to help me?" It asked as Josephus, and I walked around the inside of the stones looking each one over. What we could see now was the wear on the inside of the stones. The wear was more significant on the inside than the outside of the stones.

It was as if some unseen force was eroding the monoliths from one side. As I looked, each of the stones over Josephus's voice broke into my thoughts.

"If whatever is in this place is indeed one of the fallen. We will need to find out which of the fallen it is." He told me as I stood up from behind one of the stones.

"I think the name might be on one of these stones," I told Josephus as I looked outside of the ring of stones. It was unspoken when Josephus and I decided we could not leave without somehow making the enchantment stronger. The first night we made our camp well outside the ring of stones.

Even though we had set our camp up in the trees, a whispered voice floated to us in the air. The voice whispered to each of us; in the dark hours, the voice urged me to kill my brother. Though the whisper could be heard, any distinct words failed to make it to my ears. Throwing back my cover, I sat up to find Josephus stirring our fire back to life.

"Has the thing been whispering in your ear, little brother?" Josephus asked.

"Yes, it has been urging me to kill you while you slumber," I answered.

"It was the same for me," Josephus told me as the fire caught, and we sat down to make tea.

"It was as if in a dream. I know we were sleeping when the voice bade me end your life and set it free. Then before I woke, I laughed at its feeble attempt to corrupt me." I told Josephus as he poured the tea.

"Mine was the same; however, the thing knew about my past, of the men I have killed in battles. It kept whispering to me what is one more, just one more." As my Josephus spoke, I could see he was disturbed by the voice.

"We have to do something about this thing. At the end of my dream, if that is what we can call it, I told the creature I had been purified by the blood of Christ." Josephus turned and looked at me when I made my revelation.

"What happened then?" He asked.

"It seemed to recoil from me. I could swear the thing was scared." I answered, looking at the cup of tea warming my hands.

"Why do you ask, brother?" I asked.

"Well, in my dream, I was telling the creature I would never harm you. That you are my brother, so it would be better off killing itself. Just as I told it to go and kill itself, the thing screamed and seemed to be pulled back." As Josephus told me about his dream, I wondered if the blood of Christ hurt it.

I wish we had something to tell us how to proceed. I do not want to do anything which could see the creature freed." I said while Josephus nodded. Then we each had a thought at the same time.

"Do you think my blood on the building would hold the thing in there until someone who knows about this can come here and take care of it?" Josephus turned and looked at me, then at the building.

"I'm not sure; it didn't like the fact you have been purified by the blood of Christ. I don't think it can hurt to try." After that, Josephus and I sat waiting for the sun to show itself again.

Sitting by the fire, Josephus and I waited in silence for the dawn to come. Our moods seemed to lighten as the sun found its way back into the sky.

"We will need to study the thing in there before we do anything," Josephus said as we started to put our camp away. Standing to make sure all was as we found it, I caught a fleeting movement out of the corner of my eye. I looked over to Josephus. From the look on his face, he had seen the same activity.

Nodding to me, I watched Josephus leave our campsite. I knew he was making his way to whoever was skulking behind the boulders sitting on the top of the southern hill.

The sun had hardly moved in the sky when Josephus reappeared. In front of my brother was what looked to be an elderly hermit. It made a strange sight, Josephus so big, walking behind the bent, stooped hermit. I smiled when I could hear Josephus caution the hermit.

"Be mindful of the rocks, don't fall." Josephus cautioned the old man.

"You do realize I have been minding this site for almost fifty years, young sir; I know every stone and pebble here." The hermit scolded Josephus, which brought a bigger smile to my face.

"Now, you will tell me what has brought you both to this evil sight." The old man ordered as he looked at us from under heavy brows. I looked from my brother to the old man and then decided to tell him about finding this place.

"My brother and I are monks. We are charged with finding and protecting sacred items left behind by Christ and his family." I started. To my surprise, he lifted his head and nodded to me, so I continued.

"Our quest brought over the ocean to the south, then through the mountains. It is there in the mountains we have found more than treasures. We have found a truth others have sought to hide from the world about our savior. As we have been doing from the start of our quest. My brother and I followed clues to the next discovery. Those clues have led us to this place, whatever this place is." When I finished telling the hermit how it was, Josephus and I came to find the stone building.

"This place you have been led to is under my protection." The old man said as he leaned on his walking staff.

"My brothers and I have been charged with its upkeep for a thousand years. There were others before us; it is said their kind have long since died out, killed by good men who chiseled their evil off the door and standing stones. I remember my master telling me the men before us were here at the bidding of that things, Father." As the old man spoke, he pointed to the building.

"The ones before. Do you have any idea what they were called?" Josephus asked the old man, then helped him sit while I offered the old man a cup of tea.

"If my memory serves me correctly, they were called Yazdanism. These men were from far over the water as well. It is said they came to this place to trap and hold a great evil. The thing is there, my master told me these men believed seven angels protect this world." Josephus and I looked at each other when the hermit stopped to ask if he could have more tea. Smiling at the old man, I nodded and poured the tea for him.

"Yes, seven angels protect this world from others of their kind. Evil ones, my master told us; the others fell from their realm. Driven out by others of their kind, it had something to do with a great war. As the ones who came before believe, there are seven angels sent here to protect us from the evil ones. These angels are said to roam the world." The old man told us as he held his cup.

"Was it one of these seven who built this place?" Josephus asked.

"No, I do not think so. I was told it was built before the one who came before us." The hermit answered.

"So, do you know how old it is?" I asked, then watched as a smile crawled over the old man's face.

"Well, I always suspected it is as old as the fallen one trapped inside." When the old hermit told us he thought the thing inside was one of the fallen, we sat stunned.

"My brother and I thought it might be one of the fallen angels here. What we need to find out is which of the fallen it is. I thought its name might be on one of the stones." I was telling the old man.

"The problem is the writing on the stones is almost gone from time," Josephus said as we looked at the stones.

"It is not the passage of time that wears at the stones. It is the evil of the fallen angel scratching at them with its mind. As the stones become thinner, their power lessens." He told Josephus and me as we started to make a meal.

"How do we fix this?" I asked.

"Well, I will have to go over the scrolls and bronze plates." As the hermit told us of the bronze plates, I turned and looked at him.

"These plates have ancient writing on them; they were left to me by my master. In them, the name of the fallen should be kept. Once we find it, we should be able to strengthen the spell...." It seemed the poor old hermit wanted to say more. Josephus and I watched as the old man's face twisted; he was suffering great pain.

As Josephus and I watched, the old man leaned back and then rolled onto his side. I was shocked when my brother jumped to his feet and grabbed the old man. Josephus ran carrying the old hermit up the southern hill. As we reached the top of the hill, the aged man seemed to regain his senses.

"That thing in there can get in my head. I can hear it whispering to me. When I try to block it out, the pain is so bad I pass out," The old man told us. We decided to go to the hermit's cave while he looked for the books he thought the name of the fallen was in. I went back to our camp to gather everything and the horses.

"It whispered to Josephus and me last night while we were sleeping," I said as the old man started to rummage through a pile of scrolls.

"I was told when my order first came to this place, one would have to stand next to the cell itself for it to be heard." The old man started, then fell silent as he seemed to find what he was looking for. Josephus and I watched the old man as he turned to us, holding a batch of scrolls.

"Everything we know about the fallen in the cell is in these scrolls and on those plates," The old hermit said to us as he pushed the scrolls into Josephus's hands.

"We will bring these back when we are finished," I told the hermit.

"I will not need them back. I fear my time on this earth is coming to an end. All I ask is, when you do finish, come back here to see if I have traveled to the next life. If you find I have, please cremate this vessel," The old man asked. I was shocked when the old man asked Josephus and me to cremate his body. He smiled at us and then explained it was the custom of his people.

"We will come to see you. I hope you are here when we do," Josephus told him as we left the hermit's cave. We walked the horses back to the top of the hill, then stopped and looked over what the old man had called the cell.

That night Josephus and I sat reading the scrolls by the light of our fire. Just as my eyelids started to close for the second time and I was about to give up for sleep. Josephus sat up and looked over the flames at me.

"I think I found it," Josephus stated as he handed me a copper plate. As I read the writing, I looked up at my brother. He was right; the spell held on this copper plate could work if it was right.

The plate basically told us to find one who has been purified by the blood of one touched by god. We know Jesus was touched by god; I have been cleansed by his blood.

"It says we need the blood of one purified; I think it means you," Josephus said as he held his hands out to the fire to warm them. For the rest of the night, we read all the plates and scrolls, then reread them just to be sure nothing had been missed.

As the light of the new day found us, Josephus and I were preparing a large bowl. The bowl had to be large enough to hold all the ingredients for the spell we were going to use to keep the fallen angel in its cell.

Sitting and looking at the bowl Josephus smiled at me, then handed me his sharpened knife.

"You know what must be done, little brother," Josephus reminded me.

"I do; I just wish the plate told us how much blood I need to give," I said.

"Well, give enough so this will work; save some for you," Josephus said as he smiled at me.

"You are enjoying this way too much, brother," I told him. I knew he was worried about me, and I also knew if he could, he would take my place.

With everything in the bowl, including my blood, I read the enchantment from the copper plate. The language used in the spell was Enochian. It had died long before Joseph walked the earth. I could only hope I read the enchantment correctly. Holding the scroll over the bowl, I looked at Josephus and then started.

I had often asked Joseph why he was teaching me the language of the angels. I think he knew this day would come.

Here I was, standing in the mountains, Josephus, the only soul on earth who knew I existed. I can remember telling Joseph when I was young how I disliked my lessons. I can tell you now I still dislike reading Enochian. As I read the spell, I translated it to Latin for Josephus. We also wrote it on a new scroll for the future. On this scroll, we also drew the sigil of the spell to lock one of the fallen angels in its cell.

'Iudiciis purqari sanginem hominis sanquine nobis mundum peccatum, ordinatum persesustinuit commovebitur. Voxin perpetuum silentium inposuisset ut reprobi. In odium usque in sempiternum stetit quoniam dominus capti in hac cellula.'

I'll translate it to English, though I'm unsure if the spell would work in English.

"Blood purified by the trials of man, blood given unto the world, the punishment of this fallen one ordained by god himself will be sustained. The voice of the fallen to be forever silent. The hate of the fallen forever trapped in this cell," When I finished, Josephus and I waited for something, anything to happen. When anything failed to present itself, I looked to Josephus.

"I don't think we are the ones who will see anything happening. I do hope that thing in there will when we apply this to its cell," Josephus said as we started heading toward the stone building.

The fallen one inside the cell knew what was coming. Before we entered the ring of monolithic stones. The fallen angel started to scream the worst obscenities at Josephus and me. The sound was wrenching as it would threaten us, then curse our families and us.

"Don't you bring that vile concoction near this sacred site," The fallen screamed at us.

"Sacred site indeed, this poor piece of ground had the misfortune to be the area where you crashed to earth. It is a shame what happened to you in the war. To be wounded in such a way is terrible. Though it is no fault of yours, the evil forced upon you must be contained," I said to the voice and walked up to the door of the cell.

When I dipped my hand into the potion I carried, the fallen inside its cell cried out in anger. As I drew the sigil to lock this fallen angel in this cell, the cries of its hate and rage ceased, the corrupted angel's voice trapped in the cell, like the fallen itself.

I repeated the spell three more times on each of the cell walls. I still had some of the potion left in the bowl when the walls were finished. I looked up; Josephus must have read my mind.

"Come, little brother, I will help you onto the roof, then it will be finished," Josephus said to me. So as my brother stood with me on his shoulders, I used the last of the potion. Once we were finished, Josephus and I stood in the middle of the stones, next to a cell holding one of the fallen angels. I was surprised to hear the chirping of birds and the buzz of a bee as it passed the cell.

Without saying a word, Josephus and I turned and walked out to our horses. We wanted to be out of the valley of four hills to see the old man. I needed to tell him all went well, that the fallen was now safely locked away. As we walked our horses over the hill to the old man's cave, I was amazed at the sounds of life.

"I never realized when we first came to this place how quiet it truly was," I said to Josephus as we topped the hill.

"You know something, I could tell something was missing; it was not until you placed your hand on the door of the cell it occurred to me what," Josephus said. Nothing more was said as we walked, hoping the old man would be sitting by his fire.

The old pagan priest was sitting by his cold fire when Josephus and I reached his cave. Like the fire, the old priest had died in the night. He lay on the cold floor of his cave. I knelt by the old man and folded his arms over his sunken chest.

"I'll go and gather wood for his pyre," Josephus said as he walked out into the light of day. I looked at the cave, at the scrolls kept on a shelf. They all had the information we might need in the future. I decided the information on the scrolls and copper sheets could not be lost to the flames. So while Josephus gathered the wood necessary for the pyre, I gathered the scrolls.

We completed everything, then as the sun rose on a new day. We placed the frail remains of the pagan priest on top of the wood.

Though it might not have been a pagan prayer. Josephus and I did pray for the soul of the man who helped us in his last hours of life. For the pagan who gave his life to watch over the cell of a fallen angel gave us more than a spell to hold evil. He gave us the knowledge of his people in the end. Though his belief was different than ours, we respected the man for his sacrifice.

When we were finished praying for him, Josephus stepped forward and lit the pyre. We stayed with the flames as they consumed the old man. Josephus and I smiled as we left the cave of the old pagan, knowing his task was completed.

The night sky found us sitting by our fire, and we looked forward to resuming our quest when the sun again found the sky. Before we left the valley of the four hills, Josephus and I took one more look at the cell. The potion with my blood we used on the door was gone. During the night, it must have disappeared into the stone. I wanted to ask if this was normal on a cell of a fallen angel, then thought, who would know?"

Chapter 15

THE MOUNTAINS SEEMED to be brighter, and the birds sang sweeter as we rode along. Our horses also seemed happier as we followed the path through the mountains. For the first part of the day, Josephus and I refrained from disturbing the peace of the mountains with our voices. Both of us seemed content to listen to the creak of our leather saddles. The songs of the birds as they flitted from tree to tree.

Over the long years, I have come to enjoy the quiet times when I can just sit and contemplate the world. Smiling, I looked over to the man who I called brother.

"Let's have an early day today," I said. I watched as Josephus smiled and then nodded his head.

"I was hoping you would propose this," Josephus said as he stopped his mount. We set out our things and staked the horses where they could feed at their leisure. Winter had found its way to the valley we now camped in. We watched as the snow came closer to the foot of the mountains. I smiled as I reveled in the beauty of it all.

Like so many other nights, we set our camp up and made our meal after our evening prayers. It seemed we had decided while riding from the four hills to this place in the mountains to not speak of the fallen, so we spoke of other things.

Sitting at our fire, we talked about the past, mainly about Joseph and how he became one of the founders of the Brotherhood. The individual we talked about for great lengths was the fact Pilot was, the other man who helped start the Brotherhood.

"I would have liked to have been present at the first meeting between Pilot and Joseph," I said as we watched the moon crawl over a peak to our north.

"I as well; how could that meeting have started off, I wonder." Josephus returned as he sharpened a stick.

Throughout the night, we spoke of that first meeting and many other things. Trying to keep ourselves from wondering about the evil we left forever locked in the cell behind us. We both remembered how the creature whispered to us. How it had tried to convince each of us to kill the other. How twisted it had become over the vast span of eons instead of trying to gain its own freedom. Now it can never whisper to anyone who would stumble on the cell and stones.

During the long watch of the night, we grew quiet when we spoke of people we had lost. Then we smiled when Josephus reminded me they were still with us. They stood in heaven and watched over us; they still loved us.

It was about the time of the first light, or as some call it, the false dawn. We both saw a spark of light flash off something on the mountain to the southwest. I looked over to Josephus then we both stood. Looking at the spot where the flash was seen, we hoped to see it again. To our delight, it winked again for us, then disappeared.

"Well, the last time something winked at us out of the darkness, we found part of the greatest treasure ever," Josephus said as we stood looking at the spot halfway up the mountain.

"Yes, we did; I also learned so much; we are not in a hurry. So let us go and see what is waiting up there," I said as I pointed. The further away we rode from the cell in the four hills, the happier Josephus and I became. This seemed to be the case for our horses, also. Now we stood and looked at a spot on the side of a snow-covered mountain.

The rest of the day, we picked our way up the mountain, trying to get to the spot where we had seen the flash of light in the dawning morning. The sun was well down behind the mountains. When we reached what to us looked to be the spot where something had sparkled in the morning light.

As Josephus and I started to search the area of the mountain, I was surprised to find a cave. Its entrance was blocked by cut stones, and in the center of the wall was one stone made of crystal. This one cut stone brought Josephus and me up the side of this mountain. Someone in long years past had used rocks to block the entrance to this cave. I looked down the mountain, and I could see where our camp had been the night before. It was by sheer luck we had chosen that exact spot to camp the night before.

"What do you think is in there?" I asked Josephus as we stood looking at the wall of stones.

"There could be any number of things," Josephus answered before he could start naming things he thought could be in the cave. I suggested we should look for whatever had been left behind and why another would have called us to this spot. Turning, we headed in opposite directions. I had only made it about fifteen steps when the hilt of a sword caught my attention.

"Oh brother, I do believe I have found something," I called out to Josephus.

"Would it be a sword?" Josephus asked from the other side of the cave.

"Well, actually, yes, it would be," I answered, wondering how he could have known.

"Is it caught in a rock?" Josephus asked. To answer his question, I reached down and tried to pull out the sword. It was indeed caught in the stone of the mountain.

"Yes, it seems to be stuck fast in the stone." As I said it, I wondered how the sword could be stuck in the mountain's granite.

"Well, little brother, I seem to have the same issue here," Josephus said. I started back to where my friend and brother stood, looking down at another sword.

"Have you tried to pull this one out of the rock?" I asked. We looked at the shining sword hilt.

"I thought about it, then thought about the traps. I was going to look around to see if anything was set up." Josephus answered. We did not need to speak of it. We had been together long enough now we just went off in different directions. It wasn't long before I was calling out to Josephus.

"I think I have found something, and it is not what we were looking for, brother," I said. As Josephus came to the spot where I was on my hands and knees, looking into a small hole. He looked at me quizzically, then, without asking, he got down and looked into the hole I had found. It only took a second for Josephus to look and then pull his head back.

"Well, now, we have seen some strange and wonderful things thus far on our travels, brother. However, I do believe that is the strangest yet," Josephus said. All I could do was nod my head in agreement. Standing, we both went back to the front of the cave, our interest in finding a trap for the stuck swords pushed aside for now.

"I say we just start taking this wall down and see what happens." I offered, though he was reluctant Josephus finally gave in, and we started to remove stones. We had planned to take down the whole wall, then, at some point, we reached an unspoken agreement. Half the wall coming down would be enough for us to gain entrance into the cave.

Dropping the last stone, Josephus and I peered into the cave. The sight of trepanned skull greeted my brother and me. Why the skull had been placed to keep a watch out of the small ellipse cut into the back of the cave. Neither of us could fathom it. From where we crouched, both of us could see the skull was sitting on something. Whatever the head sat on time had turned black with age.

Without speaking about it, Josephus and I decided to remove the rest of the stones. I think it was the fact we had found a skull in a cave, and it was looking out over the mountains where we had found...well, everything. By the time we finished clearing the wall in front of the cave, night had enveloped us.

Not wanting to move away from the cave we uncovered. The two of us decided to make camp in the opening so long sealed. The unnerving part of having our camp in the cave's entrance was the skull sitting its long watch behind us.

I'm not sure when it happened. All I knew was in the dark hours of the night. Both Josephus and I were torn from our slumber by a scream. Standing beside my brother, we held our swords in hand, looking for a stranger on the mountain with us.

"You did not happen to hear what direction the scream came from, did you, brother?" I asked, trying to look in all directions at the same time.

"I was hoping you would have that answer," Josephus said as we seemed to turn in circles. About a minute after being woken up, Josephus and I turned to look into the dark maw of the cave. At first, I could have sworn something was just beyond the light of our fire. Something moving, shifting, hiding, unbeknown to me, Josephus had picked up a stone.

Just as I was going to ask my brother if he could see something. He threw the stone with all the force he could muster. The reaction was almost immediate. We could hear the stone rattling off the cave walls. Then an arrow flew out of the night, the first past my right ear. The second found its mark, hitting Josephus in the chest.

Standing across the fire from my brother, shock caused me to stare in disbelief. I was locked in my shock until Josephus dropped to his knees. Then before I knew how I had gotten to his side, I was holding Josephus easing him to the ground.

"Wait until I die, then you must pull the arrow out. For pity's sake, do not go in there until I come back, Rene. Promise me you will wait for me," Josephus pleaded. Not knowing what to do, I gave my word I would wait until he returned.

As I sat on a mountain in the cold grip of winter, outside a cave where long ago someone placed a skull. Now because of a sound and a thrown stone. I was forced to watch as my only friend and brother died.

Sitting by the fire, I held the only person in the world who knew where I was or if I ever truly existed. My heart was breaking, with my tears blinding me. I remembered the last words Josephus uttered to me. 'Pull the arrow out after I die.' Holding my brother's head in my lap. I looked at the arrow sticking out the chest of the man I called brother. For a moment, I could hear Josephus telling me to pull it out after he was dead.

Reaching for the arrow shaft, I asked Josephus to forgive me, then pulled. To my horror, the arrow wouldn't come out of the wound. Sitting on the ground with the night surrounding me, I looked up at the stars.

"Please help me do this, please." I pleaded, then tried again. I could feel the arrow move, then it seemed to get caught. Fearing I would break off the arrowhead, I stopped trying to pull it out. Trying to think of how to get the arrow from his body, I suddenly remembered Joseph. He had always told me to solve a problem; first, you must look at it from different directions.

I caught myself before I could yell, 'That's it.' Looking at the still face of my brother, I apologized for what I was about to do. Then I broke the fletching off the arrow and pushed on the broken arrow shaft with all my might. Fighting off the urge to let my stomach loose, I managed to push the arrowhead through Josephus. When

I had moved enough, I reached under my brother and grasped the arrow pulling the rest from his back.

Sitting beside my dead friend, my dead brother, I held the arrow that moments ago had been in his body. His blood steamed in the cold air of the mountain. I looked down at the arrow and then hurled it as far from myself as I could manage.

I watched the long hours of the night pass as I waited for a sign Josephus was coming back to life. I prayed for his life in the first hours; I prayed for the strength to bring him back if needed. Sometime in the night, I started to bargain for the life of my friend, my brother. I bargained with God and told the lord I was willing to give my life over to him if he would only bring Josephus back.

As the light of a new day started to show itself, I was finished bargaining. Now I just sat quietly, watching my only friend in the world for a sign he was coming back to me.

The sun was well into the sky; still, I sat with Josephus. I was starting to fear both he and Joseph were wrong about the curse. I was to the point where I was giving up hope. I looked into the cave. Looking into the cave, I could see the back of the skull. I knew I had given my word to not enter the cave until Josephus returned from death.

A sound caught my attention; at least, I thought I had heard something. Looking down the mountain, I strained to see if someone or something was making their way up to me. Just about the time I was turning back to keep watch over Josephus, the sound came again. The sound seemed to be caught between the ethereal and reality.

Sitting down beside Josephus again, I almost jumped out of my skin when the sound came for a third time. I realized my friend and brother was the cause of the sound.

Before I realized what I had done, I was standing looking down at Josephus. Again a light moan issued from my brother. Kneeling down, I opened his tunic so I could see the wound left by the arrow. To my surprise, the injury seemed to be healed entirely on the outside of his body. Looking at the sky, I smiled to the blue heavens.

For the rest of the day, I watched as my quest partner, and brother issued small sounds. As the sun sank lower, I watched as his body started to spasm. I was in fear he would thrash out and hurt himself, so I moved everything away. Then I decided to wrap Josephus in a heavy blanket. I thought it would save him some injury.

I watched as my small fire cast its light over my camp; I had eaten a light meal and prayed. Now I sat waiting for whatever was happening to Josephus to bring him back. Somewhere in the long watch of the night, I lost my battle with sleep, and it overcame me. During those hours, my brother returned to me; I will never forget that night. I lay beside Josephus, hoping I could be of some help to him. The moon was just above the mountaintop, and the stars winked down on me. I lay awake listening as Josephus fought his way back to the land of the living. I don't know where he went if or when something happened to him.

I could tell how painful it was for him to come back from wherever it was. I lay watching him hoping to help as I said, then the next thing I knew, I could hear a voice.

"Brother, for pity's sake, water, please." In my half-sleeping state, I could hear Josephus asking for water. I thought I was dreaming when the plea came a second time I launched out of my slumber.

Looking at him, I realized my friend and brother was looking at me. I leaped over the fire pit, trying to get to him so I could get whatever he wanted. Holding one of our water skins to his lips, I dribbled water into Josephus's mouth. With a slight nod, I watched as he laid back. The rest of the night, I watched as he moaned in pain. Steam rose off his face in the cold air as sweat would bead then roll down his face.

It was noon before Josephus had the strength to sit and drink on his own.

"You can never do that again; no more throwing stones into strange caves. Or any other places, or people for that matter. I don't think I can take you dying again, not again." I said to him as he lay back down and looked over at me.

"I promise no more stones, well not for a while," Josephus said as he tried to smile. I watched as he closed his eyes.

I could never tell Josephus how my heart had broke that night as I watched over his lifeless body, fearing I had lost him.

I sat vigil over the man I call brother for a day as his body was repaired by a curse thrust upon him by his father. In all my long years, I have never seen one as tortured as Josephus was. As his body was healed, he was forced to suffer the pain of death. Then the healing process, all the while, he was vulnerable.

Josephus later told me he was killed one time on a battlefield. As he lay among the dead, scavengers landed on him and the others. He had started the healing process and was coming back to life when the birds began cleaning the battlefield.

"I was healing from the wounds I had taken during the battle," Josephus started; I wanted my brother to remain silent. I didn't want him to stress himself; this is what I told myself. The truth is I didn't want to hear about his death, his torture.

"As I was healing, the scavengers were ripping flesh from my body." I dribbled more water into Josephus's mouth as he gave off a rattling laugh.

"As I lay there wishing to be dead, I thought about Prometheus." The look on my face must have told him I had no idea who this Prometheus was.

"This Prometheus was a titan, a god of some sort in ancient Greece. As the story goes, he and other Titans fought a war with the first gods of the world. This war called Titanomachy raged for ten years before Prometheus and the others were victorious. The leader of these Titans was a chap named Zeus. Zeus was the greatest of all the gods in Greece. After the war, they had peace for a time; then, as the story goes, man was created from clay. For a time man pleased the gods, but then Zeus being a fickle god, started to be cruel to man. His final act was to forbid man to have fire to cook his food with." My friend and brother seemed to be intent on telling me the story of this Prometheus.

"So, as the story goes, this Prometheus took it upon himself to steal this fire of the gods and give it to man. This angered Zeus so much that he cursed another titan to eternal torture. Zeus and some of the other gods of Greece chained Prometheus to a boulder. Then every day, an eagle would swoop in and rip out Prometheu's liver and eat it. During the night, his liver would grow back, only to have the eagle swoop in the next day. This was to go on for eternity," Josephus told me. I was relieved when he finally finished his story and fell asleep again.

Sitting on a mountain in what is now the south of France, I watched over a man cursed. I remember Josephus telling me how his father was finally killed. Sitting under the stars listening to my brother heal from the arrow, I wished I could take his pain.

In the morning, I found my brother sitting up, still wrapped in his blanket.

"How are you this morning?" I asked as he sipped tea.

"I will be able to explore the cave with you today," Josephus told me.

"Well, let's wait until the sun makes its appearance shall we?" I asked as I watched him. I could tell he was still healing. The pain caused by coming back had weakened him significantly.

Later in the morning, as he felt he could, Josephus and I walked to the cave's opening and looked in. I looked at him and then moved a stone away from his hand. This brought a chuckle from my brother.

"Oh, little brother, I will not be doing that again," Josephus said.

I just looked at him and then smiled. The two of us then turned our attention to the cave. I had been looking at the back of the skull for a day and a half.

"I need to know why the skull was placed the way it is. It would be nice to know who it was in life." I said as we moved closer to entering the cave itself. Both of us stopped just inside the cave. There we knelt down, holding our torches out, trying to spread their light out in front of us. Looking into the cave, I could see what happened when Josephus blindly threw the stone into the darkness.

When my brother picked up the stone and hurled it into the cave. Josephus inadvertently hit a crossbow, which had been set up and aimed at the entrance to the cave. It was supposed to fire at a person if they stepped on a trigger. Instead, the bow was set off by Josephus and his stone. Smiling, I told Josephus what I found. He just looked, then shook his head.

"Of course, it would be something like that. Let's be careful, just in case," Josephus cautioned, then led us further into the cave of the skull.

We took our time, took it a step at a time, always looking for another trap. Being careful took more time. I was about to point this out to Josephus when I thought, why complain. We are on a quest, and they have been known to take a lifetime. A lifetime, the thought of a single lifetime was alien to me now.

I studied the skull, looking it over and making sure there were no traps. Once I realized the skull and the sword could be moved safely. I took the skull and turned it over so I could see the front of it. We could see what had killed this man, a sword blow to the top of his head. Would have ended his life in a battle somewhere in the past. We couldn't tell how old the skull was. It could have been here for hundreds of years. A swath of bone had been hacked out of the man's head. The wound ran from over the left ear crossing the skull to the center line. It would have proved immediately fatal. This type of wound is often delivered as another is on his knees.

Stopping, I looked over at Josephus, then reached out and gently took the skull off the sword. I made sure to not disturb the sword. Something rattled inside the skull as I turned it over in my hands.

"I don't like it when things rattle around in a skull," I stated to Josephus. When I looked up at him, I could tell from my brother's smile he had something funny to say.

Holding the skull in the light from our torches, I rolled the skull back and forth in my hand. Hoping whatever rattling around inside it would fall out. To our surprise, a key fell from the left eye socket.

When something like this happens to me, I tend to ask some fundamental questions. The first is, who was this person when he still had his head attached? The second question is inevitable, who would hide a key in a skull. Was this a person of some importance and therefore held in high regard? Or did they find a skull in some dark lonely dungeon and cram the key in to hide it? If it was found, why did they bring it here?

Before I could look for the answers to those questions. I had to find out why this poor soul was left looking out the small oculus cut into the back of the cave. For a moment, Josephus and I thought it traced the path of the sun. We could see this was not right. The sun never entered the aperture in the cave as it crossed the sky.

Standing in the cave, I was still holding what was at one time some poor soul's head. I watched as Josephus studied the sword the skull had been balanced on. At first, we thought it must be of value, something of importance.

With the skull taken off of the hilt, Josephus recognized the sword. It was called a Gladius and was carried by most Roman foot soldiers.

"Well, this will not help identify who this person was in life. However, I do know why this oculus was cut into the back of this cave," Josephus stated as we watched as the stars poked through the veil of night.

Watching the stars come out one by one. Josephus and I followed Venus enter the oculus. Looking out through the portal cut into the back of the cave. Josephus and I watched as Venus traveled through what would have been the sight line of the skull as it sat balanced on the sword.

I noted the mountain peak Venus rose over. The two of us sat watching as Venus rode through the opening in the cave. As the night surrendered to the day, we noted the mountain peak Venus dropped behind as the sun rose in the east.

After the discovery of what the oculus had been cut for. Josephus and I sat by our fire, debating why Venus had been centered in the opening. Once we finished our morning prayers and had eaten, we sat across the fire from one another. It only took moments for the discussion to delve into this new mystery.

As we sipped our morning tea, Josephus and I spoke about how we would move forward from this point. We both agreed to go to the mountain Venus rose over. Once we had finished on the first mountain, we decided to travel to the mountain the group of stars set behind.

"I know that smile. What has you perked up, brother?" I asked.

"I do not know; I'm just happy to have a new direction to move in," Josephus said as he once again sipped his tea.

"A slightly warmer direction would be nice," I added.

Chapter 16

THE FOLLOWING DAY JOSEPHUS and I placed the skull back on its perch. Then we smashed the crossbow and blocked the entrance to the cave. Before Josephus and I left the cave, we said a prayer for the man who had lost his head years past.

The morning sun burned off the morning mist when we left the spot where I watched my brother die and be returned to life for the first time. I watched Josephus as we left the mountain with the cave. It seemed strange to see him in such a good spirit after his ordeal.

"You are in good spirits this afternoon, brother," I said as we rode to the southwest.

"We are moving; we have another mountain to find. I feel good about what awaits us," Josephus returned, smiling at me and then looking ahead. I just nodded, not wanting to dampen his spirit.

As we rode through the day, I was surprised by a thought.

"Brother, do you know how long it has been since we placed Joseph in his resting place?" I asked as the day once again gave itself over to the night. Josephus stopped his mount and then looked back at me.

"Little brother, I would like to tell you; however, I seem to have lost track of the days. I know when we placed Joseph into his cave, it was early spring. We rode through the summer, then reached the sea and left the holy land during winter. When we found the first rooms where we found our savior, new leaves had budded on the trees. Now the snow lay on the mountains and the high valleys." As Josephus answered my question, I looked up to see snow, once only at the very top of the mountains was now closer to the valley floor. Josephus didn't say any more. He didn't have to. It had been almost two years since we had placed Joseph in his final resting place.

Like many other nights, Josephus and I prayed for our brothers, the farmer and his wife, along with the two little girls they took in, for Mrs. Benoit and her sons. We gave thanks for what we had in our lives, for what we had found, and for what awaited us in the future.

I found traveling through the mountains took longer than one would think. When we were in the cave, I looked through the aperture. I would have thought seven days ride. Then we will be at the mountain where we watched Venus rise from.

This was the first time I had ever seen snowfall. All the lands Josephus and I had seen to this point had warm winters. Now I woke shivering from the cold that morning. Before Josephus and I mounted our horses, a flake gently landed on my hand. I stood mesmerized, watching as this tiny perfect flake melted, turning to a little drop of water from the heat of my skin.

Josephus smiled as I looked up into the heavily leaden sky. I watched as another flake floated from the sky, landing on my face. It felt as soft, as perfect as my mother's kisses on my cheek would have been before she was ripped from my life.

"Come, little brother, we will see more of this before the day is over," Josephus told me as he started out. Good to his word, it snowed all day, and the wind hurried the flakes through the mountain passes. It seemed intent to try to get all the snow to one corner of the mountains. Riding through the snowstorm, Josephus told me how the Roman military had lost a whole legion to a storm.

"This legion was at the very edge of the empire. In a place, they called Germania inferior. The way it is told, some Legatus Legionis thought his legion so powerful not even nature was a match for his men. Well, he marched his men into the forest, looking to establish a new fort. They say a terrible storm came screaming out of the north. Driving snow and ice ahead of it, following was the most terrible cold. It is said a man could freeze standing still. Now I do not know if this is all true. However, I did see the account of the lost legion. A little over four thousand men and provisions lost to the cold of the north." When Josephus finished telling me about four thousand men being taken by the snow, I wanted to be out of it.

"Forgive me, brother, what is a legatus legionis?" I asked.

"Well, little brother, this is a man usually fairly young, in his thirties, from a very well-connected family. He could have gone into the senate for whatever reason he chose to join the military." When he finished explaining what I had asked, I decided any more questions could wait until we were sitting around a nice warm fire.

Finding another cave was a stroke of luck. Josephus had seen it first and pointed it out in the failing light of the day. It was large enough for the two horses and ourselves, along with all we had to carry. Once we were out of the storm, a fire was started, and the horses fed.

"We might have to think of staying here for a while, brother. I don't know how long a storm can last here. Or how much snow can come out of the mountains." Josephus said as we watched more snow swirl in front of the cave.

Sometime during the night, I woke to add more wood to the dwindling fire. I was surprised to find the snow still swirling around, being driven by the howling wind.

When the morning came, I woke to find Josephus sitting looking out of the cave. The snow had piled up. It was now blocking half of the entrance. The horses were just outside. They seemed to be content on pawing and unearthing the mountain grasses.

"Do you think we can move on today, brother?" I asked from the fire.

"No, I don't think that would be wise; we are warm and safe. The horses can find enough grass to keep them happy. We can hunt for meat and melt the snow for water. I think we should stay right here until the spring finds us." When Josephus said we should stay, I breathed a sigh of relief. I didn't want to move out into the snow. What we had and were looking for was too important to take a chance with.

As the days came, we would talk about the past of Joseph and Mary. We wondered how the man I called father could find the strength to watch his wife. The love of his life ride off over the mountains. Then when he knew she and his grandchildren were safe, go back to the Judaean hills. Years later, taking in a young woman who was pregnant and running from her raper.

Day after day, we would pray and hunt. In the evenings, we would eat after our prayers, then sit and speak of things we might find. Storms would come adding their snow to what had fallen. The sun would come out and chase these storms off. Often our talks would center on the paintings, and I took the time to sketch what we had seen.

Josephus noticed one day, a small stream had started to open. The birds took to the branches of the tree outside our cave. Their song woke us from our evening sleep. Even our usually sleepy horses seemed to be a little more energetic.

As we stood in the sun, we watched a young deer walking through the bush. I was about to say it was nice to see life moving again when the deer startled at something.

"That was curious," Josephus said as we watched the deer move off, then stopped and looked back.

Without saying a word, I started to walk down the hill from our cave. As I moved, the young animal watched me, not knowing if I was a threat. Walking around in the bush where the deer had jumped away from, I watched my footing. I didn't know if there were snakes in this part of the world. As I rounded a large bush, I saw what startled the young deer. I felt an ache in my heart.

Looking back up the hill to the cave, I could see Josephus watching me. Looking at what I found in the snow, I wanted to weep. A young child, a boy, lay frozen in the snow and frost. I had no way of knowing how long he had been in the snow. I wished I could bring him back to life.

With a heavy heart, I walked back to the cave. Josephus stood watching me as I came up the hill.

"I've seen you like this before, brother; you found a person down there, haven't you," Josephus said as I looked back to the bush.

"Yes, it is a boy of around four or five years old," I answered, then walked inside. For some reason, the sun lost the warmth it shared with the land.

"We can not leave the child out there; he must be buried," Josephus said as he looked at the bush.

"I know," I said as I grabbed a flat stone big enough to cover the child. With the man I called brother, I walked back to where a young boy took his last step, his last breath.

For Josephus and I, it seemed the best spot to bury the child. Once the somber task of burying the child was completed, we stood over the grave.

"Lord god almighty, neither my brother nor I ever knew this innocent child or why he was out in the cold. As your humble servants, we beg you to take his soul into your grace. Give him the warmth of your everlasting love and grace. Of this, we beg you, lord, allow this child the warmth and light of your love, amen." When I finished, Josephus reached out and placed his hand on my shoulder. Later he made a simple cross and put it over the child's grave. We didn't know the poor boy's name, so his marker just stated, 'With all gods children now.'

Sitting in our cave, Josephus and I wondered who the child was and where he came from. If there were people out there missing him, how a child so young come to be by himself in the snow.

"We need to find where he came from. His people should know what became of the boy." Josephus said as we stared into the fire. I wanted to add to his statement, but I just couldn't find the words. As the days warmed, Josephus and I packed what we had, knowing soon we would have to find the family of a lost child.

Chapter 17

LEAVING OUR CAVE WAS bittersweet for Josephus and me; it brought us back to our quest. It also meant we had to find the family of the poor boy we buried. We were going to have to tell a family their son died in the cold.

The first night Josephus went to find some sign of game. I knew he had found something else when he returned to our camp.

"I do believe I have found where the boy came from," Joseph told me as he sat down.

"Is it bad?" I asked, hoping for the best.

"Yes, it is as bad; I found a wagon. A young man is lying by it. A short distance from the wagon is the body of a young lady. To my eye, I would guess they were attacked by bandits. The young man was hit with an arrow. The lady was run down by horses. I think the boy ran into the bush where the horses could not go, allowing the child to escape.

Though it took time, we couldn't leave these people where they were. Being who we were and what we were. Josephus and I gathered the young lady and man. We took the bodies back to where we had laid the young boy to rest. We placed them with who we thought to be their son.

"This family deserves justice for the evil that befell them," I stated as we placed the last of the dirt on their graves. I looked at my brother and friend to see what his reaction was. It had not escaped me; during the whole burial, Josephus had been quiet.

"Yes, they deserve justice. I am afraid in this world, justice is strictly held for the nobility," Josephus answered, anger etched on his face.

It was a fortnight before Josephus, and I rode into a small village. The people were friendly and seemed excited to have us in their settlement. For Josephus and I, this settlement was just what we needed; Josephus and I found everything we needed. It wasn't until the first night in the inn that things became odd. Josephus asked the innkeeper about the young family we found and buried.

"Oh, good sir, please, for your own health, do not ever mention those poor souls again. It was a kindness what you did for them, however. It would not be looked well upon by some around here." The innkeeper said to Josephus and me as we ate.

"The poor souls were murdered in the cold. The boy ran and froze to death; that is a murder by the most cowardly," I stated, the tone of my voice giving no room for rebuttal.

"Sirs, we all agree with you. It was a terrible thing done to those poor folks. There is nothing we or anyone can do. The man responsible for it has the ear of the crown. Around here, he is the power, and he wanted the man's wife." As the innkeeper spoke, I watched others in the room nod.

"So this landlord wanted another man's wife, and he obviously refused, so what then. When the family left, he and others followed them into the snow and killed them?" I asked as the innkeeper served others. When I looked at the people sitting in the room, I found most of them nodding their heads.

For the rest of the night, Josephus and I discussed whether it was wise to look for justice for the family. Others in the inn told us the man responsible for the family is responsible for others.

The morning found my brother and I loading the treasures on our horses. When a man rode up to us, he sat on his mount looking over our things.

"Before you leave, you will have to pay your taxes." He stated with a cruel smile on his lips.

"We own nothing to anyone saved our lord god," I stated as I mounted.

"You will give what I say." The self-important simp ordered me as he reached for my horse's reins. My reaction to his reaching for the reins was quick and caught him off guard. Before the cruel man could lay a hand on my reins, I reached out, grabbing a hand full of his hair as I pulled him out of his saddle. He crashed to the ground between our mounts.

Slipping from my mount, I could hear the man cursing as he jumped up. To my surprise, he had pulled his sword as he stood.

"Put it down, or I will be forced to take your life," I warned as Josephus watched for others who might be with him.

"You kill me; my family are the lords here!" He sneered at me.

"I do the killing; no one would ever challenge me." He finished as he stepped forward. The sneer faltered for a fleeting moment. His belief in his right to do as he wished to abandon him.

"I am going to kill you for this, then I will take everything you have as payment." He sneered. I shook my head as I drew my sword.

"I take no enjoyment in this young man, know this I will pray over your body." As I finished speaking, he lunged, trying to kill me. I watched him as he crouched down slightly before he lunged. I knew what he was going to do. Turning slightly to my left, I watched as the tip of his rapier slid past where my belly was moments before. This cruel, twisted little man did not want my death to be quick. Where he was aiming would make death an extended agonizing ordeal.

As he leaned into his lunge, I slapped his rapier out with my sword. Then I swung in with a hard left-hand punch, smashing his lips into his teeth.

I watched as a blind rage overcame the little man at being struck. In an unintelligible scream of rage, he jumped up and started the most uncoordinated attack I had ever seen. Stepping back, I waited for my opening. When he made another lunging attack. I slid my sword to the inside of his right leg, cutting the great vein.

In his rage, the spoiled son of a lord never noticed I had wounded him. It was not until his blood splashed across the dirt before him that he looked down. At the sight of the blood, he stopped, then looked at me.

"You can not do this to me, not me." The little man said as he sat in the mud.

"What would make you any different than the family you murdered?" I asked the spoiled man.

"My family owns these animals." He stated as the blood loss forced him to lay back. I looked up at my brother, who was shaking his head at the man's words.

"No man has the right to own another," Josephus stated to all those gathered around.

"Sirs, you better mount up and ride southwest. In a day's ride, you will be safe. If you stay, his family will hunt you down." The innkeeper told us as he pushed loaves of bread into my hands. We thanked the people of the village, then climbed into our saddles and rode for the mountains.

"You know, we will have to be more vigilant for others following us now," Josephus said as I looked forward to the mountain where Venus rose from.

For the first night after the skirmish in the small village, Josephus and I would only stop to rest and water the horses. Traveling through the night, dawn found us walking our mounts to give them a break. While in the village, I had taken the time to buy a pack horse from the innkeeper.

He was an older horse, a gelding, a quiet animal with a loving disposition. The older horse would walk up behind Josephus and nuzzle my brother whenever he had the chance. We walked the horses until mid-morning, then we mounted and rode.

The second night we stopped until the moon made it halfway across the sky. Then we packed up and rode until dawn when we started to walk our mounts. Josephus and I did this for three days before we stopped.

It was the morning of the fourth day when Josephus and I watched a mountain pass; we had made camp on the pass the night before. As we stood in the shadow of an overhang, we watched as a group of men stood where our fire had been.

"What do you think, brother? Are they looking for us or others?" I asked Josephus as we sat under the overhang looking back the way we had come.

"Well, they are on our trail. We have confused them by taking our mounts onto the stone plain." He answered as we watched as the four men walked around. They all stopped, and as one looked up the mountain.

"I think they know where we have gone," I said as the men started onto the stone plain.

"We can not keep running from these people," Josephus stated. I knew he was right. We were going to have to stop and make a stand.

"Do you think they will listen to the facts or reason?" I asked, then watched as Josephus shook his head.

"No, little brother, these type of men firmly believe their man had the right to do whatever he wished," Josephus said.

"So we will have to fight to be rid of them, to protect what we have," I answered.

Sitting on the mountain, Josephus and I had the element of surprise and the face we held the high ground. Now anyone who has had to fight a greater force knows one thing. You always try to force your enemy onto the low ground. We waited for the men to come to us then I stepped out.

"What, see you following me this day?" I asked from higher on the trail.

"You killed our brother, we have come to either bring you to our father, so he can pass judgment, or we can just kill you here." The oldest told me as they climbed off their horses.

"Well, your brother had it coming. I want to ask you before I send you home to your daddy. Were you involved in the murder of a young family this past winter?" I could tell by their reaction they knew the brother I killed had indeed murdered the family.

"Did you know your coward of a brother shot the father from concealment? Then rode his mount over the mother trampling her under hoof. I believe he chased the young boy into the snow, where the poor child froze to death. If this is the brother your father needs judgment for, I can assure you he is being judged as we speak. The fires of hell will keep him warm for all eternity." When I finished my speech, I could tell these men, like their brothers, held a firm belief in their right to do as they wished.

"Our father will have to live with the fact you wouldn't come back. We are going to kill you on this hill today. I will burn everything you carry. No one will ever know you were ever here." He shouted up to me as his brothers pulled out their bows.

Smiling at the brothers, I stepped behind the boulder to my left. Josephus stepped out from behind the one on the right as he loosed his first arrow. I watched as it flew true, killing one of the brothers holding a bow. We watched as the others ran for cover.

Josephus and I could hear the brothers discussing the best way to get at us. Looking over at my brother, I smiled. The men below had no idea we could hear them. Their voices carried to us on the breeze. It was also apparent they had never fought trained men.

"It is very different fighting men, not women and children, is it not? I am starting to think your whole family is filled with none other than cowards and fornicators of sheep." When I finished, I looked over at Josephus, who was staring at me.

Without warning, one of his braying laughs broke out over the mountain. My taunt had the desired effect as arrows snapped off the boulders around us.

We could hear the brothers yelling about impugning their family's honor.

"Oh, come now, you all know your family has no honor. Any family who would condone the acts of a deranged mind, such as your brothers. Have forgotten anything such as honor many years ago," Josephus shouted down to them, and another answering volley of arrows answered for them.

Josephus looked over to me and smiled as he notched an arrow and fired. I shook my head as he counted on his fingers then more arrows snapped off the boulders around us. I almost laughed out loud when Josephus picked up one of the arrows the brother fired up at us and shot it back at them.

"You must be running low on arrows; this is one of yours," Josephus shouted down to the men. This brought a chorus of angry shouts and curses from the men and another volley of arrows. Josephus picked up another of their arrows and shot back at them.

Josephus stood up and sprinted across the trail to the boulder I was hiding behind with the horses.

"What brings you over here, brother?" I asked.

"Hunger, I think it's time for a meal, something nice with bread. Oh, and tea would be nice." Josephus said as he started to get things off the horses.

"So I take it we are not concerned with the brothers down there?" I asked.

"No, not for a bit. They are sending the youngest one around the mountain to see if he can come up behind us," As Josephus spoke, I gathered dried grasses and twigs for kindling. In a short time, our fire was going, and Josephus had the last of our venison cooking. The smell of our fire and cooking meat was being carried to the men below us.

Josephus and I ate our meal, sitting away from our fire. I was watching the brothers below, wondering when they would try to attack. Josephus sat facing the opposite direction waiting for the younger brother to come around the mountain. The men below seemed to be settling in for the night. We knew they had ridden hard to catch us, so they had minimal food with them.

While waiting, I never heard Josephus notching an arrow with his bow. Until he loosed it, he had seen the youngest of the brothers come around a boulder.

Like his brothers, the youngest was not used to dealing with men who had training. Like so many other people, when he sees a campfire, he assumes we will sit by it for warmth. Josephus and I were away from the fire, so as the brother took out his bow, he aimed for what he assumed was one of us and fired.

Josephus fired his bow at the same time as the brother. When I turned, I could see the youngest of the brothers stagger back. Josephus's arrow had flown true; it hit the young man in the chest. We watched as the youngest brother sank to his knees, a confused look on his face.

Death came for the young man on the silent hooves of a nameless horse. Like his brothers before, he would have judgment passed on his soul, as we all will in the end.

"You have lost another brother. Your father is quickly running out of sons this night." Josephus yelled down the mountain.

"He has enough left to kill you." Came the answer.

Sitting with Josephus, I just shook my head at the comment. Then I thought about a question I needed to ask.

"I have a question for you," I shouted.

"Are you trying to get your brothers killed?" I asked.

"Do not try and change what you have done." Came the answer from the last two brothers.

"I have never denied what happened in the village. Your brother came in looking to rob me, and when I would not let him, he lost his temper. He then tried to kill me, I defended myself, and he died. It was really very simple. He was used to killing unarmed innocents." I called out as Josephus nodded down the hill. As the oldest brother shouted that his brother was no murderer. He once again told me how his family had the right to do what they wanted to the people they owned.

As Josephus and I moved, I answered the brothers in the night.

"Well, what happens when you meet someone you do not own as you say. What happens when a person wants to be left alone?" I asked.

"As soon as anyone enters our lands, we own them. No one has the right to say no to us. If they think they do, then we teach them differently. Like the bitch with the whelp, and her husband, she said no and slapped my brother, so we ran them down." He answered.

"So you were there?" I asked as Josephus, and I made our way down the mountain to where the two brothers sat at their fire.

"There, yes we were there the whore slapped one of us. I rode over the bitch, crushing her into the mud where she belonged." As the oldest brother recounted his trampling of the young mother, his brother laughed.

"So what you are telling my brother, and I is you and your whole family are cowards," I said as again Josephus and I moved as the brother shouted his answer.

"We are no cowards. We are lords of these lands, with all the privilege given with our title." He shouted as we moved around the boulder; they hid behind.

"We say you are cowards, now stand and be judged." When I spoke to the two brothers, it came as such a shock the brothers leaped across their fire. Standing across the fire from us, the two brothers realized they had now met men who did not care about titles.

"You do not understand; we are lords of these lands; you can not do this." The younger of the two stammered at us.

"You two do not understand; we care not for any so-called lords of any lands," Josephus answered the younger brother.

"You are going to die for the murder of our brothers." The oldest hissed through his clenched teeth.

"We are your judgment for the murder of a family, the death of an innocent. If we could spare the time, we would ride and hold your father in judgment for his actions in this." My telling the spoiled men we are judging them had the effect Josephus and I wanted. We were too close for the younger brother to use his bow. Standing with his older brother, he grabbed the sword and squared off with Josephus.

Chapter 18

I STOOD ACROSS THE fire from the oldest brother, the man who would inherit his father's title. I smiled at the killer of the unarmed, then moved to my left. He returned my smile and advanced to meet me. I watched as his smile dropped from his lips as I pulled my sword free.

"This is the blade your brother fell to. I watched him die in the mud. It was a fitting death for a pig such as he." I told my adversary as we squared off. His reaction to my defaming his brother was venomous and immediate. He ran at me, swinging his sword over head, trying to cut me down.

I stood my ground, then I stepped aside and swung my fist. Throwing my fist with my weight behind the punch had the desired effect. His nose crunched under my fist, and as his head snapped back, I kicked him in the groin. When my kick landed, the older brother doubled over, retching. I watched as he tried to retreat, his nose bleeding, dragging his sword as he held his wounded manhood with his free hand.

"Catch your breath; I will wait," I told the oldest brother as I leaned on a boulder. I watched as he would flick his gaze from where I stood to where Josephus and his brother fought.

Well, to be honest, it was where his brother fought. Josephus seemed to be bored through most of the contact. When I would not take my eyes off the older brother, the man became angry.

"All of this for some rabble, who thought herself too good for my brother. All she had to do was spread her legs, and we would have let them leave!" He shouted at me.

"All this because pigs of a family whose bloodline should have been wasted think they have the right. When you get to hell, wait for your father, then blame him." I said to the man as he stood up.

"We rule by divine right. Our rule is by God's will." As he told me God's will allowed his family to terrorize the people, I shook my head.

"I can tell you absolutely without a doubt God is disgusted with you and the others. He placed my brother and me in the village to meet your family, to end your family." As I finished what I was saying, Josephus killed the brother he faced. Just as his brother fell to Josephus, the man I faced started to move. The sound of his youngest brother falling to Josephus caused the oldest to look away. In this flash of movement, the oldest and last son of their father forfeited his life to my sword. Holding the oldest brother on my sword, I looked him in the eye as he started to beg for his life.

"You listen to me. There is no redemption for you or your brothers. The only place you are going is hell; a demon awaits you in the blackness. My brother and I know this as fact; what you never knew is we carry with us the secrets of our lord. We are monks trained to rid the world such as you." When I finished, I pulled my sword out of his body. Josephus and I watched as the oldest and last brother sank to the ground. He wept for his lost life, and during his weeping, we never once heard him cry for any of his dead brothers.

Josephus and I gathered up their horses, along with all the brothers left at their fire. We decided to keep the horses as for the brothers and what they left behind. Josephus thought we should build a great pyre and burn it all.

"If they send anyone after these four, we shouldn't leave a trail for them," Josephus said. I knew my brother was right, so we spent most of the next day gathering wood for the fire. After the winter, we found plenty of broken and dead trees to use. Once we had the pyre built, I stood beside Josephus and watched as he shot flaming arrows into the logs. Once the pyre caught and was burning, neither of us wanted to stay and watch the flames consume the brothers' bodies.

As we rode away from the pyre, the horses we kept seemed overly nervous. After a few miles, we hoped they would have settled down. That night Joseph and I went to the new horses and looked them over. What we found angered the two of us as we looked these majestic animals over. We found where they had been whipped. They had suffered terrible abuse.

"Now, boys, you are safe here with us," Josephus spoke softly to one of the geldings. The horse looked at him, and we could still see the fear in the horse. They all stood still and let us care for them. Like our horses, they enjoyed the attention.

"They are good horses; there is no need to beat them. Animals like these will kill themselves for a kind master." My brother told me as we brought the horses fresh grass.

After our evening prayers Josephus and I sat down for our meal. We watched as the horses nodded off, all standing together. For the four horses we gathered from the four brothers, they seemed to crave contact with their new friends.

As the days turned into weeks, our new horses came to trust us. We switched out riding horses day by day, and one day the big bay came to me. I never called him; all I did was pick up my saddle. I was going to walk over to him, but I stood still as he walked up to me. I knew he loved to have his ears scratched, so I took some time and did just that.

The snow pulled back to the top of the mountains, and nature started the dance of life. I marveled at this as we passed over the hills and through the passes. Mothers with babies follow them through the fresh grass. One night when we had decided to stop, I became enthralled watching a mother black bear. She had two balls of black fur running around, Josephus and I laughed as she tried to get them to follow her. I pointed to one of the cubs as it scooted just out of reach of its mother.

"That has got to be the boy cub," I stated, then watched as the little ball of fur jumped on the other cub. Josephus and I watched and laughed at the antics the bear cub tried as they crossed the valley.

The sunset brought out all the colors God intended when he started his creation. We sat beside our fire and watched with wonder as the snow at the peaks blossomed with the orange and reds of the setting sun. We could not look away as the reds slowly turned into the royal colors of blues, then purples. Sitting beside our fire. Josephus and I stopped watching the peaks of the mountains when the stars began to appear.

"When the night begins this way, I know everything will be fine. Everything will work out for us and the treasure, little brother," Josephus said as he lay down. I looked over at my brother. I knew sometime in the future, we would have to part. I couldn't tell him this, for I also knew if I did, he would never leave me. Then our savior and the other treasures we found would be in danger.

So day after day, night after night, we moved. Always following the map copied from caves and from a boulder. A boulder sitting under a small lake, where our brothers hid it centuries before. Moving to the mountain shown to us by a skull in a cave guarding a secret path to a church.

As the weeks passed, Josephus and I followed the path shown to us. We marveled at the beauty in the mountains and the high alpine valleys. It was one of these high alpine valleys my brother looked down upon from a high ridge.

Josephus and I were surprised to see sheep in the valley below us. We watched the sheep, knowing there must be a shepherd close by. Sitting on our horses, Josephus and I watched as two young men stood looking up at us. One of the boys looked panicked and then ran to the east.

I waved to the shepherd, who still watched us from the valley. To my relief, the boy raised his arm and waved back, then ran after the other boy. Josephus and I decided to see where the boy was running to, and we turned and rode to the east. As we rode on the ridge, I could see the boys running in the valley below. The ridge overlooked a settlement in the valley below; we could make out huts where people lived.

We could see two of the huts had smoke rising out of chimneys. My brother and I sat on the ridge in sight for the whole settlement to see before we started to move down into it.

"It would be nice if they had some mutton to sell. If not, potatoes and such will be welcomed." Josephus was saying as we slowly made our way down from the ridge to the settlement.

People came to their doors and windows, most of the people looked friendly. Some even gave us a slight wave. The only person who seemed to have misgivings about our arrival was a large man. This large man stood beside a forge and anvil. He looked suspiciously as Josephus and I stopped in front of his shop, then climbed off our horses.

"Excuse me, sir, would you have the time to look at this horse. I think he has a bad shoe." I said as I walked over to the big bay.

"Before I do anything, can you pay for services?" He asked, folding his big arms.

"Yes, sir, we can pay. Also, we were wondering if there would be foodstuffs for sale?" Josephus asked as he slid off his horse.

"Forgive my gruff husband. He recognized these horses. They belonged to the bastards who call themselves lords. Their father is related to the king to the north of us. He holds no power here, though the way his seed strutted around doing as they please, one would think he did." A sturdy lady of about fifty said as she brought lunch to her husband.

"How is it you men came to have these poor horses." The blacksmith asked as he took a drink of water.

"The brothers you spoke of killed a family this last winter. We found and buried them, and my brother and I prayed over the poor souls. One of the brothers tried to lay hands on what we consider holy. I warned him to leave us be, but he didn't listen. He pulled his sword, and I pulled mine; I'm here." When I finished telling the blacksmith what had happened, he smiled.

"Well, if you did one, then you will have to watch for his brothers." The wife said as another man walked over to see what we were discussing.

"Oh, we met his four brothers on the side of a mountain almost a fortnight past. These were their horses. Now we travel with them; they seem happier with us." Josephus finished as the man stopped.

"This man here raises the sheep you saw down the valley. We have others who raise all the vegetables and grow wheat to make flour. If you need salt, we have a family who lives on the other side of the mountain. They mine salt from the ground; personally, I would not leave the warmth of the sun for what waits below." The blacksmith told us about the others in the settlement. He seemed proud of the life the families were making here in the mountains.

"Thank you for your help," Josephus said as he shook the men's hands. The blacksmith led the big bay over to a hitching post. Then the big man gently coaxed the horse to raise his hoof so he could examine the shoe.

"The shoe has come loose; I can reshoe him if you wish." The blacksmith said as he patted my horse.

"I think that will be for the best; I do not want him to throw a shoe out there," I said as the beefy blacksmith nodded, then turned and went to his shop.

Josephus and I stayed in the mountain settlement for the night. Then in the morning, with our new supplies brought to us, we paid the people, smiled, said our goodbyes, then rode away from the settlement. Again we rode into our quest, knowing there was a small church with someone buried we needed to find.

Josephus and I spoke of the clues we had found so far and where they had led us so far. The beauty of the land we rode in took my breath away on more than one occasion. We smiled at the beauty of this creation, given to a most favored child. During the nights, we looked into the firmament as the stars appeared. One memorable night we sat and watched as streaks of light blazed their way across the sky; it was then we knew God sat and smiled on this world.

"What do you think they are?" I asked as Josephus and I sat silenced by the beauty we were allowed to witness.

"I do not know; it seems the stars themselves are falling to earth," He said as we continued to watch. I never said anything; I gave a silent prayer, hoping some would stay in the sky.

The day after we watched the lights flash across the sky, Josephus and I sat overlooking a small stone church. Just as it was depicted in the painting, this small church sat on the edge of a cliff. From where we stood, we could see what seemed to be a marker.

Chapter 19

SITTING ON A FLAT STONE ledge overlooking the rocky valley set high in the mountains, I looked for a path to descend. When Josephus pointed a narrow winding path, I knew we would have to walk the horses to the bottom. Walking to where the trail started, I looked down, then back to my brother.

The only way to the bottom, to the church where we hoped the key would unlock something, was a stony path we were forced to take. We both worried about the horses as the path twisted around more significant obstacles set in the way. I stopped at a small stream and then checked the horses. Josephus checked with me; he wondered if our old horses were taking the path well.

I know, like myself, Josephus worried about our newest horses. I would hear him speaking to them as we followed the path down. Once we checked and calmed the horses, we started down the path again. Like myself, I know Josephus kept watching the sun as it made its trip across the sky.

We knew the path would be untraceable in the dark of the night. One misplaced step, and a thousand-foot drop waited for us. I wanted to hurry, to be off this path before the sun finished its daily travel. Looking back at our horses, it did not take long to see they were going as fast as they could. If one slipped on a rock and thrashed around, they could kick another horse or Josephus and myself. Up in the mountains was no place to be with a horse trying to regain its footing. The day went slowly, step by step, one turn in the path at a time.

We watched the sun as it crawled lower and lower. On more than one occasion, I looked back to Josephus, who would shrug his big shoulders. It was his way of telling me he didn't think we were going to make it to the bottom before the sun sank out of the sky.

I started to hope for a flat place on the path where we could set up a camp. A place where we could picket the horses, a place where they would be safe for the night.

I was confused when I found myself looking at a flat plain. I could not believe we made it just as the sun fell behind the mountains. The small stone church stood at the edge of the plain. I turned and looked back up the path we had just come down. Just to be sure, we had made it all the way down.

The stars started to poke their way through the blanket of the night by the time we reached the small church. While Josephus and I were excited to begin exploring the church, we knew doing so at night could prove dangerous. So we took care of the horses, then ourselves.

"I know you have thoughts about what could be waiting for us," I said. Josephus and I started when a cry came to us on the wind. The sound was so unnerving; both man and beast resting beside the church stood stock still. For a moment, it seemed even the breeze stopped in anticipation of danger. I looked to Josephus, hoping he would know what made the cry.

"Do not look to me, little brother. I have no idea what made that sound," Josephus told me. We looked into the night. It seemed just as we became comfortable with the idea, it had been a passing bird of some kind. We settled down again, only to be brought up standing by the same sound. Looking around the corner of the church, I tried to find the direction the cry was coming from. It seemed to be all around us; it came from everywhere and nowhere. Going to the horses, I tried to comfort them, to settle them. When the cry stopped, they would settle quickly.

The warbling cry sounded three more times that first night. That first night Josephus and I said our nightly prayers, then ate a cold meal. We never thought about gathering wood for our fire as we traversed the path down to the church.

Setting our camp on the high stony pass of a mountain. Where a church was shown to us by a painting. A painting on a wall, in a cave on another mountain pass. The direction of this church was given to us by a skull, with a key, in a cave on another mountain.

The church's front door opened over the precipice between it and another mountain. Now as we sat in the night, the ground was eerily lit by the stars above us.

Josephus and I were awake as the sky above us started to show the first signs that night was once again losing the battle with the coming day. As the sky lightened with the retreating night, Josephus started to gather our camp together. Our horses nibbled the rough grass cropping up between the stones of the high pass.

"Well little brother, what shall we find this day?" Josephus asked me as I stood.

"I do not know, something wonderful, I hope," I answered as we both turned to look at the church.

Standing next to the church, Josephus and I looked around the corner. The front of the building was indeed right at the precipice. Turning, we walked around the church to the other side. The marker we first saw in the painting, we both realized this marker was more than a place of burial. As we looked the marked stone over, we both could see a tomb depicted on it.

This strange tomb sat in a grove of trees. A lone man sat upon the tomb, his head hanging in despair. In the background, we could see another man. The man in the background was looking into the sky beseechingly to the heavens.

"What do you make of this brother?" I asked Josephus. I watched as my brother shook his head, then shrugged his big shoulders.

"I have no idea what this depicts; at this point in our quest, I believe Joseph knew his love and family would be safe. Knowing this, Joseph turned to go home," Josephus told me of his suspicion; I looked at the stone again.

"Something about the man looking to the heavens bothers me," I told my brother and quest mate. I could not tell Josephus what bothered me about the man looking to the heavens. Gathering parchment and charcoal, I drew what the marker depicted.

Once I was finished with the marker, Josephus and I moved on to the church. I wanted to try the front door to see if it was locked. If it was, would the key we had found in the skull unlock the door?

My thinking was if it did indeed unlock the heavy wooden door of the church, then it was probably Joseph who was there. Walking toward the corner of the church, Josephus and I looked at the front of the small building.

Then we looked over the edge, down into the canyon below. Now I have been in the mountains for some time by then and have seen the world from high vistas. This time, however, when I looked over the edge, my stomach tightened up, and my knees wanted to buckle.

"Well, this a bit disconcerting," I said as I took a step back.

"To say the least." Josephus returned and then edged his way onto a narrow walkway leading to the door. I watched him as he shuffled his way to the church door.

"Well, little brother, we have a problem," Josephus said when he reached the door.

"Just one, well, let's have it, brother," I said mockingly, for which I was rewarded by Josephus sticking his tongue out at me.

"Our problem is the door; it only opens outward." When Josephus told me how the door opened, I looked over the edge.

"Can we open it with the key?" I asked.

"No, it is some kind of puzzle lock. This is going to take some time and a lot of thinking," Josephus said as I watched, holding my breath as Josephus made his way back to where I stood.

Standing at the side of the church, I looked the wall over. I know I must have looked foolish, standing with my nose so close to the stones of the building. I had an idea we were missing something so fundamental. As I moved my gaze over the heavy stones making up the wall, a pattern formed.

As the sun lowered, the pattern became clear. Standing in the golden light of the late afternoon, I found something that made me sit down.

"What great thing have you found, little brother?" Josephus asked when he saw me sit with my back to the church wall.

Try as I might, I couldn't speak for a moment. Sitting there, I would open my mouth to speak. The only sound I would produce was a croaking sound. Looking at me, Josephus walked to the wall and placed his face against it as I had. After a few moments, he to sat down, shaking his head.

"Did you see it?" I asked when I was able to speak.

"Are you asking me about the banner?" Josephus asked me. As I was nodding, neither of us could believe it. Here on this little stone church, in the middle of an unknown pass. High in the mountains separating the land of the Franks from the land of the Basques.

Etched into the wall of the church was a sheaf of wheat. Hidden behind the wheat was a wolf. When I first saw the sheaf of wheat, I was confused as to what it meant. Then I remembered my days with Joseph and his teachings. The bundle of wheat is the banner of one of the twelve tribes of Israel. It is the banner for the tribe of Joseph, was it meant to be a message from Joseph?

"The wolf confuses me, though," Josephus was saying when I returned from remembering my lessons with Joseph.

"Well, you are going to think me at a loss of my senses. If I remember correctly, the wolf is the banner for one of the lost tribes of Israel," As I said it, Josephus looked at me as if I had lost all my senses.

"No brother, I to think what I am about to say senseless. However, I believe the wolf is meant to be the tribe of Benjamin. The cursed tribe of Israel. The tribe of Benjamin lost the battle and was punished for their ways. Judah, Manasseh, Ephraim, and Gad, along with the other tribes of Israel, forbade the men of Benjamin to take wives from the other tribes." I recounted the lesson Joseph had taught me so many years before.

"Now, after some time, the leaders of Israel allowed the men of Benjamin to take wives to save their tribe. Many families of Benjamin left Israel. It was never recorded where they intended to go," I said. When I finished, I looked back at the marker as the light faded from the day.

"I think this is going to see us here for quite a while." I agreed with my brother, neither of us knew how long we would be at the church.

As we sat by our fire the second night, our conversation turned to Joseph. We had always thought he went back to the holy land to keep others from following his Mary.

"We have been together over two years now, brother, and I often wonder why Joseph would have gone back to the holy land?" I asked as we watched the night sky.

"I often wondered the same thing. I asked Joseph many times what would have convinced him to leave his love and grandchildren." Josephus started, then fell silent, leaving me hanging on the edge of an answer.

"What did he tell you, brother?" I asked, wanting an answer.

"He never did; Joseph would change the conversation to another area of our day. I think remembering his love and the children and how he left them was painful for him. If the truth is told, I don't think it was his choice to leave Mary."

"Well, I know Joseph would not have left them if he had a choice. It must have been for their safety. Something or someone must have brought him news of danger if he were to stay." There was no way I could know any of the past, or what had taken place. However, from what I knew about Joseph, I know in my heart he would not have abandoned his family.

"I always thought the same way." Josephus agreed as the stars danced overhead.

The stars slowly crawled across the blanket of the night. Josephus and I watched as the sun fought the ink of night back to the corners of the world. Again we stood looking at the church; I wanted to study the three walls. If there was an etching on one wall, there could be more on the others.

As the sun rose from the east as god had intended from the dawn of time. We were standing at the east wall as the sun came up. Josephus and I closely watched the wall for the shadow of any etching to show us.

I held my breath with the anticipation of a promise, what could be, what would be. As the morning sun crawled higher into the azure sky of the mountains.

Standing with Josephus, I craved there be another etching on the church's east wall. As the sun rose higher, my dismayed grew, turning. I looked at my brother.

"I can not see anything more," I said, the disappointment evident in my voice.

"Not on this wall, little brother. Remember, there are three other walls for us to explore." When Josephus reminded me of the other walls. I had to hold myself back from running around the church.

Before I reached the church's west wall, I knew it was the wall where the door stood. Watching the sun crawl across the sky. We were forced to wait until the sun reached its highest point before any etchings could be seen.

To both our surprise, the west wall held etchings on either side of the door. I did not realize I had stepped out onto the narrow walkway to study the etchings.

"Be careful little brother," Josephus warned me as he reached out to keep me from stepping backward.

"This is the same as the painting. It shows a man on a ship. The ship is on a vast ocean. In the background, I can make out a great beast. It seems to be following the ship. A storm looming just behind the beast." I described the etching to Josephus as I shuffled my way off the walkway.

Sitting by the ashes of last night's fire, I drew the etching on the east wall beside the door. Josephus sat and looked over the drawings from the east wall and the marker stone.

"What do you think little brother, could all this be linked. Could this be what Joseph is trying to tell us, something from all those many centuries ago?" Josephus asked me, then stood. I looked up, wondering why he had never waited for me to answer.

"Where are you going, brother?" I asked as Josephus started to walk towards the church.

"I think I know the answer to the puzzle lock, to open the door." He answered as I stood up.

"What brought you to this answer?" I asked.

"You know Joseph and the lengths he has gone to up to this point to protect Mary and the children. You know what might happen if you are wrong." I told my brother as we walked towards the church. I turned and ran back to our campfire. I wanted the chest holding our savior and the book with all the information about his family with Josephus and myself.

I don't know why I wanted the chest with me. I just picked it up and followed Josephus.

"I understand how dangerous this is. I also believe I have the answer." Knowing he was going to try his answer, I just smiled and hoped he wouldn't be hurt again. I stood at the corner of the west wall by the etching of the man on the ship. As Josephus passed the etching, he started out onto the narrow walkway. I watched as Josephus reached the door and studied the puzzle lock.

It seemed to happen so fast, one second Josephus was standing at the door looking at the lock. The next moment I heard a click, and the door swung open, almost knocking him over the brink.

I yelled out for my brother, for a moment, both Josephus and I thought he was going over the edge. Only his reaching out and grasping the edge of the door kept him from falling.

"By all that's holy, would you be more careful," I said to my brother as he righted himself.

"That was close little brother." Was all Josephus could say as he looked down into the nothingness. I ran around the church so I could enter without stepping over the abyss. Josephus and I stepped into the church together. I did not realize I still carried the chest with the mortal remains of Jesus.

Just as we stepped over the threshold of the entrance, we both heard a faint click. Before we could move, the heavy wooden door slammed shut, and four snapping sounds were heard from the door. Turning, I tried to open the door, to no avail.

"I do believe we are trapped in here unless you have thought of the answer lock to get out," I said to Josephus as he shrugged. I turned in a circle I tried to take in as much as possible.

Standing in front of the door at the west wall of the church. The first thing to come to our attention was the two effigies on the floor. Walking over to these effigies, Josephus and I kneeled by them. I placed the chest holding our savior, along with the rest of the treasures at the head of the images, then wiped away the dust from the inscriptions.

"Everything is written in old Hebrew," Josephus said as he ran the tips of his fingers over the script.

"Um, brother, I can read old Hebrew," I said out loud, still trying to grasp what I was reading, of who it said these effigies were of.

"Well, little brother, do not keep me in suspense."

"These effigies are of a husband and wife. These should not be here. These people should be far, far from this place," I said as I touched the brow of one.

"Come now, Rene, tell me so I can have that same shocked look on my face," Josephus said with a smile.

"These effigies are of Anna and Joachim. You know the mother and father of Mary, the mother of...." I was explaining when my brother threw a biscuit at me.

"I do know who Mary was," Josephus said as I tossed his biscuit back to him. We sat beside the carved stone depicting the mother and father of the holiest woman to ever walk the earth. A woman who was picked at birth to be the mother of gods only earthly son. His voice to us directly, to show his love for us. Then what did we do? We killed his son.

"How can these be here? Surely her mother and father are not under here?" Josephus asked as he looked over at me.

"No, I do not actually think her mother and father are here. I think these are here to pay them homage. These people knew what their daughter and grandson would be. They lived their life as normally as could be expected." I told my brother as we stood.

"We need more light in here, look for some torches or something," Josephus said as we felt our way deeper into the church. The further we moved into the church, the darker it became. I was shuffling along when I almost fell into what felt like a small ditch. Seeing that I was in a church in the middle of the mountains between the Franks and Basque. I didn't think it would be a ditch, more than likely I would find a drainage trench cut in the floor, for spring runoff.

How wrong I was when I knelt down to feel the bottom of the trench; my fingers touched oil. Pulling my hand back, I smelled the tips of my fingers. To my surprise, the oil carried no smell; I tried to think of oil with no scent.

Looking around I tried to find Josephus, it had become a private joke of sorts. Every time I found a trench with oil in it, I lit it. I would always look to ensure my brother wasn't standing in it. However, if he was close I would lite it to scare him, I thought it was great fun.

Taking another look around, I could see Josephus by the effigies of Anna and Joachim. Pulling out my flint and striker, it took only two flashes with the flint to ignite the oil. I stood watching the flame race around the entirety of the church's floor.

I looked around the small church, along with the two effigies Josephus and I found when we entered. I was shocked when I looked toward the altar and found a simple stone chest.

Standing by the burning oil I looked at the chest as it sat on a raised alter. A small nave held a robe; time had faded the colors of the robe. Looking back at the now locked door, I found Josephus kneeling down, studying the floor.

As the flames flickered, I could see etchings on the church walls. These etchings were much clearer, though time was no different on the inside of the church. There was no weather, so the etchings were as clear as the day they had been carved into the stone.

It showed clearly the life of Mary of Nazareth. It showed her being betrothed to Joseph. Their engagement, her being visited by the angel Gabriel. This was when Mary was told she would become the mother of man's savior. Gods living son was to be born unto her. The etching revealed how Mary worried about her betrothal to Joseph. The etching told of her life to the point she gave birth to Jesus.

"I don't understand why it would end at the birth; she did so much more," Josephus said as we both looked the wall over, hoping there was more. Looking at the wall, I wished there were more etchings, that more of Mary's life was told on these walls. I had forgotten about the tomb I had found when I lit the oil.

"Little brother, what about the chest you found earlier?" Josephus asked as we turned around. I looked at Josephus, then back to the chest, then at the altar and the stone chest on it.

We looked at the altar first; I walked around it looking for a trap of some sort. As I searched the altar, I found nothing to worry about. So we turned our attention to the stone chest, it was about the same size as the one we carried everywhere Josephus and I went.

I looked back to where the chest sat. I wanted to go and move it to the center of the church. Josephus must have caught me looking at the chest before I could move to retrieve it. Josephus walked to it and had it moved to the center of the church.

Again we walked around the stone chest on the altar. I used my hand to wipe the dust from the stone chest; to my surprise, I found writing. It was in old Hebrew. I read the text and then looked up at Josephus.

"This is a turn I was not expecting," I said as I looked back at the writing, thinking I must have read it wrong.

"This says we are standing in the church built for Mary, for her final resting place," I told Josephus. I looked up at my brother as I read the last line." The strange thing is, this does not make any sense, it says here this was built so she could, at last, know peace," I read out loud. I looked at Josephus.

"What do you mean, at last, know peace?" He asked as he looked over the chest.

"Well, I'm not sure. It just says. This holy place has been sanctified by a son taken, for everlasting peace of a loved mother."

When I finished reading the script, Josephus and I looked the chest over again.

"If she is not here, then where?" Josephus asked. I know how foolish I must have looked as I looked around the church.

"We know those two by the entrance are to represent her parents. Does that mean the one in the middle is Jesus?" I asked as we stood at the altar.

"No, I don't think so; I might be wrong. I think it's Joseph." When he told me what he thought, I looked at Josephus and nodded.

"Your right; I think she had this place built for herself as a place of safety after her death. Then something changed. Something didn't make this sanctuary safe any longer," I said.

"Maybe they found out about the traitor. No Joseph had taken care of him long before this." Josephus recounted, then he turned and looked at me.

"What, what is it?" I asked, knowing he had a thought.

"I think Mary wanted to go back to Joseph; however, she knew she couldn't. I think she had this built hoping they could be together in the end. Then they saw something that caused her to abandon her final resting place," Josephus said as we turned in a circle, wondering what they could have seen.

"Let us go and have a meal. We can resume our contemplation by the night's fire." Josephus said as he turned toward the door. I was about to remind my brother about the puzzle, then waited. I wanted to see if he knew the exit puzzle. I had thought about it the whole time we were in the church of Mary. I had solved the word that gave us entrance to the church, then knew the exit answer.

As it turned out, so did Josephus; the answers were two names. To enter the church, you had to spell the name of Christ's son. To exit the church, the daughter's name had to be entered, both in old Hebrew.

For the time being, we decided to leave the chest holding our savior along with the scrolls with the names of the children and the family lineage in the church for safety.

It was nice to be out in the fresh air of the mountains again. Standing beside the church, Josephus and I could see a new horse standing with ours. A man sat at our fire, a pot steamed, showing he was cooking something.

"It feels a bit ominous, us coming out of the church only to find a stranger sitting cooking soup," I said to Josephus as we walked toward the stranger.

"Well, I do not think he wants to fight. Well if it was myself, I wouldn't have made soup." He answered as we neared the stranger.

"Good afternoon," Josephus called out as we walked into our camp.

"Good afternoon...brothers." The stranger said as he turned to look at us

Chapter 20

THIS STRANGER CALLING us brothers went from feeling ominous to feeling dangerous. When he turned to look at Josephus and me, there was hate and loathing in his gaze.

"Well, what brings you to our camp this day." I could not believe how calm Josephus was as he asked the stranger a question.

"I am here to retrieve what belongs to my masters." The stranger said as he stood. The large pot still steamed over the fire, and seeing this man, my hunger deserted me.

"You can give me what you have found, so I can return it to its rightful owners. Then we can have soup and go our way. You will be alive. Or you can try and keep it from me, and you will die. I'll have it anyway." The stranger told us, smiling the whole time.

"First, you need to tell us what it is you think we have?" I said to him; as I spoke, I could see the skin around his eyes tighten. While he might be a skilled fighter, his emotions betray him. Both Josephus and I knew he was not used to being defied. Asking him a question was an act of defiance.

"You know what you have; you know it belongs to others. I am not going to ask again. Either you give me what you have taken, or I will take it from you." The stranger ordered. I could see the rage building in the man. He kicked the pot off the fire when Josephus laughed at the order.

"We have left it in the church where it will be safe if you do not have the right answers for the puzzle lock on the door. Well, everything we have found will be safe for all time." I told the stranger as his rage at being defied grew in him.

Smiling at him, I took another step toward the man. My movement seemed strange to him, as I moved forward, he took a step to the side. It was as if he wanted to keep a distance between us.

I then took another step towards the stranger who had found us in the mountains. As I took my step, he threw off his cloak, revealing throwing knives. As his cloak dropped from his shoulders, Josephus and I took the last steps running at the man. For the stranger to use his knives properly, the would-be killer needed to have space between him and us, his targets.

Both Josephus and I sought to deprive him of the space he needed. As we closed the ground with the assassin. The stranger took a step backward, a rock rolled under his foot. I watched as the man fell, thinking he would surrender when he hit the ground. A greater surprise came to me when Josephus raced past me. I watched my brother kick the stranger in the head as he landed on his back.

The man twitched and then became still. I watched for the movement of his chest. Nothing Josephus killed the stranger with one kick to the back of his head.

"Look, look at the pot; look what he was cooking." My brother stammered. I looked down to where Josephus's finger pointed at the pot the stranger had knocked over. I felt my stomach turn in on itself, spilling out of the pot were hands. Human hands, he had been boiling human hands.

"What was he doing? He wasn't going to eat that. Tell me he wouldn't eat it." I said as the shock of what I was looking at struck me.

"No, I don't think he was going to eat it. I believe he was going to try and feed it to you." Josephus told me as he turned to look at the pot.

"What, you can not be serious?" I asked.

"Why in the name of all that is holy would he want me to eat that?" I questioned.

"It is a spell, with the flesh of man and the blood from the birth of a bastard, along with some other items. They think your purification can be reversed." Josephus told me as we searched the stranger's belongings.

We removed the knives from the man who found us. I walked away from the camp to try and dig a hole in the mountain. I quickly learned I was wasting my time and energy, so Josephus and I opted for the abyss. We said a simple prayer over the man. Then threw him out into nothingness, and neither of us tried to see where the body went. Knowing he was boiling human parts, along with blood, was enough not to care about his resting place.

Sitting by the fire, going over what we had found from the stranger. I came across a scroll; it had been written two years before. Whoever wrote the scroll told of how they discovered the home of Joseph. They had found the house empty and abandoned. They feared the father had died before they found him.

The writer told of how he had asked around he had found out the old man had adopted a male child. It goes on to tell of how one day, Joseph's neighbors went to check on him after he had been missed. Only to find the house empty. It seemed they moved overnight.

"Why would they be looking for Joseph? Nobody knew who he was." Josephus asked. I wished I knew. I did not have an answer for my brother; all I could do was read on.

Once the man found out Joseph had either moved or died, he sent word back. He stayed in Joseph's house, waiting for orders to come telling him his next course of action.

"This scroll tells of how the stranger ended up here at our camp. It seems the man had stayed in Joseph's house until another came to him with orders. The man who found Joseph's house kept records of everything they did. Everywhere they went, everyone, they spoke to while searching for me. It says here they knew about the bastard boy he adopted." As I read the scroll, the thought of some strangers knowing I was a bastard angered me.

"So who cares if they know about your past? It is only the present and future that matter." Josephus said to me he was right, of course.

"It says here the man who came here and the other managed to find where we came ashore in the first village where we bought our horses. The one from Joseph's house calls himself Alpheus. The man who came here was called Ursus. Alpheus writes he had to keep Ursus from killing the brother of the innkeeper." As I read the accounts of the two, who had been set on our trail. I could see Josephus starting to gather a meal for us.

"The innkeeper and the others in the village refused these two any service. They were forced to walk out of the village, and they waited in the forest. Then when things became quiet, they crept into the village and stole two horses along with saddles." I stopped putting the scroll down. I was having a hard time believing men followed us across the water into the mountains. Then I thought about the farmer and his wife. When I looked up at my brother, I could see worry on his face.

"The farmer and his wife, the two little ones?" Josephus asked as he turned and looked at me. Picking up the scroll again, I read on, trying to find any mention of the farm.

"It says they tried to follow us into the mountains. However, they could not find our exact route. They took what seemed the most logical. Now they did find where we camped. They searched the area to see why we had spent days there. It says here they never found what held our interest, so they moved on." I read from the scroll.

"The next object they came to was the statue of the brother. The one called Ursus wanted to destroy the statue, but Alpheus again had to stop him. He says here, the one he travels with raged at the statue of the brother. It seemed he had destroyed a sword. This Ursus hacked at the stone until he broke a sword." I read as Josephus cooked some mutton with tea.

"It seems they stayed at the brother for three days trying to learn its secrets. When they failed to open the shield the statue of the brother held, they could see the seams and knew it had opened. Alpheus concluded we had found the statue first and had taken out the treasures." As I read, I looked up at my brother; he was smiling. He had the same conclusion I had. These men sent after us had no idea what they were looking for.

"Keep reading, little brother; we need to know what happened to this Alpheus," Josephus said to me as he dished out the mutton. The scroll was a record of the places the two men found as they tried to follow us around the mountains.

"It seems they were greatly confused as to why we would camp by the small lake," I told Josephus as I read the scroll.

"Did they think to look in the lake for the boulder under the water?" Josephus asked as I chewed some of the mutton.

"Well, if I'm reading this properly, they did realize there was something in the lake. However, they came to a conclusion whatever was under the water was destroyed by the landslide." I told Josephus. I smiled, thinking they had found us by chance.

"After they left the lake of the boulder, they rode into a small town. It is here they heard a man talking about the two strangers who saved his little girl from slavery. They sat and talked to this man; he told them of all the girls we had saved. When they asked him which direction we had gone, the man told them northwest. Said we were on a holy pilgrimage. It seems people wanted to help the men find us. They were now telling people we all were brothers of the same order." When I told Josephus, the men who hunted us lied to people. The assassins sent to kill the two of us told the good people we helped that we were in the same order; he shook his head.

"Giving a falsehood is a sin. To do it with malice takes it to another level," Josephus said. All I could do was agree with my brother.

"Well, after they left the town, the man they spoke with had a bad feeling about them. So he sent word to others to keep quiet about us. As they met other people they would ask about us. When folks in the villages and towns of the mountains said they never saw us, this Ursus would become angry. Then like us, they became stuck when winter came to the mountains." I recounted their story from the scroll.

"This Alpheus fella became sick; it says here he couldn't breathe properly. He ran a high fever." I told Josephus of the illness one of the men sent to find us caught.

"In the last entry, the handwriting was shaking; it talks about how the person would have liked to see Rome one last time." When I finished, I looked up at Josephus as he sat looking at me.

"Well, is that the last of it? Does the other take up the quill and keep the record or..." Josephus never finished the sentence. He didn't have to.

"Something is bothering me; whose hands are those?" I asked as we both looked over to the macabre site. Getting up, we both walked over to the hands. All spilled out of the overturned pot they were being boiled in. I used my sword to put the hands back in the pot.

"Do we bury these or toss them over the side?" I asked as Josephus stood the pot back up.

"Well, on this matter, I can not say. I just hope these hands do not belong to any of the people we met along our path." I agreed with my brother as we wondered what to do. That night as the moon rose over the mountains, we decided to throw the pot with its contents over the side.

The following day we entered the church for the last time. We knew Mary had been here, though she intended this to be her final resting place. Something drove her from it; now it held something in a stone chest. Looking the chest over, we could see where the lid was held down.

With some effort, we pried the lid off the chest; grinning up at us was a skull. Two scrolls were rolled up, one on either side of the skull.

"I am becoming a bit weary at opening something up only to find a grinning skull looking back at us, brother," I said as Josephus reached to remove the skull. As he lifted it over the edge of the chest, it slid apart down the center. Before I could stop myself, I reached out to catch one side before it could fall.

"What happened?" I asked. I knew Josephus did not drop the skull.

"It was broken in half when it was placed in the chest. Something fell out of it when the halves came apart." Josephus said. Looking in the chest, I found another key. We had one from the first skull in the cave with the aperture showing Venus. Now we had two keys.

"It is another key," I told Josephus as he set half of the skull down. It was only then I realized I was still holding the other half of someone's former head. I put half the skull down, then wiped my hand on my cloak. Looking back into the stone chest, I reached in and removed the scrolls. It was then we found a keyhole. Josephus looked at me and then smiled.

"Try the first key; see if it works." Josephus urged me. So I did; pulling the first key out, I held my breath as I placed the key into the hole and turned.

When I turned the key, Josephus and I heard a series of clicks. Looking at Josephus, we both took a step back and waited for whatever was going to happen. With no fanfare, a small door slid aside, revealing a set of stairs dropping into the mountain. As the door slid aside, it revealed a symbol.

Chapter 21

♍

I LOOKED BACK TO JOSEPHUS, who was at this time reaching for the symbol. Like myself, he felt the overwhelming need to touch it. Again I looked down the stairs leading into the darkness of the living mountain. We knew whatever room was down there could not be very big. If it went to the west, it would extend no further than the face of the cliff. Finding a dried torch, I asked Josephus to light it from the oil. He took the torch and went to light it. I smiled when he made me promise not to move from the step I stood on.

When the light from the torch showed us our way, it didn't take long before we found hanging bronze bowls filled with floating wicks. These wicks were floating in the same oil that filled the small trench upstairs. Neither the bowls nor the channel had any odor to the oil.

More of the passage we were in was revealed to us as we lit the oil lamps. As we looked around, we found the walls held paintings showing the mountains the two Marys traveled through with the children. The last image showed the two women with the babies and the brothers sent to guard them. In the background, it showed a lone man standing at the edge of a mountain.

"It's the painting from the cave with the traitor, just seen from the perspective of Mary," I said as Josephus and I reached out and gently touched the painting. Then for the second time in my life, a surge coursed through me. It was so powerful I could not pull my hand back from the painting. I could hear someone screaming. I realized it was my screams as the power brought on visions of a future.

As the power coursed through me, it ripped screams of anguish from me; I could feel Josephus pulling at me. Through it all, I could hear his plea for it to let go of me.

I watched the vision as the power held me fast. I could see the dark fortress on a mount. A young man looked over a valley at it; he walked his horse up a lonely road last used to imprison the men in this place. Now he was looking for treasure for the church. This young man was going to be the savior of the glory we held dear. I knew I was dead, even though I was going to mentor this young man. Then the vision changed; I watched as a ship sailed away from a shore I stood on. Josephus was standing on the deck, and tears ran down my face.

The vision flashed, and Josephus stood on a new land. Men with brown skin watched him as he stood on a strange shore, the chest between his feet. A small island off the coast of a big island. Great floating vessels of ice passed by his redoubt as the years passed slowly by my brother. Again the power coursing through me flashed, and I was standing next to the young man. A new chest at his feet, waves lapped at a shore, he watched as a storm broke on the horizon. I could hear my screams as the power tore them from my throat.

Josephus was pulling, trying desperately to break the grasp the surge had on me. Then just as suddenly as the power that held me so firmly released me, I collapsed into Josephus's arms. Every bone in my body hurt, and my teeth seemed to take on the taste of brass. The muscles in my legs jumped with spasms as Josephus held me.

"Brother, I don't know what it is about these paintings. From now on, you touch them," I said, trying to make light of what had happened.

"If you don't stop doing that, I am going to beat you until your arms fall off," Josephus told me as he looked at my hands.

"I have to tell you of the vision I had while the power had me. However, I would like to wait until I'm sure I can walk, and I would like to see the rest of this tunnel we are in," I told Josephus as he laid me back on the floor.

"After that, you want to see the rest of the passage...little brother...Rene, if you reach out to touch anything, the only power you will feel will be my fist. Am I making myself heard?" Josephus asked; he was so worried he was yelling at this point.

"I hear and understand, big brother," I told him as I struggled to stand, the muscles in my back and legs still twitching.

The rest of the passage held other paintings of the mountains and the path we were on. The last image in the gallery was of a church.

The church we were standing under right now. It was in the background, the mountains behind it. Holy light fell over the church, and a dove could be seen landing. The dove seemed to watch as a procession moved off into the distance. A coffin is being carried at the head of the line. A lone man wearing a tunic with the insignia of the order on it stood at the church weeping. Behind the church, a dark figure waited for the lone brother.

"This one explains why Mary is not here; someone she feared found her. She was afraid they would find the grandchildren, as her last wish she had herself removed." I recounted.

"Removed to where we need to find her," Josephus said as he looked around. I assumed he was looking for another painting. Something to tell where to start, a clue as to where she wanted her remains to be taken. To be hidden to await until she could be reunited with her son.

"When she was taken from this place, I wonder if she was dead. I know what the painting shows, think about it." I said as we turned and looked at the painting again.

"Ok, let's say she was alive. Would she go back to Jerusalem?" I asked looking at the painting, then shaking my head.

"We know she would never go back there. What about Ephesus?" I asked and looked at Josephus.

"Well, it is said there is a church. It is said to hold her remains under it." He answered then shook his head.

"If that were so, Joseph would have gone and taken her away." When Josephus finished I stood looking at the painting nodding.

"We need to look at the other paintings again. I think the clue to where she might be is in one of them." I said, I had no more than said the words when Josephus turned and looked at me.

"Rene, if your hands leave your sides, I will have to carry you out of here," Josephus said. Looking at my brother, I believed his warning.

"I will not touch a thing, I give you my word," I told Josephus. I watched as my brother smiled, then we made our way back down the passage.

As we traced the passage back to the stairs, the paintings gave no clue where Mary might have been forced to flee to. Turning I looked at the stairs, smiling, then I tapped Josephus on the shoulder.

"Look at the stairs; there is an etching on the steps," I said as Josephus turned and looked.

"Do you think this is the last part of the puzzle?" He asked as we looked at each step.

The etchings show an island; it was far to the north of the church. It showed the procession as it moved out of the mountains onto open ground. As the procession moved along, it was attacked. Many who were taking Mary to where she could be safe died, and still others took up their positions. On the top step of the stairs, the etching showed a great wall. It showed the island cut in half by this wall.

Looking at the last etching on the stairs, I shook my head.

"A wall? I have never heard of a wall cutting an island in half." I told Josephus, at this point in our quest, I was hoping we hadn't come up against a puzzle we could not solve.

"I have, I have been beyond this wall," Josephus said. I watched as my brother reached out with his hand and touched the wall etching.

"What bothers you about this place, brother?" I asked as I watched him.

"It is a land of beauty, fertile fields where one could grow enough he would never have to worry. Sheep become fat in this place, their wool shines with the dew of the morning. It's a beautiful place, I was sent to this place with my unit because of the people who live beyond that wall." Josephus remembered as his fingers traced the wall.

"So you went to this place; it sounds like a fine country," I said, wondering why Josephus seemed stunned as to why Mary would want to go here.

"It is not the land the Roman army feared beyond this wall. It is the people they feared; the generals threw countless men at the people beyond the wall. They are called Picts, a more fearsome fighters I have never seen. If they took our mother beyond that wall, then we have to be careful," Josephus said. I could tell it was not fear he spoke with; it was adoration. Josephus had great respect for the people beyond that wall. I just nodded then we climbed the stairs.

Removing the key caused the stairs to be hidden once again. I watched as Josephus put the key halfway into the keyhole, then he bent it over snapping it off. Looking up at my brother, I knew he did this so no one would ever be able to solve the secrets of the stairs.

We each stopped and looked around the church for the last time. We knew our savior's mother had been here, that she had walked around this very room. I watched as Josephus again spelled out the name of the daughter and the door opened. The sun was welcomed as we stepped out onto the narrow ledge.

It seemed sad to me to be carrying the chest holding our savor's remains. We were taking Jesus away from where his mother should have been safe. Now we stood and watched as the door swung shut for the last time. Standing in the sunlight, despair fell over me as the door to the church swung shut.

Josephus pulled his sword out and, with one mighty swing of his blade, smashed the puzzle lock. Seconds after, his blade smashed the locking device. The narrow pathway under our feet started to slip into the abyss.

We started to run for the side of the church. Though I do not like to remember it. I was forced to toss the chest and jump the last bit of the path so as not to fall in. Josephus gave a mighty leap, landing across my legs. Reaching back I grasped his tunic holding on fearing I would lose my brother with the rocks.

"Well, that was unexpected!" He exclaimed as I turned to look at him. For the briefest of moments, I was at a loss for words.

"Unexpected...unexpected, we have been following a quest that has seen us find hidden rooms where the smallest of keys have unlocked tones of stone...a statue of a brother holding treasures in a puzzle box...where paintings tell of the life of our savior nobody knows about...about how the fallen came to be...and this was unexpected...brother if I am not to reach out and touch any paintings we find. Then you are not allowed to hit things with your sword, hammer...rocks...anything before you ask!" As I spoke, I watched as Josephus's big smile started to form on his face.

"So what do you want to do now?" He asked as we stood up and looked over the edge of what was short minutes ago a path.

"Well, let us get a fresh start in the morning. Do you think we should go back to the settlement?" I asked. I worried that the assassin who found Josephus and I had come through the settlement.

"Yes, I would like to make sure the people are in good health," Josephus answered as we walked back to our camp and our quest.

Chapter 22

THE NEXT MORNING FOUND us back on the winding path where short days ago had brought us down to the church. This time, however, we were leaving the church. We now had a new heading, a new place to try to reach in the quest for Mary.

When we reached the top of the path, where we had not so long ago, we sat on our horses. Looking down at the building, we thought our quest was coming to a close. Now it seemed our hopes of reuniting a mother with her son were further afield.

I remember looking over at my brother and wondering why he was smiling. When I asked Josephus about it, he turned and looked at me.

"We get to keep our adventure for a bit longer, and we also know Mary is safe where ever she is," Josephus said.

"Um, brother, Joseph had left us clues to our destination up to this point. Now we are well and truly on our own; this worries me," I said. Josephus, who, for all our worry, just sat on his mount smiling.

"It is what we were meant for, little brother, so it is what we will do." Josephus returned as we rode through the mountains.

Our first stop was at the mountain settlement. As we arrived, the blacksmith greeted us. Knowing us, the settlement was warmer than our first introduction. We were glad the people had never seen the strange man, who found his way to our camp by the church. The following day Josephus and I shook hands and left the small settlement. We headed north, wanting to find the route Mary and the others may have used.

"We know Mary and the others have gone their separate ways by this point. We know the daughter is with a good family and has gotten the best of everything. The son, however, went with his mother and Mary; where did they go. We needed to find her to bring her and Jesus together, to bring them to our order.

The first day we rode through the mountains, I had a strange feeling, an urge. It felt as if I was being pulled to some unknown destiny. This intense urge, the pull as I called it, had become urgent by the time we had stopped for the night. As we ate after our prayers, Josephus speculated about what the future held for us. As we spoke of the future and what we might find. I told my brother of the urge, the pull I had been feeling all day. Now as we camped by a large crack in the mountain, the pull was almost overpowering. Our horses seemed unsettled when we first arrived and only quieted once Josephus and I moved them away from the crack.

The sky lightened in the morning, though the sun hadn't yet crested the horizon. We decided we should get going and see what was pulling at me. The horses seemed calmer this morning, they went willingly as Josephus and I entered the crevice.

Josephus stepped in front of me as we emerged from the crevice. We both stopped and were shocked at what we found. Standing against a sheer wall of the mountains behind us, we looked out over a valley. This valley was effectively cut off from the rest of the world.

"What do you hear, little brother?" Josephus asked as we stood still.

"I don't think I hear anything," I answered.

"Right, there is no sound, no life sounds, nothing," Josephus said as we stood and looked around the valley.

Standing at the start of the valley, Josephus and I could feel the weight of whatever was here. Stepping out into the grass of the valley, I could swear something was watching us. I could feel its rage, its hatred; it emitted unbridled loathing. For the next few hours, Josephus and I stayed with the horses as we explored.

"I think we should leave soon. We can come back in the morning," Josephus said. I agreed with him this place was a burden to be in. The malice I could feel had started to sap my will, my strength. Looking back to the crevice leading out of the valley, my brother and I gasped in surprise.

On the face of the mountain, above the crevice leading to the outside world. A blackened blaze in the shape of a giant wing stood in sharp contrast to the light grey granite of the mountain.

I looked at Josephus; he was standing with his jaw hanging open. We knew what this had to be. We wondered if the creature could be trapped. Imprisoned the same as the first fallen we encountered. Standing where we were, we could make out the whole shape of the wing. Standing looking up at the shape left on the mountain, my brother and I could only wonder how hot the creature must have been to leave a mark like that.

As the cursed angel fell from heaven, the impact with the mountain melted the hard rock into the shape of the wing. Standing there with the setting sun, Josephus and I could make out individual feathers that would have been on the wing. We both could see the cave at the opposite end of the valley.

"We will come back tomorrow, little brother; for now, let us be free of this place," Josephus said. I nodded and started to head back to where we came into the valley.

That night we asked to be cleansed of whatever was in the valley. After our meal, I asked Josephus what he thought might be lurking in there. We discussed it until night came, and sleep claimed us both. As the night crept on, horrid dreams of death and torture chased my brother and me.

As the stars wheeled overhead, nightmares caused us to jump. We woke to check on each other, for the sights in our dreams convinced one of us had died in the worst imaginable ways.

When at last, the daylight found the edge of the world again. It found Josephus and me sitting by our dead campfire, exhausted from a night filled with torturous dreams.

As the horizon turned grey with the dawning day, neither Josephus nor I wanted to eat. We sat as the rain patted down around us. Once we finished our morning prayers, we gathered the horses and again looked into the crevice.

Standing in our camp looking into the crevice, it took longer to gather our courage that morning. I looked at my brother, then nodded, and we started into the crack. Unlike the day before, Josephus and I knew where we wanted to go. The cave at the other end of the valley seemed to be waiting for us.

Walking through the long grass of the hidden valley Josephus and I noticed the horses wouldn't eat. Before we reached the face of the mountain with the cave. I thought I could see a crumbled shelter.

"Is it my eyes, brother, or was that at one time a house?" I asked, pointing to a pile of sun-bleached polls. Josephus turned and looked to where I was pointing.

"Well, it seems it was a shelter. I wonder who would live here?" Josephus asked as we started towards what was left of the shelter. Going over what was left, we could tell it had once been lived in. Josephus and I could see what had at one time been a blanket. There were smashed clay jars. I went to look at a large copper pot. I looked up at my brother and shrugged my shoulders. Behind the shelter, we found the bones of a donkey and old leather bags for the animal on the ground.

Walking around the shelter Josephus called out to me, he said he had found something. When I joined my brother, we both stared down the bones of who we thought had lived here.

"That would explain the donkey. It would seem this man had tied the poor animal, then walked around the house and died." Josephus surmised.

"Let us do what is right by this poor soul," I said as we looked for the best place to bury the bones.

Once we had picked a place Josephus and I buried the last human resident of the valley. Once we became used to the lack of sound in the valley, it became almost peaceful. It wasn't until we tried to place a cross over the grave that Josephus and I learned there was a force there.

As I place the cross marking the grave, a fierce wind howled through the valley. At times it seemed to carry a cry of anguish on it. I looked at Josephus, I wanted to ask a question. I just couldn't find my voice. Together we looked towards the cave again.

"We need to go there; whatever holds sway over this valley, we need to find it," I said as I took the first step, then another as I moved on. Each step became easier. Before I realized it, I was standing at the opening of the cave. On each side of the opening were drawings. On the left side of the cave entrance was a winged creature.

It seemed to be soaring over the valley, its wings spread wide. On the right side of the cave, the painting showed the same creature lying in the valley, its wings broken and burnt, its body bent, twisted, and deformed. Looking back at the horses and then at Josephus, I nodded as we both entered the cave.

The first thing to come to us was an underlying smell of decay, it was more than rotted flesh. The smell was more than death. There was something under the odor, something genuinely foul. Josephus said if the scent was stronger it would remind him of the sewers of Rome in the spring when they would overflow. When Josephus told me about the sewers overflowing, I was glad I had never visited Rome.

As we walked into the cave, we found the floor littered with bones. I wondered what kind of animal bones they were until I kicked a human skull. Again I could not help thinking about how many former heads I had found so far. The answer disturbed me.

"Well, we know who, or whatever, was here wasn't picky about what it ate," Josephus said as he looked at the bones. Pulling my sword, I stopped to light a torch. I nodded to my brother and then heard his sword slide from its scabbard. With our torches, we walked through the bones, hoping whatever seemed to have an appetite for the flesh of men had moved on from this place. I expected the thing to be dead.

It didn't take long for us to find the creature. As we stood looking over the grotesque bones, neither Josephus nor myself knew what to think.

The thing lying in the cave was enormous; the skull was twenty times the size of an average man. Standing, we looked over the bones and came to the same conclusion. Whatever this thing was, it was gigantic. Walking around the skeleton, I found one of its weapons.

"I think this was its sword," I said to my brother as I knelt down to get a better look.

"Do not touch anything," Josephus said. I remember turning to see what had him concerned. I found him pointing to a group of paintings on the wall behind the bones.

"What are they about?" I asked as I walked toward him.

"These paintings were done by that evil thing," Josephus said as he flung his arm to indicate the bones lying in the cave.

"This first painting talks about Lucifer and his injuries, about how Michael and the others tried to reason with Lucifer. Lucifer, driven insane by the evil infesting him chose to fall, along with the other angels.

"What is? This is an evil thing, brother; I can feel this is not what we are here to find. Whatever it is, we need to go deeper into the cave." I said as I stepped over the bones again.

As the torches lit our way further into the darkness, I could feel something ancient, something genuinely evil knew Josephus and I were in the cave. I looked back to the man I called brother. I knew he was cursed to wander the earth until he could reunite the mother and son. I knew we wouldn't find anything good in this cave, only evil.

"Something waits for us in there," I told Josephus as I pointed to a gigantic doorway, then stepped into a room.

Chapter 23

FOR A MOMENT, WE STOOD shocked; our minds couldn't comprehend what we were seeing. I blinked, thinking my eyes were playing a trick on me.

Josephus reached out and touched my arm. I don't know if it was to stop me from going any closer or if he needed to steady himself; I never asked.

A giant cage sat in the center of this room. The cell was enormous. It looked big enough to hold fifty horses and their riders. Before we entered the room, Josephus and I held our torches high to try and spread their light further into the inky darkness of the rock.

"What in the name of the holy father was that built to hold?" Josephus asked. I stood looking at the cage. I could see something lying in the center of the cell. Both Josephus and I stepped into the room, holding the cell. I still stared at whatever was lying on the floor of the cage while my brother looked behind and above us.

"There was once a battle in this room, a fierce battle," Josephus said as I turned to see what he was looking at. The walls were scared with cuts that looked made from great swords. Even the floor had deep cuts carved in it. Once our eyes became accustomed to the gloom, we could see gouges everywhere.

"Whatever fought down here was forced into the cage; it lived for eons in there," I said as I pointed to whatever was still lying in the cage. Walking around the cell, we tried to see it from every angle.

When I looked away from the cage, I could make out a shape against a wall of the room.

Looking at Josephus, I nodded to the object. He shrugged, showing he didn't know what it might be. Slowly walking over to what the gloom of the cave conspired to hide from me, I gasped with shock when it became apparent.

"What is it, little brother?" Josephus asked from behind me.

"It's a great arm, an arm not from a man, though," I answered as I pushed at it with my sword.

"There is still flesh on it," I whispered to Josephus; he walked towards me and the arm. Laying a staff length away from the arm was a great sword; it lay shining on the floor. The blade was covered with a black substance.

"I think this might belong to whoever left their arm behind," Josephus said as he knelt down to examine the arm.

"By the look at that arm, I wouldn't call whatever left it behind a who; it was most certainly a what or a thing," I said as we stared at the clawed hand.

Walking to the sword, I looked it over, trying to see if it was a trap. After a moment, I decided it wasn't, then knelt down, thinking something as big as the sword would be heavy. I grasped the hilt and then almost fell backward as I picked up the sword. It seemed to be nearly weightless; I looked at Josephus.

"You're getting stronger little brother." He said as he smiled at me.

"Not this strong; it weighs almost nothing, nothing at all," I said as I walked over to him. Josephus held the sword by the hilt and tested its weight.

"This is a marvel, something so big yet so light." I decided we would take the sword with us, for it had a feeling of great good about it.

Standing in the room with the sword Josephus and I both looked at the cage again. I needed to know what was lying on its floor. I looked at the cave floor and saw a channel running around the cage. Kneeling, I ran my finger along the canal and realized it was filled with oil. Looking at Josephus, I nodded and touched my torch to the oil.

The flames raced around the cage. The light from the fire threw light throughout the room. The thing on the floor could be seen clearly now, along with what was left in the cage.

A gigantic single black feather lay in the center of the cage. As the flames of the oil steadied, I looked up and found a giant hanging from the ceiling. Giving a cry, I grabbed Josephus and jumped back.

"What in the name of the holy mother is that?" I asked as my brother, and I stood looking up into the twisted visage of the monster. To us, it seemed the monster at the start of the cave had a brother, and it was hanging from a great chain.

"I think these things are a type of Nephilim. One sent here to guard something terrible, something so evil it corrupted them. I think they fought each other to the delight of whatever was in there." I said as I reached out with my sword to poke the foot of the giant.

"Do you think they were its jailers, or could they have come break whatever was in there out?" Josephus asked as he walked over to the flaming channel. The lite smoke coming off the flames smelled sweet. It was then I realized what the oil was.

"It's anointing oil, holy oil," I said as Josephus, and I looked at each other.

"Whatever was in the cage was being held by something holy," Josephus said as we stepped back from the flames.

"You may think I have lost my senses, brother, but I think what was here was another of the fallen. A follower of Lucifer, still following Lucifer's plan, the fallen took on human form. Then this evil thing took a human wife. The poor woman then gave birth to the two abominations we see here." I surmised.

"The second painting seems to agree with you. There is a name on the painting; I hope the painting is wrong. It calls the fallen Azazel." Josephus told me.

"It speaks of how near death Azazel was when he found this valley. As Azazel fell, he watched the family who had called this area home. Azazel knew if he could regain enough strength, he could take human form. Once he was in human form, he could marry the daughter and have children. These bones we see here are the product of that evil act. This thing was a Nephilim. A terrible creature born of the fallen and the daughters of man." As Josephus finished, he spat on the paintings.

"I have heard about these Nephilim. It was a grand plan by Satan to corrupt the bloodline of man. In his twisted way of thinking, Lucifer set the fallen loose on the world of man, hoping to stop the coming of the Messiah." I said as I looked at the bones again.

"If that be so, then where is the evil thing? We know angels don't die of old age; they are celestials. They can be killed by another angel with a special blade." Josephus said.

"How else can we explain these two," I said as I pushed the foot of the hanging Nephilim, the giant chain creaking.

"Also, there is only one black feather left in the cage. That was enough to draw me here to this room." I added as we stood looking past the flames to the lone feather lying in the cage.

"Do you think this feather is what is left of Azazel? Could the injuries he sustained in the war have rotted him away to nothing?" I asked.

"I don't think it's what's left of him. I think it was left as a warning. Remember what we trapped in stone back at the four hills." Josephus reminded me as I headed out of the room.

Going to the horses, I retrieved a fresh scroll and my charcoal. I planned to draw the scene in the room below the cave when Josephus came running from the cave.

"The feather is spinning in the center of the cage." He shouted to me as he ran.

"How is that possible?" I asked without thinking. Then a great wind hit us. The gust was so intense I feared I would be blown away. Josephus and I watched as a gathering of black clouds blotched out the sun, turning the day to dusk in a matter of moments. The gathering of the clouds reminded me of the moment Christ died on the cross. At the very moment of his death, a great gathering of the blackest clouds gathered above the hill of skulls. They blocked out the sun causing the day to turn to night.

"I think we should be out of this valley before they let loose," I said as we climbed into our saddles.

"Do not look back, little brother, lest the gates of hell open up to swallow us," Josephus said as we kicked our horses into a hard run, racing for the crevice out of the valley. I never realized I still carried the great sword I had found in the room where Azazel was once held.

Once we reached the crevice, Josephus and I turned to take one last look at the valley hidden in the mountains. As we turned, another gust of wind sought to drive us through the crevice. Neither Josephus nor I wished to argue with whatever power caused the winds. We rode away from the valley, happy to be free of the evil stain Azazel left behind as he crashed to earth.

Over the years, I have spent many a night discussing what haunted the little valley between the mountains. Josephus and I have our own theory about what it was we found. What power caused the feather to start to spin in the cage. As we spoke about that day, Josephus and I knew we had come in contact with absolute evil, a wanting evil, for the second time.

Chapter 24

JOSEPHUS AND I LEFT the valley hidden inside a mountain, and our horses seemed happy. They would break into a canter if we did not keep a reign on them. As we went, our days were spent looking for hidden clues to show us we were on the right path. Days turned into weeks, and those days grew shorter and shorter. Until the frosts came back to the land.

One cold clear day Josephus and I sat on a river bank. We watched a village across the river. As we watched the village, no sound floated to us on the breeze. There were no children, no dogs, not even birds chirping as they made their way through the trees. Josephus nodded to a church sitting on the edge of the village.

"Should we go to the church and ask what happened here?" I asked. Josephus nodded as we started to walk our horses into the slow-moving river. We exited the river at the opposite end of the village of the church. As we walked through the village, my brother and I knew something was terribly wrong.

The shops look as if the owners had just picked up and left. Clothing still sat on tables. As we walked past the butcher, no smell of rotting meat came to us. The meat was left out so long that rot and insects had stripped the bones of flesh. The blacksmith left his tools out in the open to rust.

All the doors hung open nothing was locked or even closed. We tied our horses to a rail at the foot of the stairs. Standing at the foot of the stairs, Josephus and I looked at the doors of the church. We were shocked to find a symbol carved into the church's front doors.

As we stood at the foot of the stairs, Josephus and I stood shocked by the carved third seal of Solomon.

"What in gods name was happening here for this to be carved into these doors?" Josephus asked, his voice breaking in on my thoughts.

"This seal is the third of the forty-four seals of Solomon. It's the Pentacle of Jupiter, meant to protect against an enemy or evil lingering around oneself or the home," I said as I recalled my days with Joseph. The two of us stood in front of the church, still looking at the carved key of Solomon.

"Do you feel anything, little brother?" Josephus asked as I moved forward.

"No, I don't feel anything, nothing evil, nothing good either," I said as I took another step. Before I realized it, we were both standing at the door. Josephus and I stood and looked back at the village; it seemed to be caught out of time. It was a place meant for the lives of families; now it sat dead, rotting.

I grasped the handle of the church doors, said a small prayer then pushed the doors open.

The scene Josephus and I found caused both of us to step back. I recall gasping in shock at the sight of the church filled with dead people.

Standing at the open door, Josephus and I looked at each other. Though neither of us wanted to enter the church, we knew whatever happened to the people of the village would need to be explained. So we steeled ourselves, then took the first step into what had become a mausoleum. As we walked up the center aisle, we looked at the people sitting and lying on the pews.

"There is no sign of violence; no harm befell these people," Josephus whispered as we stopped to check some of the villagers.

In the choir, we could see who we thought would be the priest sitting in a chair. His flesh had long ago left his bones. Like the people who came here for his help, he was nothing but bones.

"What kind of madness could have driven these people to sit here and die?" I asked, not expecting an answer. When Josephus stepped beside me and tapped my shoulder, I almost cried out in fright; he pointed along a wall. I looked at another group of symbols; these were not the key of Solomon.

Under the symbols were the bones of the children. In desperation, their parents tried to save the children from whatever evil they thought was stalking their village. In the living quarters of the priest, Josephus and I found a type of census taken one hundred years before we found the church.

It talked about how sheep started to die, and two weeks later, the priest wrote about milk cows going dry. Pigs began to attack each other killing the piglets, mice, and rats never seen before invading food stores. Everything the rats and mice touched had to be destroyed; the priest feared the black death.

Then a young girl was thrown into a fit. The priest reported she would speak in a language never heard before. He wrote the girl could contort herself into unbelievable positions. To the priest, it was apparent a witch or demon had invaded their village.

At first, people moved to other villages in the Languedoc. When people in those villages found out where the newcomers were from, they would force the people out. They feared the demon or witch would follow them to their town. With no other place to go, the villagers would be forced to return to their homes.

Eventually, things became so bad they locked themselves in the church. The priest carved the key of Solomon on the doors, hoping to fend off the evil. The last entry into the census book talked about how they were hearing scraping and scratching on the church walls.

Fearing for their children and what would happen to them if evil somehow gained entrance to the church. The priest and some of the fathers carved symbols into the wall and floor of the church and then sat the children in them. Then with the help of the mothers, the older children braved the outdoors one last time to go into the forest to gather as much wolfsbane as they could find. I heard Josephus gasp when I read aloud the mothers were to pick wolfsbane.

"What is it? Why do the mothers gathering whatever wolfsbane is bother you?" I asked as Josephus took the book from me.

Josephus and I turned pages of the book, hoping something else was writing.

"Wolfsbane is a strong poison. I think the mothers feared evil so much they poisoned the children. Rather than letting the evil they feared to have the children, they killed them," Josephus told me what he thought the priest and the parents of the children did. We both hoped there would be more in the book. To our dismay, we found nothing.

Looking back at the remains of the village, we both wondered how long the parents sat in this church with their dead children before thirst and starvation took them.

"What should we do about this?" I asked my brother, who looked woefully at the small bones of the children.

"We'll take the census with us. We may have a brother who will know what to do about it. As for the people, I think we should cremate them here in the church," Josephus offered; I nodded, agreeing with him.

Walking out into the bright sunlight seemed an insult to the people still sitting in the church. The villagers died hoping evil would not be able to enter. Josephus grasped my shoulder as he spoke in a low whisper.

"We must be vigilant, brother. If we do this, whatever evil drove these people to sit and die could be nearby," Josephus said.

"Then let us pray we will be safe and be gone from this place," I said, throwing a lit torch into the church.

As the flames raced through the church Josephus and I said a prayer for the people in the church. We asked for protection as we rode our horses back into the forests gathered around the foot of the mountains.

For the next fortnight, Josephus and I rode north the days grew colder. We woke one-morning snow was gently falling. We both knew it would soon be time to find shelter again to sit and watch the snows pass. As we rode out of the mountains into another valley, Josephus stopped. Curious, I rode up beside my brother, wondering what sight had stopped him.

"If this has been abandoned, I think we should shelter here for the winter," Josephus said as we sat looking over a small farm.

"Why would anyone leave this?" I asked. Without a word, Josephus and I started forward, watching for any sign the farmer was around. We reached the house. I called out, hoping someone was around, but I never received an answer to my calls.

I watched as Josephus knocked on the door, then entered the small house. Turning, he shook his head, telling me nobody was at home. I started to walk around the house, heading for a small barn. At the back of the house, I found two small markers. A name was on each with a date.

Standing at the graves, I called to my brother; as he came around the house, he stopped at the markers with me.

"Well, we now know it was not abandoned. The poor souls passed two years ago," I told Josephus as he stood beside me.

"The house has been cleaned; everything was taken out of it. There is a table, chairs, bed frames, and such. Anything one could call keepsakes has been removed." Josephus told me as we walked to the barn.

The barn had also been cleaned, and no hay was left in it. All the tack for horses hung on the walls. Thankfully no horses or cows had been left either. Looking around, Josephus and I decided to stay. Actually, it was the turn of the season that guided our hand to stay. When we walked out of the barn, the wind had started blowing in from the north. It now drove snow and ice pellets into our faces.

Spending winter in the house with our horses safe in the barn was a kindness. Hunting in the fields was good. The horses could find good grass under the snow during the day. Josephus spent his days working on the great sword found in the cave. I spent days committing the bloodline to memory.

I was shocked one morning to wake up to find water running from the roof of our shelter. Two weeks later, Josephus and I cleaned the little house for the last time. Then rode away, giving a silent thank you to the husband and wife buried behind it.

Chapter 25

LEAVING THE MOUNTAINS of southern France, Josephus and I rode through small villages and larger towns. It seemed wherever we rode, people took an interest in us. Some of it was out of country curiosity, then there were the ones who thought we may have money.

One night three men came to our camp. They were sure they could rob Josephus and me without any trouble.

"We know you two are alone; if you hand over your gold and other valuables, we will let you live." The leader of the thieves said from the darkness of the night. I could make out his form in the dark of the night.

I heard a gasp of pain when my dagger sailed out of the inky night. The thief who was speaking gasped when the blade I had thrown hit him in the chest, stopping his heart. The other two wanted to run and hide when Josephus stepped out of the darkness.

This was the only time we were forced to fight off a thief, or any form of a highwayman. For the rest of our trip, we decided to stay away from towns. We seemed to garner too much attention from the wrong sort.

I remember we stopped and asked a fisherman if he had ever heard of a great island to the west. He looked at me, then at Josephus, and nodded his head.

"If you want to go to that awful place filled with barbarians, you first need to go to Cancale. There you can pay for passage to the islands. From the second island, you will need to find another boat to take you to the island. We thanked the man and went on our way, looking for a sign to Cancale.

Four days later, we rode into the town of Cancale. It only took a few moments to find a man willing to take Josephus and me, along with our horses and belongings, to the islands. Later that day, as we loaded, I watched as a man dressed in dark robes slowly walked towards us.

"What do you make of this brother?" I asked as the man lifted a hand towards us.

"I'm not sure; let us be our guard," Josephus answered as the man lifted his other hand to show he was unarmed.

"Brothers, I bring news of the gravest kind." The stranger started.

"It is not safe for you or what you carry here. Make care to hasten your departure from these shores." The stranger quickly turned and walked into the crowded market.

"That was a bit more than ominous," I said as Josephus loaded the chest. We both stood at the railing of the small ship, silently urging the winds to fill our sails and take us from this place. As the little ship started to leave the port, I could make out a group of men questioning other captains of other vessels at the dock.

"Do you think the stranger was a brother?" I asked Josephus.

"He could have been; his warning seemed in earnest, though," Josephus answered as our ship rolled over another in the endless waves.

Watching where we had just left, I wondered if I should have stayed on the shore and let my brother carry on without me. Then I remembered the shore I stood on in the painting was barren. I seemed to be the only one present as Josephus sailed off for lands unknown.

The following day the captain told us this was the island he would drop us off. He gave us the name of another captain who would take us the rest of the way. The sun was barely over the horizon when the crew lowered the sails. Bringing us into the dock, in short order, Josephus and I were on the dock. Our captain pointed to the ship his friend captained.

Before the sun had climbed into the morning sky, we had our passage booked on another ship. Our horses, Josephus with myself and the chest, were onboard. I watched the sun climb into the sky, hoping to get underway. I was about to ask the captain what the hold-up was when he turned and gave an order.

His men started to untie the ship from the dock, then the sails rose on the masts. I could feel the wind fill the sails, pushing us to a new place. A safer place, I hoped, where we would find the mother of our savior.

A day later, I watched as the land slowly appeared from heavy fog. Men shouted and grappled with the lines as we glided into the dock. Wasting no time, Josephus and I guided our horses off the ship with all we had in the world. Then picking a direction, we headed away from the town of Poole.

"We want to keep heading north. Also, we want to avoid any large towns." Josephus reminded me traveling fast in this country would wear out our mounts. We needed to save our horses. We couldn't exhaust them.

"We do not know this place. We could stumble into anything, brother. Or run afoul of a king or some law," Josephus told me.

"When the Roman army arrived, Britannia was made up of many kingdoms. To the east and controlling, the most significant part of the island was the Anglo Saxons. To the south was Wessex, and in the center of the island was Mercia, with Britons to the west. North was Northumbria; still further north was the lands of the Pictish people.

"For the most part, little brother, if we keep to the small places, we should be safe." Josephus was telling me as we rode north. For the first day, all was well. On the morning of the second day, I started to feel myself being pulled in one direction. The last time I felt the urge, the pull brought us to the valley. Where Azazel had crashed to earth all those untellable thousands of years ago. Now a great worry crept into me as I wondered what this pull was leading my brother and me to next?

North forever north, I could not explain it to Josephus. He would ask what was pulling me, and I would only shrug my shoulders. Even when we had to stop and rest the horses, the incessant pulling was there. I could see Josephus was becoming concerned for me. One day, the constant pulling caused me great pain in my head. Josephus came to me.

"I wish I could take this from you, little brother," Josephus told me as I knelt beside the road retching into the bushes.

"I shall be fine when we reach whatever it is we are to find," I told him as I stood.

"We need to get north; we need to find what it is that pulls at you," Josephus said as he looked down the road we were on. That was the only time the urge, the pull, affected me in such a way as to make me sick. From then on, I felt the continuous desire to be on the move. Day after day, we traveled. As the sun would set, Josephus and I would stop for the evening.

Days turned into fortnights, and these turned into months. Still, the sun would find my brother and me on some road or path, always heading north.

Then one night, I caught Josephus looking at a ruin. Sitting in the moonlight, I wondered why my brother was so enthralled with the crumbling walls.

"What has you so enthralled with this place, brother?" I asked as I stood beside him.

"Well, little brother, many hundreds of years past, I stood near here, watching as people went about their lives. This place was at one time called Vindolanda. Near here is a wall Hadrian ordered built to mark the boundary of civilized man," Josephus said. It seemed so strange when my brother would remind me how old he was. It seemed stranger to me; I would one day be telling stories like this to other brothers.

Smiling, Josephus looked at me, then mounted his horse and started north again. As the sun rose above the world, it found Josephus and I across the wall an emperor had built as a boundary.

"The pull is becoming stronger; it seems the further north we go, the stronger it becomes," I told Josephus as we rode through the days. The days came and fell behind, and the nights would crawl by as the stars showed us our path. Then one morning, we stood at another wall; looking to the south, I smiled at my brother.

"Apparently, without you, the Roman army made an advance." I laughed when Josephus looked at me, acting hurt.

"Well, this is later; you can tell by the flimsy construction." Josephus sniffed and then laughed as we found a place to cross the wall.

"The pull just became stronger again. It seems every time we cross one of these barriers, it pulls harder on me." I told Josephus, who was becoming concerned.

"Are you in pain?" He asked as we rode off into the unknown lands.

"No, it is not painful anymore, it is very insistent though. I don't think I could stop for very long." As I told Josephus I could not stop, he looked at me and nodded.

"Then let us find this spot; let us see what is pulling at you," Josephus said. So we rode north, always north. Josephus and I were surprised the day we found an odd site. As we sat looking up a hill, we saw stones standing atop it. They stood there like a splendid crown, each holding vigil, waiting for a mighty king to return.

Each day we rode north, the pull was ever-present. It was a consonant even when we stopped for the night. During my sleep, I could feel the force as it invaded my dreams, urging, pleading with me to carry on.

One day as we rode the pull stopped, it happened so suddenly that I almost fell from my horse. As I turned in my saddle, I looked around, then at Josephus.

"Something has happened or will happen," I said as I dismounted.

"What do you mean? What do you know?" Josephus asked as he slipped to the ground.

"The pull I've been feeling for so long just suddenly stopped," I told Josephus looking around. We stood on a hillside overlooking a long body of water, a lake as it were. Behind us was the hilltop and, beyond that, a forest with beautiful fields. The land was idyllic; we saw villages and people farming the land. For the most part, they would look suspiciously at Josephus and me as we passed by.

As we stood overlooking this body of water, I could make out a boat of some kind fishing the waters. Josephus walked to the shore of the lake and waved to the men in the boat. I watched as they rowed over far enough so they could speak to him. Once they had answered what Josephus had asked, the men nodded and rowed back out on the water.

"Well, what did they have to tell you, brother?" I asked.

"The men were friendly. They told me this lake is called Loch Linnhe. If we ride along its banks, either way, we will find towns. I asked them if there was a way to cross the lake short of swimming it. They said we would be able to find a ferry to take us to the other side at a village called Corrow."

"It still seems odd the pull I've been feeling for so long has stopped here. Maybe it is a sign we were meant to stop here for a time." I told Josephus, the two of us looking at the lake.

"If it were up to me, I would like it here. The horses can feed and put some fat back on them. We can fish and gather supplies for whatever comes next." I nodded as my brother listed the benefits of this area.

I just thought stopping and staying in one spot after years of being constantly on the move would be a luxury. It seemed the only time we stopped was for the snows of winter. Josephus and I chose a small wooded area beside the lake to set our camp up in.

It was a beautiful little copse of trees. The breeze coming off the lake would rustle the leaves. I started to nap in the shade of the trees; in the evenings, Josephus and I would eat what the waters gave us and talk of the past. Sometimes the conversation would turn to the future. Every day we waved to the men as they fished the waters, trying to feed their families and have enough to sell for coin.

Josephus and I had been beside the lake for two fortnights when a man dressed in dark brown robes stood on top of the hill. He waved to us and then started to run down the hill by the time he reached our camp. Josephus and I had our weapons ready for whatever the stranger tried.

"I hope you have a very good reason for running to us this way, stranger!" Josephus said as I turned to look over the water. The fishermen were rowing away, wanting to avoid getting involved in whatever was happening on the shore.

"Brothers, brothers." Standing with our swords drawn, Josephus and I readied ourselves for a fight. We could see the man was disheveled; to us, it looked as if he had been running for some time.

"Stop, or we will defend ourselves!" Josephus shouted. The tone of his voice brought the man to a sliding stop.

"I come with a warning from the land of the Franks." The man said as he looked around.

"Give us the warning," I said as I turned to look out over the water again. The man slowly sat on the ground panting; his robes looked as if they would slide over his shoulders and fall to the ground if he stood too fast.

"The church has fallen into ruination. The men who steer it walk further from Christ's path each day. They know about the brotherhood and hunt us at every turn. The treasures must never find their way to Rome. Our Abbott sends word, you must find the holy mother. You two brothers must take her and the rest of the treasures as far from the church this earth will allow. Josephus, Rene, I am a brother, though not a warrior. Please heed my words, for I bring them from Dagobert. Save the family, save the treasures."

As our disheveled brother finished speaking, Josephus and I watched as he took out a flask and drank from it. I stared as a tear rolled down the man's cheek, then he looked to the heavens and softly asked.

"Lord god, can you forgive me for the life I have taken from you." the brother said. Josephus and I walked to the brother; we helped him to a log so he could lay back against it and rest.

"What was in the flask, brother?" Josephus asked as we laid the man down.

"It was a potent mixture of hemlock. Each brother who was sent out into the world to find you had this with them. Once the message was delivered, we swore to take our lives so the church could never make us speak of it." He told us as he smiled, knowing he was dying. Josephus and I sat with our unknown brother, waiting for the inevitable.

For the rest of the night, Josephus and I sat beside a brother we never had a chance to know. Hemlock poisoning is a terrible way to die. We watched over the brother through the hours of the night. Drying his perpetration as he drifted from the light we know as life, into the unknown darkness of death.

The morning found us burying our unknown brother at the top of the hill. In our prayers, Josephus and I begged god would see his sacrifice and forgive him. We hoped he would be permitted to enter the gates of heaven.

"I wonder how many brothers have been sent into the world looking for us?" Josephus asked as we sat down to make tea.

"I shudder to think of the number," I answered as a small group of men topped the hill behind our camp and started towards us. After the night we had with a brother sent to find us and the message given. Josephus and I were ready for the men as they rode down the hill.

As the men rode, I could see one of them starting to pull his sword free of its scabbard. I grabbed our crossbow, fitting a bolt and drawing it to my shoulder. Josephus called to the leader of the men.

"Sir, if I were you, I would think this over before you start something you cannot finish." As my brother spoke, I could see one of the men slide from his mount. The others did the same, planting their feet firmly on the ground. The man and his companions smiled at us as they pulled their swords.

"The priest at the church in the next town told us he would pay a great sum for your heads and what you carry." The leader of the men told us.

"Would you be so kind as to tell us what this man looks like before we are forced to kill you all?" Josephus asked the leader. I almost laughed when the man's eyes widened at the question.

"Come now, it is a sincere question," I said as Josephus stepped forward. I watched as the first man to pull his sword stepped forward. I put the bolt from the crossbow through his skull, killing the man faster than one could blink an eye.

Then before another word could be uttered, one of the men swung his sword, and Josephus cut him down. Two other men ran forward into my blade, and the leader watched his men die. They fell to the ground as chaff blew in the wind. He stood stiff-legged, looking at the carnage at his feet.

The man who had led the four, now dead, their blood splashed across the grass behind our camp. This lone man stood trembling, his sword rattling against a piece of wood at his feet.

"You are going to tell us who wants our heads and what we carry. If you tell us and give us your word, well, then you can go." I told the frightened man. Josephus stepped to the side of the man. Josephus using his gloved hand, grabbed the former leader's sword. I watched as my brother took the sword from the man and threw it into the lake.

"My brother has given you a chance to live after this. If I were you, I would take it and live a long quiet life somewhere other than here." Josephus told the man as he sat down.

Once the former leader of the dead men strewn about us started to talk, he couldn't stop until he had finished his story.

"If that is all, you can leave, however, know this, if we ever see your face again, we will kill you on sight." As I warned the man he stood and walked towards his horse. I looked to our mounts as they munched the long grass away from the recently dead.

The sound of the long grass brushing a boot caught my attention. I watched as the man we let go ran at me, his belt knife held low. Josephus was about to shout a warning when the man and I came together. I used my sword to block the knife attack from the man. Then I felt his heart flutter as my dagger pierced the flesh under his left arm.

"We let you go; why would you do this?" I asked the man as he sank to the ground.

"I took the priest's coin." Was all the man said as his blood spilled onto the earth.

I stood looking at the five men sent to find us. I looked at Josephus, and I could see the anger written on his face.

"I think we should go and find this priest; I have a few questions that have a terrible need to be answered," Josephus said. We said a prayer for the men. For the rest of the day, Josephus and I packed our camp up; we used two of the horses our attackers brought with them. The others we gave to the fishermen when we saw them in the morning.

We explained what had happened and where the horses came from. One of the men looked the animals over, and he told us the horses had been abused. They would be good animals once they had a good home. We were happy to see the horses going to a place where they would be treated kindly.

As the sun rose the following day, it found Josephus and me on our way to find a priest. Once our business was finished with the priest. Josephus and I would have to find a way across the loch we wished to call home for a while longer.

This was the first time my brother and I were forced to leave an area we wanted to stay in. I remembered the church of Mary, sitting at the edge of a cliff. Josephus and I left that wonderful place only after we had found what was needed. The madman we had found sitting at our fire told us the church leaders were after Josephus and me. Even then, my brother and I stayed to finish finding what was hidden.

That night as the moon showed us our route, we found the church the highwayman told us about. The church was a simple rectangular building. On the east end of the building sat an altar where the high cross was held. To the west end of the building sat a small house. A faint light spilled out of the only window beside the door.

As Josephus and I walked toward the home of the priest, we made sure to stay in the shadows. The movement caused us to stop. We watched the grounds of the church, then I whispered to my brother.

"Normally, I would say let us wait until daylight; seeing what has happened, I think the dark hours of the night could be better," I said;

we stood and ready ourselves as we watched from the darkness. The priest walked from his church to the small house. We watched as the priest turned and then made the sign of the cross on his chest before he entered the house. Taking another look around the area Josephus and I started towards the house again. This time we knew the priest who sent men to kill us, now stood in his house.

Chapter 26

TO ANNOUNCE OURSELVES, Josephus took two quick steps and then kicked the door off its latch. The priest looked in horror as his door flew off its hinges.

"What is the meaning of this?" The priest demanded as Josephus grabbed him. I watched as my large brother threw the priest over the dining table. The black-robed priest crashed to the floor at my feet.

Standing, I looked down at the man who spoke of god to others. Then would order the murder of men he had never laid eyes on. Josephus and I had been targeted by others in another land. I smiled at the priest, then knelt down so I could look at the man eye to eye.

"You send highwaymen to rob us of our lives, and you ask what this is about," I said to the man of god.

"All you carry belongs to the church. You carry a lie that would see the end of our savior's good work." The priest said as he tried to get up, only to be knocked down again by Josephus.

"What we carry belongs to all those who believe; we carry the truth. We have other truths with us. If you wish, we can show them to you. So you will also know the truth about the men who corrupt his church." I told the priest as I let him stand,

"I know the truth; I do not need the lies of Satan. If you repent and give all you have found to the church, I promise your death will be a kindness. You can still be allowed into heaven; the holy father has ordained it." The priest begged us. I could tell by his fervent need for us to believe what he said as truth that he genuinely believed what he was saying.

"You do realize it is not the church who controls the gates of heaven," I said to the man who was now on his knees pleading for us to leave the treasure with him.

"The holy church is charged with all holy items left by our savior and those who called themselves his family. Whatever he left on this earth belongs to the church. The holy father is the voice of god on earth." the priest said. Josephus looked at me, knowing we could never reason with a zealot.

I wanted to weep for the man, this priest. He was so entrenched in his belief in the church that he could see no other way. As we looked at the man who thought nothing of our lives, I wished for him to change so I wouldn't have to do the inevitable.

"You have been corrupted by Satan, the great deceiver, if you confess to me and turn over what you carry. You can stay here in peace. I will uphold your lives." The priest begged us as Josephus, and I changed positions.

"Well, my good priest, it seems you have no idea who we are," Josephus said to the kneeling man.

"I am the son of the Roman soldier Longinus, the cursed soldier who ran the holy spear into our savior." As Josephus told the priest who he was, I could see the man turning red from rage.

"There is no hope for you. The lowest bowels of hell are too good for you. That creature took our savior from this world; if I could, I would see you die." The priest hissed at my brother.

"Well, you could never see me die; such is the curse Jesus uttered on the cross that terrible day. He cursed my father to live until he returned. Well, as it turns out, we can die. When my father found a way to die, the curse was passed onto me, so I could fulfill our savior's last wish. Jesus wanted to be reunited with his mother and his wife. Also, so his children could be safe." As Josephus told the priest,

Jesus was married and had fathered children. The supposed holy man kneeling in front of us went into unintelligible screaming fit.

Silently I slid my dagger from my belt, then grabbed the priest by the head and slid my blade into his skull at the point where it connected with his spine.

His death was quick and merciful; this is something I do not think he would have afforded my brother and me. Looking around the house, I concluded that the priest would have shipped Josephus and me off to Rome so we could be tortured. The highwaymen were a means to an end, a way to get what he wanted for the church.

Walking out into the night, Josephus and I looked up to the stars. "How has it come to this? Joseph warned us this may happen. I never thought it would be like this. We must take everything far away from these shores." I told Josephus as he stood nodding in the moonlight.

When we reached the horses, I stumbled, and the pull came back. It was more insistent than before, urgent, compelling.

"Brother, it is back; the pull is back. It is so much worse than before. I know where it is; we must go. It is a group of islands far to the north. There we will find her; she is waiting for us in a cave." As I spoke, Josephus came to me and helped me into my saddle.

For the next day, we rode north, and we stopped when the moon hit the highest point of its nightly voyage across the stars. Then as the sun found the edge of the world, we would set off again. On our fourth day, we came across a small village where we could buy food. We were also able to find out about the islands we were looking for.

The farmers and others we spoke to along the way were not Christian. This fact didn't bother Josephus and me; we met these people and respected them. Though we knew what was coming in the future. These people would be forced to convert, or they and their families would be put to the sword. These good people who lived on the land farming would give us information on the waters we faced, along with added advice.

"You had better find shelter before the winds from the north come and lay on the land." One man told us as he clucked to his horse, then the rattle of his wagon drowned out his last words to us. As we turned our horses to the north once again, I turned and watched as the man and his wagon sank out of sight behind a low hill.

"I wish we could have made out his last words before the winds blew them away," I said to Josephus, who looked back and watched as the old man and his wagon drifted out of sight.

"Do you think them of importance?" He asked me.

"Any information we can gather in this land is important to us and what we carry. I returned, looking ahead. At times like this, I wish I could see the future. When I told Josephus of my wish, he laughed and said that would be cheating.

The days drifted into weeks, and as we rode north, we could see the change of the seasons marching toward us. One day we woke to a bitter frost; it lay on our blankets, on the horses. It covered everything; everything saved the chest where we carried the treasure.

"We had better find a shelter for the horses and us. We may have left it too long already." Josephus said as we stood shivering in the cold morning.

While we had been in the mountains of southern France, we had been spared winter's bitter bite for the most part. As Josephus and I traveled further into the northern lands. We found the cold became worse. After loading our horses Josephus and I climbed a low hill to see the land.

As we looked at the land laid down by god, then covered through the night with the frost of an impending winter. We wondered how much time we had before the winds of winter would come. The colors of autumn started to fall weeks before the wind could be felt.

For the next three days, Josephus and I looked for a cave or abandoned shelter we could use for our needs. Truth be told, I was becoming disheartened while riding along a small stream. Josephus looked up and saw more tall flat stones standing at the top of a hill. My brother and I looked at the stones, then decided to go and investigate them.

We topped the hill to look at the stones standing in a circle. Josephus and I walked around them, each still holding the chisel marks from a long-forgotten man. We still didn't know what or why people would take the time and energy to stand these remarkable stones in circles.

"Whoever or whatever people made these circles must have been doing it for some sort of ritual," Josephus said as he ran one of his hands over the stones.

"You don't think the pagans around here practiced sacrifice?" I asked as I stepped into the stones looking at the ground. Hoping not to see human bones.

"No, I don't think they would on humans; they might have on sheep or other animals," Josephus answered as I used my sword to part the long grass inside the stone circle. When I stepped out of the stones, I looked back through the stones. I could see a dark opening of a cave.

"Oh brother, I can see a cave. Do you want to go and see if it will suit our needs, or should we carry on?" I asked as I looked and smiled at Josephus.

It did not take long to see others had lived in this cave and from the paintings on the walls and ceiling. It was apparent people had called this place home for a very long time. As we moved our things into the cave, we found a stone used to grind flax into crude flour. It was used for such a long time it was hollowed out. We saw many flint chippings from early people for making tools.

The next thing Josephus and I had to do was to build a wall at the opening of our cave. This did not take long, seeing we were next to a great forest. As we worked, the nights grew colder, and the frost stayed longer on the grass every day. I was happy to see a bear feeding and trying to get fat for his long sleep.

"I saw a bear today; it was down by the stream, and it looked good and fat," I told Josephus as we sat by our fire in the cave.

"Tomorrow, we will have to see if he comes back; his meat and the fat from his body will be needed. I think we are in for a bad winter this far north, brother." He told me as the winds howled through the gaps in our log wall.

"I'm going to see if I can use mud and grasses to close the gaps in our wall," I said as a shiver chattered my teeth together.

The next day Josephus went off to find the bear while I dug dirt and cut the long reeds beside the stream. With the horses, I was able to haul enough of the mixture back to cover half of our wall. That night it was noticeably warmer in the cave.

"I don't want to cover the whole wall with mud; I'm thinking, what if we need to see out," I said as Josephus looked the wall over.

"We should cut notches in the logs; these we can uncover if needed. When we don't need them, we can cover it over again." As Josephus looked out through a crack, he saw something that caused him to pull his head back.

"What is it, brother?" I asked.

"Three men are standing by the stones looking this way." As he spoke, I walked toward the wall we built and looked out another crack. I was surprised to see the men standing by the stones. Each was dressed in a long robe with a hood covering his head. A tall walking staff was held in their hands, and on the front of the robes was a design of some kind. The design reminded me of the different orders of the church. I hoped it was a mark of their order or church.

As we watched the men, one of them lifted his hand and pointed to the log wall Josephus, and I built, blocking the front of the cave.

"I wish we could hear what they were saying," Josephus said as we watched them.

"Why don't we go and see what they are doing?" I asked. As I spoke, one of the men stepped away from the others and started to walk toward our cave. Before I could say anything, Josephus stepped through the door. When the stranger saw Josephus, he stopped, turned, and looked back to his friends and then back to Josephus. I could tell the man was afraid of Josephus. What I wanted to know was if he was fearful of my brother for his size? Or was he afraid of him because he stepped out of the cave? I watched as Josephus raised his hand in a friendly wave. I was relieved when the older man copied him, then moved forward. I watched the others as they watched.

Josephus and the older man talked for some time, then gave a slight bow. I watched as the others turned and walked over to the top of the hill. Josephus stood where he had talked to the old man. When the others disappeared over the hill, he turned and returned to the cave.

"What did the old man have to say?" I asked as Josephus held his hands out to warm them by the fire.

"Well, they were shocked to see anyone in this cave. It seems this cave has been part of the stones for as long as their stories go. I told him we were on a quest seeking the truths of the past. That seemed to satisfy the old fella; he said we were welcome to stay here for the winter. He also told me this would be their last pilgrimage to the Stones for the year. Once they left, no one should be coming here until the spring thaw."

"So do we believe him or..." I added, looking at my brother,

"He seemed truthful...however, I think we should be the ever-vigilant little brother," Josephus said. Knowing my brother was right, I nodded and turned to look at the wall.

As the days marched on, Josephus and I cut and gathered all the grass we could. We found wild straw the horses seemed to like, along with wild oats. Then it happened, one morning, we woke to find it had started to snow during the night. When I opened the door to our cave, the howling wind blew snow in. I shut the door, standing with my back to it; I looked to be trying to keep an enemy out.

Chapter 27

"DON'T LOOK NOW, BROTHER; winter has arrived, and it wants in," I said then we laughed.

"How much snow has fallen?" Josephus asked as I looked out again. I smiled at the amount on the ground in such a short time seemed absurd to me.

"Well, it is past my knees," I told Josephus as I looked up the hill to the stones. It was then I saw something move behind one of the stones. Again, I opened the door to look out, then shut it slowly, hoping whoever was at the stones would think I had not seen him.

"The old man you spoke to, he said no one should be here until the spring?" I asked Josephus.

"That is what he said; why, what did you see, little brother?"

"I just saw someone duck behind one of the stones; whoever it is, they are trying to hide," I said as I walked back to gather my cloak and weapons.

I watched as Josephus walked to the wall and lifted one of the viewports. Standing there, I watched as he looked out into the storm and then turned.

"I don't think you will need that." He told me, pointing to my sword.

"Are you sure?" I asked, wondering what he had seen. Josephus opened the door and called out into the snow.

"Come to the door; you will be safe and warm here!" Josephus called into the storm.

I watched my brother as he made a come here motion to someone outside.

"Do not worry, we are monks; you will be safe with us, come and get warm by our fire." Josephus pleaded with whoever was outside. He didn't have to yell now to be heard, so I took it as a sign whoever was out there in this storm was closer. Then to my utter amazement, a small boy staggered into Josephus's outstretched arms.

Standing with the boy in his arms, Josephus turned with a look of complete shock on his face.

"Why is this child wandering around in this weather?" I asked as we laid the boy down by the fire and covered him with blankets. It wasn't until the afternoon the boy woke and looked around we could tell he was frightened of us.

"You are safe here, lad; we will not hurt you," Josephus told the boy as he handed him a bit of roasted duck.

The boy started to speak in a rapid, clipped speech. It was so utterly different from what we had encountered in the mountains of France; for a moment, it escaped me.

With the purification of the blood, the language came to me, and I was able to understand the boy. I would listen and then ask a question of him, all the while translating for Josephus.

When the boy had finished telling what had happened. Why he had been forced into the cold and snow of the night. He, along with his mother, father, and two sisters, had been traveling with their house servants. The family had been en route from the north to their southern stronghold for the winter. They left late because of a raiding party his father and his kinsmen had been forced to deal with.

His father had gotten back later than planned. He had wanted to wait for the storm to pass. It was his kinsmen who came with the word a more significant force than they had dealt with was on the way to kill his family.

"It seems our little friend here is royalty. His father was a king of some sort. So his father needed to get his family to safety, and decided to use the storm as a means to cover their escape." I translated so Josephus could keep up.

"Sometime during the storm, they ran into another raiding party. Our little friend became separated from his family and lost his way in the snow." I walked over to the wall we built and looked out into the snow. Standing there, I wondered if he was being tracked as the snow fell. In a very short time, it would be almost impossible to find his tracks.

His mother and father, if they were still alive, would they think their son dead. Taken or lost and freezing to death in the snow. I looked at my brother as he heated soup for the boy.

"We have to find out if his mother and father are alive and if any of his family survived," I said as I walked over to the fire.

"I was thinking the same; if they did survive, I could not imagine what they are going through," Josephus answered. The child was looking at the two of us as he sipped his soup. When I told the boy we needed to find his family, he smiled and nodded. I asked the boy what direction he and his family had traveled from and were going.

Both Josephus and I were shocked by the level of information he had. Then he explained that as the only son and heir to his father's throne, he needed to know everything to make him safe.

Josephus and I discussed what we were going to have to do. We decided it would be better if I went to find the family. It was because I could talk to them and bring them back to get their child. So I saddled a horse with a word of caution from the boy to watch for the man with the long axe. I walked out into the snow.

Heading north and east, I watched the horizon for a smoke trail. It would give me forewarning of a campfire, of a possible enemy. The sun had started to slide towards the trees when the first sign of man showed itself.

I could smell the campfire before I came upon it. Four men sat around the fire, and a large carriage sat behind them. Inside the carriage, I could see the frightened faces of two girls, one slightly older than the other. A man was chained to one of the wheels, and six fine-looking horses were tethered to the trees beyond. An older lady was being forced to serve the men their meal.

As I watched, one of the men being served yelled out in anger and slapped the woman. His reaction to her enraged me; as he stood to kick her, I fired my crossbow. The bolt flew true, killing the bastard as it cleaved his heart in half. The other men sitting around the fire leaped to their feet as their dead friend fell face-first into the fire.

The three remaining men stood and grabbed their swords. They fell into panic as another bolt from my crossbow flew out of the night and took a second man through the head.

Standing in the tree line, the remaining two looked around, wondering how many stood in the night waiting to kill them. As I loosed another bolt from my crossbow, I watched as a third fell to my attack.

Then I walked into the camp. The fourth and final man stood looking in shock at his friends, all killed by one young man. The fight was short and brutal. It ended with the fourth killer lying in the snow, his head some feet away from his neck.

I looked at the woman as she knelt beside the man tied to the wagon wheel. When I reached the woman, I knelt down, handing her my knife, hoping it would be a gesture of trust. I stepped back and waited for her to free the man.

"You would give me a knife?" She asked as she started to cut the ropes.

"You need it to free your husband, and some protection always makes one feel better," I answered as I pulled the man off the fire, hoping to stop the smell of burning flesh. She looked at her husband as the ropes came free. I walked into the forest and came back with my horse. I watched as the man stood, checked his wife, and nodded to the girls in the wagon.

"Are you and your wife missing a young boy?" I asked the man. I watched as the woman covered her mouth, a tear rolling down her cheek.

"We are; this is a terrible day. Would you take us to his body...." The father started to ask.

"Body, there is no body; he is with my brother. He found us, so we took him in; he is in good health." When I told the mother and father of the boy that he was alive, I watched as the large man walked over to me. He placed his hands on my shoulders and looked into my eyes.

"My boy lives, truly lives?" The King asked as if he couldn't believe what I told him.

"I am a monk and can not lie; your boy lives and is with my brother. When I left, he was having some soup made with duck fat." I answered to his booming laugh, his wife holding him.

"That sounds like my boy, always eating." Then another laugh. As fast as we could, we hooked the team of horses up to the wagon, then left the area heading for the cave where Josephus waited for my return.

The snow was getting deeper as the hours passed. The horses struggled to pull the wagon through the drifts. As I led the family to their son, I worried if the wagon would make it. Then out of the snow and wind, the stones stood like a beacon. Happily, I turned to the west, knowing the cave was mere steps away. As the face of the cave materialized out of the snow, I could see Josephus standing with the boy.

When the father saw his son standing in the snow wrapped in a blanket, he jumped from the wagon and ran to the boy scooping him up into his arms. His mother and two sisters ran to the child they thought was lost to violence and the cold of winter.

The family seemed so grateful when we asked them inside where it was warm, and food could be made. Sitting around the fire, I asked the father what it was about the men holding them.

"I rule this part of the world; it has been so since my father's death. Though it should have been my brother, he was found unfit. He has an evil in him, a need to hurt, to kill in the worst way. My family has ruled over the lands to the north of the island of Mull. It has been this way for generations. My wife's people are a great family and rule the South. Her uncle is a great man, and I have fought for him before. To make a lasting peace, my father and her uncle betrothed us. So the families can become one, it worked so our families are now one. Everyone is happy about this, except for my older brother. He wants to kill my son and me." The father told me. I looked at the boy's mother as she checked over him to be sure he was okay.

"The King is my uncle. He would never allow his only nephew to be killed in the winter snows." She said as her daughters hugged their little brother.

"Our king is a man who believes the old feudal ways need to be left in the past." The boy's father told us as he watched his son squirm under his sister's hugs. As I watched the boy's mother care for her son, the old anger at the theft of my mother's love crept in. Then I smiled; the bitterness lingered for a short time, then passed. What I was left with was a warm feeling knowing I had saved this young boy.

As the day turned into night, I sat with Josephus and the boy's father discussing what the family would do. Josephus and I were shocked when the father told us they still needed to get to the South for their winter home. Then as the father stood to go see his boy, Josephus and I spoke quietly.

Before long, we had a choice, we could let this family go off into the teeth of winter. Their enemies, who think nothing of killing a child, still hunt them. Or we could go with them to help protect the boy and the family.

"What of the pull Rene?" Josephus asked me as we came to the same decision.

"Well, the pull seems to want me to go with this family. It had something to do with the boy." I told him as we watched the family.

"My brother and I can not let you go without protection, so if it is agreeable, we will travel with you as protection." When I told the father, Josephus, and I wanted to travel with the family as protection, he smiled and shook our hands.

"I would be a fool to say no." He said as his wife and the children all smiled.

Chapter 28

MORNING FOUND US ALL leaving the cave, which Josephus and I thought would be our home for the winter. The storm stopped during the night, so the sun brightened the world. The blinding white of the snow caused us to squint into the glare.

It came as a shock to Josephus and me when we realized the family we had promised to protect was heading back to Corrow.

"Do you think any are looking for us there?" I asked Josephus.

"The church has no hold here. It is just sending priests they deem expendable to far-off lands." He answered as we looked ahead, wondering what we would find.

It was well into the third day as Josephus and I watched from a hill; a small group of men was watching the road from the forest on either side of the road. I looked back to the family my brother, and I had given our word to help.

"Should we go tell them, or should we just go and ask these men if they are waiting for the family or us?" I asked as Josephus smiled; it was this smile I had come to know when he wanted to ask a question.

"So, I take it we are just going to walk in there and see what is what," I said as we started down the hill; it did not take long before we knew what the men were doing.

Josephus walked out onto the road and smiled at the first man. This first man yelled at my brother to leave the area, or he would kill him. Josephus being the man he was, took this as an invitation.

The others stood and laughed at Josephus when he smiled again and waved to the fellow who threatened him.

The big man who told Josephus he was going to kill him walked out onto the road. He looked at my brother, shrugged his big shoulders, then attacked Josephus. The fight was short. As the man ran at Josephus, he drew his sword only to be met mid-stride. Unlike the Scotsmen, Josephus's sword was made from the finest metal. Also, my brother had hundreds of years of experience wielding it. The fight was over in mere moments. The Scotsman lay dead on the road. His blood staining the mud and snow, his clansmen stood to either side of the road. The shock of losing their leader silenced them. Standing beside my brother, we watched the men.

Josephus's sword still dripped the blood of their leader. I turned slightly when I heard the rattling of the carriage. Josephus and I never took our eyes off the men who stood around the body of their dead leader. None looked up when the carriage stopped. Bhaltair, the father of the boy who shared his father's name, stepped down from the carriage.

Josephus and I watched the men as he walked toward us. Bhaltair looked down at the dead man lying at our feet, and he shook his head. Then Bhaltair looked at the men, who had, a short while ago, waited to kill him and his family. As he started to speak, I translated for Josephus, who stood with his sword in hand.

"Is this what it is to be? Do you men really want a tyrant as a leader? I know my brother was older than I am; my father named me his heir. Only because he knew what my brother was, I want you men to sit and listen. I am going to tell you of the past, a past my father hid. I was a boy no older than my son is now." Bhaltair started as he looked back to his son sitting atop the carriage holding the reigns.

"My father sat in our stronghold. I will admit there were times my father did not always work with the welfare of his subjects at heart. More times than I can remember, he would work for his own interests. However, when it came to my father's attention to what my brother was doing. Well, even he couldn't ignore his eldest son's sickness. Word had gotten to the King about my brother taking girls and boys from villages. These young people would be taken to a cave, tortured, and killed in the worst ways one could imagine." As Bhaltair told the men why his brother had been passed over by his father, the men paled. Bhaltair cleared his throat and continued.

"When my father asked my brother why he was doing such things. My brother told my father it was his right to do whatever he wished with the little animals. As he explained to my father and mother, it was his right to take the children of their subjects and torture them to death. My mother left the room; the shame of her firstborn and what he was, broke my mother's heart." Bhaltair stood looking at each of the men.

"My father shook with shame and rage, and my brother laughed at our father when he was told he didn't have the right." These clansmen had followed their lieges brother, who sought to kill their rightful ruler, and all looked at the ground.

None now looked at the body of Bhaltair's brother as it grew cold on the road. Three of the men looked sick; I think they knew their former leader was sick and demented.

"My father, for once worried over his subjects, sent word to the King. My father told the King what his son was doing to the children of the highlands. The King, in turn, sent a man he trusted to decide the fate of my brother. This man had been sent to other parts of the kingdom. He held members of ruling families to account. When my brother was told he would have to answer for his crimes, he again laughed at our father." As Bhaltair told these men, his brother was going to be held to account for his actions. The men looked up. We could tell this was the first time they had heard this.

"When the day came, my brother was ordered to my father's great room. My brother ran, knowing he would be held responsible and made to answer for his crimes. I was named my father's heir, and my father ordered my brother's name be struck from the family's records. The servants of the family were ordered to never speak of him again. My brother's rooms were cleared and sealed. My father ordered the families he had hurt to be brought to the stronghold. The King ordered compensation for the families. I saw a different side of my father that day. He stood and told the families there was no amount he could think of. No amount could bring back the love of a stolen child. The families all stood in my father's great room and nodded; husbands tried to comfort their sobbing wives. My mother stood with them and wept for what her eldest son had taken. Even my father stood shaking with grief and rage. My father went so far as to striped my brother of his protection, so if he was found. He could be tried and hung for his crimes." The men sat on the side of the road, shaking their heads.

"He only lived in the memories of those who worked for my father before his death. I had been waiting for the time when my brother would come back; I knew he would get word of our father's death. My wife and I knew he would try something." When Bhaltair finished telling the story of his brother. Why his brother had lost his place and family name, the men all turned, wanting to go home.

"You men have hunted my family, almost causing my son to be lost, to die in the winds of winter. If not for these good monks, my heir would have been lost, as would have been my life. You have all committed a crime against the crown. This can not go unpunished." Bhaltair said as the men all stood, knowing what their ruler said was true. Each man waited for their sentence to be death; they knew it had to be so.

Smiling to myself and Josephus, Bhaltair looked at the men.

"If you men will swear fealty to my house to my heirs and the King from this day forth. I will consider this act as over and shall be forgotten. When you swear your fealty to my family, I must have you all at my call. You will have to move your families to our stronghold on the island of Mull." Bhaltair told the men. I looked to Josephus and then the men who all knelt on the road. Each man stood after he had sworn his oath to Bhaltair and his family.

Only one stood away from the others, his head bowed.

"Will you not swear fealty to my house?" Bhaltair asked. I could see this one man was conflicted about what he must do.

"My lord, I would swear and be so happy to have my wife and child on Mull." He answered. We all could tell there was a reason he would not be right there.

"Lord, forgive my brother, please; he is the youngest of us, and our father is not long for this earth. Our mother went last snow, and father will not see the end of this winter." One of the older men said as he placed a hand on his brother's shoulder.

"Kneel and give me your oath, then go and take care of your father. Once you have fulfilled your duty as the youngest, come to me on Mull." Bhaltair told the youngest of the men, who looked up at his lord smiling. He knelt in front of Bhaltair, holding onto his cloak. The youngest swore his fealty.

"My lord, from this day forth, my life is yours; I will give it willingly for you and your heirs." Bhaltair touched the young man with his sword and then asked him to rise.

"Go to your family, be safe." The lord of the islands and highlands said to his man.

"Thank you, lord; I will return with my wife and son." The young man said as he looked at his brother.

"I will bring your family, brother; I give you my word; all will be looked after till then." The two men shared a brief hug.

Standing, we watched as the younger brother rode to the north. Back to his family and that of his brothers, I turned and looked at the man they called lord. Bhaltair smiled at his own son, then looked at the men he could have beheaded for their part in his brother's act.

"Well, men, let us get this trip over so you all can get your families to the stronghold." An arrow flew out of the night as Bhaltair finished speaking. The bowman missed the lord by the thickness of his tunic. Before any of the men standing around Bhaltair could act. Josephus and I grabbed the lord and ran him back to the heavy carriage.

I took up the station on top of the carriage while Josephus took the reigns. With all the breath my brother could muster, he yelled out his signal to the horses. With a slap of the reigns, the team of six burst into a flat-out run. The men, by this time, were on their mounts, running beside the carriage to protect it from the unseen bowman.

As I turned with my crossbow, I watched as the younger brother reappeared and dove his horse into the bush. Looking at Josephus, I smiled as he shook his head, then I jumped from the carriage. Jumping to my feet, I ran to the spot where I watched the young man crash into the bushes.

I could hear the sounds of a struggle as the two men fought. I rushed to the side of the younger brother. When the man who had hidden in the brush looked up, he smiled at me and pulled a knife from his belt.

"Well, shall it be one at a time, or will you both fight me at the same time?" He asked, then stood.

"Oh, it will not be a fight, you will do something foolish, and I will be forced to kill you," I told the bowman as he looked around.

"What makes you think you are good enough to kill me?" The bowman asked as the shadow of doubt crawled across his face. I looked at the killer. I shook my head.

"You do not have to do this; the lord is kind." The younger brother said as he lowered his sword.

"No lord is kind. They are fat inbred monsters; they all deserve to die." The bowman spat at us as he looked at his sword lying on the ground.

"If that is how you feel, pick up your sword. Let us start this so I can get the lord and his family to their home." As the bowman reached for his sword, I turned to the young man standing beside me.

"You are not to interfere with this," I told him; I smiled when he started to protest.

"You are in service to the lord; in this matter, I speak for the lord, and you will honor what I say." When I spoke, the bowman looked at me; what he saw frightened him. The man standing with his sword in hand knew he faced a knight. A man trained in the arts of killing with all manners of weapons. The young man who swore his oath to the lord nodded his head and stepped back.

"Bowman, I will let you yield; you do not have to die this night. I will hold your honor, however, if you do not yield if you go forth with this foolish endeavor. You will die this cold night." I watched as the bowman looked at his sword and then back to me. He shook his head, then raised his sword and ran at me.

Stepping forward, I brought my sword up, forcing the bowman to raise his weapon to parry my action. As his sword came up, I swung my hard left fist to his ear. As he fell from the blow, I could see the fog of the blow wash over him. Stepping back, I waited for the bowman to clear his head. I watched the man get back to his feet; we all could see the bowman needed to use his sword to steady himself.

"Again, bowman, if you yield, this will end, and you will live. If you insist, I will not offer you kindness again." I said as I could hear the others moving in the bush.

"I will not take any kindness from you or the one who calls himself lord." The bowman shot back as the blood running from his smashed ear froze on his neck.

Again I watched as the man tried to rush me; this time, I knew I would be forced to kill him. As he ran at me once again, I was able to slap his blade to his inside and step behind him. With one stroke of my sword, I cleaved his skull in half. The momentum of his rush caused the dead body of the bowman to take two more steps before he fell.

Josephus stepped up beside me in the bush, the light of the moon showing the steam of the bow man's blood as it drained from the hideous wound. The others and the lord stood behind me; all were quiet.

"Lord, if you and the others will carry on, my brother and I will bury this man," I asked Bhaltair as he stepped beside me.

"You wish to show this man kindness, even after he tried to kill me and you?" Bhaltair asked.

"It is our way; this is something we must do, lord," I answered as the others started to make their way back to the road.

"I will have the men tie your mounts here. We will wait on the other side of the loch." Bhaltair told us, then he placed his hands on my shoulders and smiled.

"It is a kindness such as this we need more of in this land." Then the lord turned and walked back to the road.

Chapter 29

THE FERRYMEN WERE WAITING for Josephus and me when we reached the dock. They told us Bhaltair left a message they would be waiting in the town. Josephus looked at me and shrugged. We wondered if the priest we had killed had been found. As we reached the other side of the loch, we could see one of the men waiting.

"Something is going on here; it seems some sort of holy man was killed. His purse and coin have been taken, the Lord is concerned highwaymen are about." We walked our mounts along the lone street leading from the dock.

"Where did this take place?" Josephus asked as we mounted.

"Where he lived, by the place where he told people they were all bad." I smiled as the man told us the priest spent his days telling people whose families had lived on this land for thousands of years what they believed in was horrible, evil.

As we walked our horses up to what was left of the church. It seems the locals started taking the stones from the church when they thought it was abandoned. They only took the stone from the building. They never touch the cross. The locals thought it would bring bad luck if they touched it.

"It seems the people did not go near the house. One of the older women told the Lady the man who lived there had whipped a lad for touching the church once." One of the men told me.

"Now, do you wonder why he was killed?" I asked Bhaltair as he walked over to Josephus and me.

"No, it is no wonder he was put down. The locals have many stories of his actions towards the young people in the town." Looking at the house and what was left of the church, I shook my head. Then I turned to the local people who waited to see if there would be a punishment.

"Lord, it is your choice. However, I would let these good people take the rest of this building. Hopefully, they will make better use of the stone. The cross should be left as a reminder. The house turned into an office of your representative; this way, your rule will be here also." When I made my suggestion Bhaltair turned, he looked at me and then at the house.

"Who would I leave here? This is still two fort nights from my home." He said as we all turned to look at the men with us.

"Lord, if I may be so bold. My younger brother rides home to see our father. When he comes to you in the spring, I know he would be a good man to represent your interests here. You see, my Lord, my brother is kind by nature and loyal to a fault. You never asked why we followed your brother." The oldest among the men told Bhaltair as we stood in the yard of the church.

"I was going to ask, then thought it better if you men tell me in your time," Bhaltair said as the men all looked to the eldest among them.

"Well, Lord, your brother came to our village during a terrible time. Four children had gone missing, he told us who he was, and he was tracking an ancient evil. He informed us his father had charged him with ridding the land of this evil. He said while he was out tracking this evil, you had killed your father and stolen his title." As the oldest man finished, another took up his story.

"At first, we felt bad for him, though we did not follow him. Then he returned to us, and he told us he had killed the evil. He wept when he told us he was too late to save any of the children. We asked him to take us to the bodies so we could bury them. He did;

we stood there as mothers wailed to the skies grieving for the loss of their children. It was then we swore to help your brother gain his titles back. If we had only known what he was, what he really was." When the man finished telling how he and the others came to be with Bhaltairs brother.

"The thing you men have to understand is my brother was a monster. He could lie as easily as most tell the truth, easier, I think." It was then Bhaltair turned to a villager.

"Who is the headman here?" He asked.

"I would be the one most look to here, Lord." A man said as he stepped from the crowd.

"You and the others can have the stone from this building. The house is not to be touched." Bhaltair ordered as the man stood before him.

"It will be so, Lord." The man said as he twisted his hat in his hands. We watched as the crowd gave a bow to the Lord of the lands.

As the sun rose over the hills, it found Josephus and me on the road. We rode with the men who now protected the Lord of the land and his family. Bhaltair was correct when he told us we had to travel for two fortnights to reach the home on the island of Mull.

Winter had set in with its fierce winds as they drove the snow into every crack and crevice. The cold bit into the flesh if one left his skin exposed. Standing on the ramparts one day, I turned to look at my brother.

"I do miss the deserts at times like this, brother," I said, then chuckled.

"I hate to say it, little brother, but I am afraid something may fall off if we linger out here any longer." We laughed and then stood looking out over the cold grey waters of the bay.

"Little brother, we know what is coming. We know Mary is nearby; the thing we call the pull has told you so. We also know the church has strayed. We can not have Jesus and Mary together. For now, he is safe with us, and so is the bloodline." As Josephus spoke of what we both knew to be the truth, I knew what was coming. Though neither one of us wanted to admit it. Our years of being together were coming to an end.

"I know, brother, with the coming of spring, you are going to have to take our savior and go west," I told Josephus. As I spoke the words, I could feel my heart breaking at the loss of my brother.

"We are going to need the help of Bhaltair," Josephus said as we turned to walk back into the keep. I nodded as one of the guards opened the door for us.

Standing in the great room Josephus and I stood by the central fire, warming our hands. I was worried about how to ask the Lord for his help, sending my brother away over the water.

"You men have saved my family and me. Whatever it is you wish, just ask; if I can help, it will be yours."

"A ship, my lord, one large enough to cross the waters to the west," Josephus asked as he sat down at a table.

"You wish to see what is to the west. In my younger days, I would stand on the ramparts looking west." Josephus and I watched as Bhaltair stroked his beard and then smiled.

"Yes, you will have your ship. All I ask is if you come back to this land, you tell me what you find there." Both Josephus and I stood and bowed to our benefactor. As weather would allow, the ship was worked on, the keel being the first to be laid. As Josephus and I watched, the ship slowly took shape. Then as the snow resided further from the water, I knew our time together was growing short.

Spring was on us when the ship was finished. Its masts held the canvas sails, the rigging set. The workmen took one last look at their trade and then walked back to their homes.

As I stood with my brother, I hated to look at the ship given to us. If I could, I would have set fire to it as it floated beside the dock.

"Little brother, we have been together for so many years. I hate to leave you, though we both know the church is now hunting us. I will follow the sun to wherever it leads. There our savior will be safe. I have made another bloodline up. The names on it will lead nowhere. You must find the holy mother; you must decide where you are going to protect her, hide her." As Josephus spoke, I knew what I was going to do. Who I was going to tell of the holy family. Bhaltair and his wife had been sitting in the evenings as I told them the story of Christ's life.

"Josephus, as you sail to the west, remember you have a brother in the world. You are not alone. You have family, a brother who loves you." I said, then I helped the man I had been traveling with for the last fifty years load the chest. The chest holding what we had found, what we had wept over, the chest we had sworn to die to protect. The chest contains the earthly remains of our savior, his bloodline, and two of the vile of his blood.

The painting in the church of Mary came rushing back to me. As I stood on the rocks overlooking the bay on the island of Mull. I watched as my brother sailed out to the sea. I could see him standing at the stern of the ship, waving to me. Tears fell from my chin as I raised my arm to wave back, knowing I would never see him again.

It was the one part of the vision I had never told Josephus. When I reached out to touch the painting in the passage under the church of Mary in the mountain. My vision had foreseen this, Josephus sailing away to live with and protect our savior. The one part of the vision I had to keep from my brother, or he would never leave me, was my death.

I knew I had to die, to suffer the same injury Lucifer had suffered, the evil. Then another would come along, I learned how I would die, and I knew when. I just had to be strong enough to let it happen.

Chapter 30

BHALTAIR WOULD COME and sit with me in the evenings. One evening as the summer night brought the stars, I asked him to call his wife.

"I have been with you for the winter, and now summer claimed the seas and the land. I have to go and find one who was lost many hundreds of years ago. When I return, if I return, I will tell you a story most would not believe. This story is of a man whose love for his fellow man assured his torture and death." As I sat and explained to the lord and lady of the land I needed to go. I could see a question being held back by the lady.

"For you to find this lost one, how long do you think it will take to come back to us?" She asked as Bhaltair stood and paced in front of the fire. Looking at the lord and his wife, the family Josephus and I had saved from a demented older brother.

"It could be as long as a year. I hope it is not so long." I said as Bhaltair turned and smiled.

"I can not stop you, nor would I try; you have to do this. You have to find this lost one?" Bhaltair asked as he sat back down.

"I do; it is a matter of honor for myself. I gave my oath many years ago to do this." I told him I knew he was a good man when he nodded and placed his hands on my shoulders.

"Then go, find whoever it is you seek, then when your oath is fulfilled, return here." I thanked my friend and his wife for their support.

The morning's first light found me on my horse, and I led two more pack horses. I had everything I would need for my journey to wherever the pull led me. I waited for the large flat ferry to take me to the mainland.

As I climbed the hill, I stopped and looked back over the water. I knew I would not be able to see anyone from this side of the loch. However, it was nice to think Bhaltair and his family were there, waving me off safe in their stronghold.

I quickly learned to let the pull guide me, not to fight against it. I rode through the land of the Picts, and for the most part, I kept away from any settlements. Josephus had taught me well if I needed to enter a settlement for provisions. I would take time to watch the people learn if they would welcome a stranger or be hostile.

The summer found people working hard. They had to get everything ready for the coming of winter. Life here in this northern land, at this time, was hard. It held little forgiveness for being idle. I rode through the summer days, the heat welcome after the long grey of winter.

I stopped by a lake one afternoon. I smiled as I thought about Josephus and how he would try to catch a fish. As the sun started to sink, I smiled when a large fish jumped out of the water.

As I looked up from the water, I found two men standing on the opposite bank. I felt uncomfortable with how the men seemed to be trying to keep my attention. Looking around, I caught a glimpse of two others sneaking through the wood beside my camp. As I started to walk back to my horses, one of the men stepped out of the trees.

"We are going to have these horses for taxes you have not paid." He ordered as the other stepped from the shadows.

"You will have nothing here if you do not leave now. You will not be leaving." The first man stiffened at my implication of his death.

"You need to be taught where you stand. These lands are our lands; we claim all." He said as he placed his hand on the hilt of his sword and smiled. His smile faltered when I smiled back and pulled my sword, then shook off my cloak. I knew it would take time for the men on the opposite bank to make their way over. So I needed to deal with the two standing in front of me before the others could be involved.

As I stepped forward, the first man ran at me. Our swords gave a mighty clang as they met. From the corner of my eye, I could see the second man standing with a bow. He was waiting for his friend to push me away, so he could have a clean killing shot with his bow. What he was not expecting was when I shoved the first man away, I pulled my dagger and threw it.

The sun glinted off the razor-sharp blade. Then, before either of my attackers could blink, the dagger pierced the bowman. My aim was true; the bowman died, a shocked, confused look on his face. Standing facing the first man, I watched as his face changed colors. He was in a state of rage when he yelled about his brother and ran straight at me.

His attack was so intense I was battered back, then I found his pattern. My counterattack took his hand off at the wrist, though he still held his sword. When my counter took his left hand, the shock of the injury stopped him. In this flash of time, I stepped to the side, running my sword between his ribs.

I could hear the two from the other side of the river splashing out of the water. I pulled my sword free of the first of my attackers. Number three and four slid to a stop on the grass water streamed off their swords.

"You have killed our brothers." The bigger of the two hissed through his clenched teeth.

"Yes, they tried to take what did not belong to them," I stated and shrugged, then looked at the two facing me now.

"I am going to cut you to pieces." The bigger of the two said as he started to slowly wave his sword back and forth. I watched him as he moved towards me. I shook my head. It seemed these four brothers had been used to robbing softer men. As the bigger one moved towards me, I could see his brother moving to the side.

As the bigger one raised his sword, his brother took his signal and ran at me. Spinning out of reach of the smaller brother's sword, I trust my sword out. It found his belly and opened a large wound in his gut.

The scream he gave off was disturbing, bringing his brother to a stop. Then he looked at me; I could see his anger; unlike his brother, the last brother controlled his rage.

"Three of my brothers, you have killed three. You killed three for some grubby horses." He hissed at me as he passed back and forth.

"Yes, I never wanted this, I would have ridden away, and your brothers would still be alive. You all wanted this. You all came looking to take what did not belong to you." I answered him, and he stopped and looked at me. I could tell my answer baffled him.

"We do not need the permission of any such as you to take what we want." He said as he raised his sword; he ran at me. This last fight was over in three moves. I held onto the last brother as I lowered him to the earth. Like his brothers, his last look was one of confusion and hate. His last words reminded me of a spoiled child.

"You can not do this; we take what we want, we take...." The final brother never finished what he was saying. I watched what little light he had left in his eyes fade away as death took him.

It didn't take long to dispose of the bodies. I placed them in a hollow under a large tree. Walking over to the man I had stabbed through the stomach, I watched as he whimpered.

"That is a terrible wound," I said as I sat beside him. He looked up; all the color drained from his face with blood loss and pain.

"You should have just given us what we wanted." He said as he tried to keep his viscera from spilling across his lap.

"Why, why should people have to give up what they have. Why is it you seem to think you deserve anything?" I asked, hoping to get an answer before this last brother slipped into death's embrace.

"Before our father left, he told my brothers, and I kill all who do not pay." Death claimed this last brother as he uttered these last words. I placed him with his brothers then gathered my things and rode away. For a long time, I would think about the brothers about what the last one said to me, how his father told them to make everyone pay, and what kind of man he was.

The pull kept me heading north, so north I rode. I watched as the days grew shorter, and the nights claimed the land more and more. The good green things of gods creation started to fade. The once green things began to turn color, and I marveled at the reds, the oranges. As I rode, I kept watch out for stag, rabbits, and all manners of creatures.

Then one day, I stood looking out over an ocean, the great rocks making up this land behind me. I looked at the three horses I led and my supplies. I was utterly at a loss on how I was going to get them across this water. The pull I had been following had brought me to this place. It seemed to cry for me to cross the water, to keep moving north.

Looking back the way I came, I decided the pull had not taken me wrong so far, so again, I surrendered to it. I watched the sea as I rode above the shore, I knew I was going to have to cross it at some point. Then one day, I rounded a point of land and stopped.

I found I was looking at a village, its homes all sitting along the shore. Boats of various sizes had been pulled up above the water line. Larger two and three-masted ships were tied to a large dock.

As the wind blew off the frigid grey waters, it raced over the land bringing shouts of men as they loaded and unloaded the ships. A young boy noticed me standing watching the docks and village; I smiled as he walked over to me.

"Are you waiting for someone?" The young boy asked, then looked towards the dock.

"I am watching," I answered as I looked down at him.

"What are you watching for?" The boy asked

"To see which ship I want to approach about sailing to the lands north of here," I said as the boy scratched his chin. I smiled, knowing he had seen his father do this in contemplation. Now his young son mimicked his father.

"My father is down at the dock. I could take you to him." I smiled and nodded for the young lad to lead on. Soon I was introduced to a tall, slender man. He smiled at the boy and then tussled his hair.

"Go on now, son; Mother will be worried over you. Tell her I will be home soon. Now sir, what is it you require?" The boy's father asked as he watched his son run home.

"Passage to an island north of here," I stated as the men finished unloading a ship.

"At this time of year, you want to go to the islands north of here?" The father questioned.

"Yes, it is something I need to do. Is there a chance of booking a passage?" I asked, then watched as the father of the boy scratched his chin.

"Yes, the captain of this ship will take you if he is going where you are. Though I warn you, sir, winter is most unforgiving here. North of here, it is murderous." As he warned me of the winter, a large man stepped off the ship.

"Captain, this good sir wished to travel north." The father called to the man. To my surprise, the captain smiled and walked over to me.

"Well, if you can pay, I will be happy to take you to the island." The captain told me as he looked my horses over; before he could ask, I smiled.

"Yes, I would be taking my horses along. If the price is right, I can pay." The captain's smile broadened when he found someone to haggle with. He clapped a big hand on my shoulder when I offered to pay for a meal while we agreed on a price. Before our meal was over, the captain and I decided on payment for taking myself and my three horses to the island of Sealtainn.

I stabled my horses for three days as the ship was loaded. On the last day, we brought my horses on board, and it was decided they would have to stay on deck. I agreed, and to our surprise, the horses seemed to enjoy the fresh air.

"We will see the shore of Sealtainn in less than a fortnight if the wind stays with us." The captain told me as we left the protection of the harbor and headed out to sea.

The voyage was unremarkable for the most part. I was amazed at how cold the water was. As I sailed over the frigid waters, I often wondered how Josephus was? How his voyage to some far-off land had been? I knew Josephus, my lost brother, was looking at the stars, thinking about my part of our quest.

The days passed as we watched more and more birds flying south. I remember the first morning I woke to shiver uncontrollably. I rubbed my hands together, trying to rid them of the cold before I walked onto the deck. I went to my horses and broke the ice from their water buckets. Then stood and watched as the men used wooden mallets to break the ice from around the rigging.

"The cold has come early this season; we will arrive in the morning. I hope wherever it is you are going, you find it fast." The captain told me as he barked out to his first mate. Good to his word, the captain and crew had their ship docked in the morning.

Riding away from the docks, I turned to take one last look. I wondered how long it would be until I saw another person. Before I knew it, Josephus had again entered my thoughts, and I was wondering if he was alone somewhere in the world.

The pull guided me north. This time it seemed to take me into the heart of this island. The days melded together as I rode my way across this land. Days became shorter and shorter as the nights grew longer and colder. I knew it would only be a matter of short days before the snow came to this land. As it was, I had to break the ice at the edges of watering holes for my horses to drink.

I lost track of time as I traveled, I knew one day the pull turned and I started to travel west. I was surprised when I had to skirt a vast headland. I traveled faster as the pull was more urgent now. Whatever the force, 'the pull' seemed to know the snow was coming.

As it were, I wouldn't have enough supplies to survive the winter. Though if I were, to be honest, my only concern was finding the holy Mother. I rode past over the headlands for three days, midway through the third day I stopped.

I was looking at a round foundation of some sort. Whatever building sat on this foundation was long forgotten by man. A short wall now stood where at one time some lost soul had built a defensive structure.

Wrapped in my cloak, I walked around the foundation and stopped when my sight fell upon a tower. A tremendous circular tower stood out against the vista of the sea behind it. Gathering the reigns of my horses, I walked them through what would have been a gate in the distant past. As I walked towards the tower, I could feel this was what I had been looking for. All this time, all these many miles. All these many lands from the home I knew as a boy to this frozen land of the north. I could see the end.

Chapter 31

WHEN I DROPPED THE reigns, I reached out with my hand and laid my palm flat on the tower. It was then a surge of power coursed through my body.

This was by far the strongest I had felt to date. I could hear my screams ripped from the intense pain echoing off the granite of the tower. Then as fast as the surge came, it was gone. I lay on the ground panting, racked with pain. The muscles in my legs and back twitched.

As I lay on the ground, I looked over to where my horses stood, watching me. When I finally found the strength to stand, I walked over to them. My pack horses shied from my touch; I couldn't blame them. My mount came to me and nuzzled my outstretched hand.

This time as I walked around the stone tower, I kept my hands at my side. I had come to the conclusion one of those power surges a day was more than enough. It was on the west side of the tower I came across what looked to be the only way into the structure.

Looking at the door, I couldn't see any way for it to be locked. I slowly reached out with my finger and gently touched the heavy latch. As my finger touched the heavy latch, I jumped back, expecting another surge of power to grip my fingers.

What happened was a stone rolled under my boot, and I fell. As I lay on the rocky ground, I shook my head and then looked over to my horses again. They all stood their ears forward, looking at me.

Secretly, I wished to hear one of Josephus's braying laughs breaking the silence of the land.

I walked back to the door; this time, I reached out and pushed the heavy latch down. To my surprise, the heavy door moved, the hinges protested the use. Standing in the open doorway, I wondered how long the tower had been sealed. When was the last time sunlight spilled into the tower, across the floor, up the wall?

After I had gathered what I thought I would need from my horses, I walked into the dark interior of the stones. I lit a torch to chase the shadows back into the tower's stone.

I would have to choose to go left or right in this passage. The light of day spilling across the stone floor splashed up the wall I faced; the granite of this tower was dark. I wondered who had built this place, why they had built it, was the holy mother here, hidden, safe?

Right, I decided to go to my right as I walked around what I assumed was a protected interior. I came to a set of stairs. I looked back the way I just came. I would follow the stairs after I explored the base of this tower. So I turned around and then walked back to the doorway. As I walked past the door, I glanced outside; there were my horses. They stood looking at the doorway, closer than before I had disappeared.

Walking in the passageway, the light from my torch showed me a painting on the wall. Josephus had warned me once while we were in the passage under the church of Mary. His words rang through the time spent riding with him and the winter apart.

'If you touch anything else, the next thing you will feel will be my fist.'

Thinking back to the times I had with my brother gave me the strength to carry on. Now standing in the stone tower, I wish he was here with me. I caught myself smiling as I stood in front of the painting, my hands at my side.

All at once I felt I was being watched; looking around, I found I was alone. Smiling, I reached out, placing my fingers on the painting. I braced myself for the surge of power I knew was coming.

Standing with the dark granite surrounding me, no surge tore through me. I heard a humming sound then, and to my amazement, I watched what had taken place here so many centuries past. I stood watching a scene; this scene had taken place centuries before I stood in the tower.

Standing with my hand on the painting, I watched Mary lead a procession to this place. It was here she told her followers she was to be entombed upon her death. As the holy mother turned to look out to sea, her gaze fell on a small island offshore.

Time seemed to flash then I was watching this tower being built. Mary was being attended to by three women. I could tell she was ill with age.

Again time moved, a bright flash took my breath. I stood on the small island. I watched as men and women carried the body of Mary into her resting place. Tears streamed from my eyes as I walked down into the tomb I was to find.

Time flashed again, and men in long boats came to this land. They tried to live here using the stone tower. They left after a season when everything they planted died. Their stock died, and the walls they built fell to ruin. The long house burnt down, and the leader of these men said the land was cursed. They were the last to set foot on this land until I came along.

Walking out into the daylight refreshed me; still, my horses stood looking at the door. Looking at the sky, I knew I would have to spend the winter in this place.

As the days wore on, I had to make what I found into a shelter for the coming winter. Time was short, so I would have to make the best of every minute of each day I had left. I would be awake before the sun was up in the morning. I would work until the moon was halfway across the night sky.

This was my life for a month, then the day came when I woke to find ice pellets blowing across the land. Winter had arrived, and I had gotten most of what I wanted done. My horses were inside the tower, and I had found another doorway through the interior wall.

As the storm hammered at the tower's walls, I felt safe inside. I found stairs leading to the top of the tower. I looked at a doorway I knew led out onto the top of the tower. From this point, I could see over the water to the island in the painting on the wall by the entrance to the tower. The island I knew to be Mary's last resting place. The island I was going to have to go to. All so I could disturb the holy mothers resting place to save her.

Winter crawled by this far north. It seemed the seasons were at consonant odds over this unforgiving land. When spring finally won its hard-fought victory over winter, it brought blossoms from the frost. I turned my horses loose upon the fresh grass of the spring.

Winter had been harder on them than I had planned. My second-pack horse had died a month ago. I knew the poor thing was sick, so I removed him from the others. Then one morning, I found it dead; such was life in this land.

Standing on the tower, I looked out over the water. The island stood dark against the blue sky of day. My exploring proved fruitful; I had found a path long unused and overgrown with moss, which led to the rocky shore of this land. Sitting on the path, I watched as the waves of this sea crashed against this land's armored shores.

The island sat two hundred feet from me. I could swim it, I thought. Then I watched the waves again, and I gave up the thought of swimming. As I watched the island, I could see why Mary had chosen the island.

From what I could see, the soil on the island was too thin to grow anything on saved course hard grass. It was made up of the same dark granite as the tower I lived in. Looking along the shore, I found a cave at the high tide mark. I looked up the path and then along the coast. I decided I would have enough time to explore the cave before the water came in.

As I entered the cave, I waited. The first reason I stopped was to let my eyes become used to the dark. The second reason was I hoped not to set off a trap of some sort. Taking my time as I walked through the cave, I found the back of the cave had been made impassable by large trees. I couldn't guess the age of the trees; the bark was stripped from them, and at one end, what was left of the roots pointed to the water.

With as much strength as I could muster, I managed to shift one of the trees enough to gain entry beyond. The sight greeting my eyes shocked me. Sitting in a cradle made of rock was a small sailboat.

Beyond the small sailboat, the floor of the cave started to rise. Going to the sailboat, I looked it over, not that I knew much about sailing. I knew I would have to check to see if the bottom of the boat was damaged, and if it was, then I would have to learn how to repair it.

The boat itself sat above the floor of the cave in what looked to be a cradle of some sort. Its sails were all folded in the bottom, and ropes sat coiled on the sails. In the middle of the boat sat a small structure. It had a little roof and a small door on the front.

Leaving the boat, I walked further into the cave. The floor of the cave kept rising. It was about fifty paces from the boat, and my hand brushed a torch mounted on the cave wall. Pulling my flint out, I managed to light the torch. The feeble light it gave off showed me other torches.

Surprise washed over me as I came to the end of the cave. Only to find a doorway. Looking at another heavy latch, I reached out and lifted it. I found myself standing under the stairs at the bottom of the tower I had called home all winter.

Looking back along the dark tunnel, I smile. I now knew how I was going to get to the island. My plan fell into place the following day...well, if truth be told, it was not exactly the next day. In reality, the next day, I tried to get the ropes through the tackle of the sailboat. The day ended with the sail rumpled on the bottom of the boat. Where it had been neatly folded when I arrived in the morning. It was when in frustration, I gave up and decided to go and start my evening meal. As I was about to leave the boat, I stared at the tunnel wall. My frustration was to the point I was about to throw something.

As I stared at the wall, trying to calm myself, a faded drawing danced in the torchlight. As I walked over to it, I could make out lines. For a fleeting moment, I thought I was looking at another map. Then it became clear this was a drawing of how the rigging on the boat went together. I could feel the smile breaking out on my face, then I looked at the tunnel's ceiling. My voice echoed back to me from the end of the tunnel when I whispered.

'Still looking after me, are you, father?' Joseph never answered. I always liked to think he was watching me smiling.

The following days seemed to go by faster and faster, then came the morning. I had brought my pack horse into the tunnel. With the broken trees cleared out of the tunnel, getting the sailboat to the shore was a quick process. I showed my horse the path back to the top of the cliff. Like any other horse, he wanted to be back with his kind and started up without my aid.

Sitting in the boat, I watched as the water rose on the shore. I made sure the boat was pulled far enough out. This way, the tide would pick it and me up, and I could sail to the island. At this point, I had gathered everything I needed. Everything I had brought with me when I came to this place. I would not be returning to the tower, to my horses. They were free now. I planned on sailing back to the island of Mull to Bhaltair and his family.

It did not take as long as I thought once the tide picked up my sailboat. I was pulling it on the shore of the island where the tomb was. Tying the boat, just in case I was on this island longer than planned.

Leaving the shore, I recalled the painting in the passage in the tower. Standing on the shore of the island, I looked at the dark rock making up the island; I was astounded. I found I was looking at a winding staircase. It made its way through the shattered boulders guarding the shore.

Starting up the stairs, I watched the boulders for a sign of a trap. Before I realized it, I was standing at the top of the island, looking back at the tower. I could see my horses in the field content with the course grass. I turned in a slow circle, trying to find a sign of the tomb.

A thought came to me, had I misread the painting in the passage. It was then I looked at my feet. I started to think I would not be able to do this without Josephus at my side. On the last stone of the staircase, between my feet, was the symbol of the virgin.

Looking out over the flat top of the island, I started to search for other stones with symbols on them. When I realized my shadow had begun to get longer, I knew I would be on this island longer than expected.

Returning to the boat, I gathered what I needed for the night. I pulled the boat higher on the shore and tied it so another tide wouldn't take it away. I can say, for the first time, I was worried about being stranded on that island.

For three days, I followed the flat stones with the astrological sign for the virgin. These signs were in a spiral that covered the whole top of the island. At the center of the spiral was, well, nothing. Just a bit of sparse tough grass. As I looked over to the tower, I could see my horses. They pulled at the same grass I stood on; standing there, I watched the loyal animals. It was then it hit me, remove the grass.

Getting on my hands and knees, I started pulling at the grass. It was about the third handful of grass when a clump of the island's soil came loose. I could see a large flat black stone under the thin ground.

I brushed the rest of the soil and grass from the stone. I looked down at the stone I had uncovered. It had the same symbol I had been following around the island for three days. Now I stood and looked at the mark; the difference was on this stone, it was not alone. As I stood looking at the stone, I could make out rows of honey bees to the right of the center. Walking around the stone, I stopped when I saw the carved skull and crossed bones.

What was the mark of a master mason doing on what was the sealed lid of the Holy Mother's tomb? I knew from my time with Joseph and Josephus the men of the stone were hunted by the men of the church. Now I stood at Mary's tomb on an island in a land where even the mighty Roman army failed. Looking at a symbol of another brotherhood hunted and killed by men of the church.

Getting on my hands and knees, I crawled around the stone. Searching for a way to lift the stone, short of breaking it. I was about to give up when I felt a lump in the grass. Carefully I pulled the grass away from the lump, then swept the light soil away.

To my surprise, I was looking at four interlocking wheels. On each wheel were numbers, all written in Hebrew.

I sat down and looked at the wheels; their numbers held little meaning for me. Reaching over, I started to clear more of the grass away from the area. I wanted to ensure there was nothing else I had to worry about.

I was about to stop clearing when with one last handful of grass, another stone came into sight. Pulling still more grass out of the ground, I watched as letters started to appear. By the time I had the last stone uncovered, I was looking at eight letters.

I looked down at the eight letters. If someone could have seen me, they would have thought I was praying. In a way, I was praying

I would be able to decipher this enigma. I looked at the four interlocking wheels of the lid. Then I looked back to the letters on the second stone, then back to the wheels.

Chapter 32

I ALMOST SHOUTED WHEN the answer came to me. It was a code, four wheels, two numbers per wheel. Eight letters, two letters per wheel. All I had to do was come up with how to convert the letters to numbers. Then I would have to get the numbers in order on the right wheel.

Then the answer came to me as if by magic. In the center wheel, I had to turn it until the letters O and V lined up with the west wheel and the numbers twenty-two and twenty-one lined up. When I did this, a resounding clunk could be heard below the lid.

Bolstered in my resolve, I then twisted the center wheel again. This time I lined up the letters U and V, then turned the north wheel until the numbers fifteen and one lined up. I heard another heavy clunk from under the lid, and unlike the first time, I felt the lock give way.

I stood back and wondered what would happen when the third and the fourth lock gave way. Would the top of the hill cave into the tomb and bury everything, me included? Kneeling at the stone, I looked out over the water. I smile when I see both horses standing at the cliff's edge, watching me.

For the third time, I turned the center wheel until the symbols for O and A lined up. Then I turned the east wheel until the numbers 19 and 22 lined up. The stone shook when the third lock gave way. From below, where I knelt, I could hear something heavy fall. Then all was silent; for a moment, I couldn't bring myself to move.

Kneeling on the stone, I looked at the center wheel and then the south wheel. Before I realized what I was doing turned the center wheel to the symbols for V and S, then the south wheel to the numbers fifteen and twenty-two. Quickly I stood and jumped off the stone, fearing I was about to fall into the tomb. As I jumped off the stone, I could hear the heavy clunk, then a rattling of stones as they fell. Then the stone I had been trying to pry loose swung open as if on a hinge.

Shocked, I found I was looking into the dark passage, long ago sealed from the light of day. Now the sunlight struggled to penetrate it; I took one step towards the tunnel, knowing I would have to enter it sooner rather than later. I looked at the sky, then at the tower across the water. Grabbing one of my torches, I looked into the darkness.

I took a deep breath and stepped out of the sunlight. The flickering light given by my lone torch was welcome. I was only thirteen strides into the passage when I came to a staircase. Looking back to the entrance of the passage, I again steeled myself.

The staircase was built out of the living rock of the island. It took me down, down into the bowels of the island. As I went down, I found torches long ago left by the last people to be on these stairs. At the bottom of the stairs, I found an oil lamp, its wick still floating. Using my torch, I lit the lamp, and with its light, I found others. I lit all I found as I went into a passage under the stairs.

Holding my torch, I could see a stone sarcophagus. I thought it had to be holding the Holy Mother. I took my time and started to walk around the sarcophagus.

As I circled the sarcophagus, a shelf built into the wall came into view. On the shelf, I could make out remains. Walking over to the shelf, I knelt beside the remains and read the inscription.

'Here lay his mother, her earthly remains, the son given to mankind so he could wash away the stain of our sins.' As I knelt, I felt my tears as they fall to the floor of the tomb. Then a thought came to me if Mary lays here. Who was in the sarcophagus, and why is it in this holy place?

Looking around, I had to find something to hold Mary while I traveled with her. It was then I remembered there was a chest sitting by the sarcophagus. This chest reminded me of the one Josephus had sailed to the West with. Walking around the large stone sarcophagus, I soon became fascinated with it. For a second, I forgot where I was, and before I could stop myself, I reached out to brush the dust from a plaque.

The surge of power that hit me was exponentially more powerful than any of the other times before. As my fingers touched the side of the sarcophagus, the power lifted me off my feet. I hovered in the air, my body seized by the unseen force.

Faintly I could make out screams, the sound of the surging power covering up all other sounds. It was then I realized the screams were mine. The energy coursing through my body was so great I feared the surge was trying to tear my soul in half.

I do not know how long I was gripped by the surge. I can remember waking up on the floor of the chamber. My torch burned out my body ached as if I had been thrown down a mountain. Looking at the sarcophagus, I knew what lay hidden inside. I also knew this great thing could never find its way into the hands of man.

As the surge flowed through me, I could see it inside the stones. Its lid tightly closed, the wings of two angels still pointed at each other. The stone tablets with God's words are still hidden inside its gold walls. The most incredible power to be bestowed on mankind waiting to be released.

Picking myself up, I walked over to the chest I had seen earlier. Then gently placed the holy mother inside it. Looking back at the sarcophagus, I dreaded what lay inside its granite walls. I did not dread the word of God placed on the two granite tablets by his hand. What I dreaded was the power within the sarcophagus, the power of gods will. It was this power that, if man ever found it, could end this world.

I knew I couldn't leave this tomb the way I had found it. I knew what was coming, while I was trapped in the surge I was shown the future, of the evil times coming, of men and women who think themselves given divine right to rule.

Far into the future, there will be men so corrupted by the lust for power. They will murder millions of men, women, and children. All on the whims of a madman; it is this madman who I need to stop. If he was to ever get his hands on the ark of the covenant. The world would be lost to his insanity in his last desperate gambit to rule over all the peoples of the earth. This little madman would see the world turned to ash rather than leave its people in peace.

The ark showed me a trap; once tripped, this trap would collapse the whole island into the sea. I had to stop before I left the gloom of the tunnel. The chest I carried seemed to weigh nothing as I stood in the grey of the tunnel; looking at the sunshine streaming into the tunnel, I was forced to squint.

As soon as I left the tunnel, I turned to look at the tower across the water. To my surprise, my horses were still there. As I watched them, they turned and started to move further inland. Watching them leave the tower, I wished them luck; I know it was silly. They were good horses, and I hoped they would run free together until old age took them.

Leaving the chest with the holy mother in it by the tunnel. I went to my sailboat and made it ready for a quick departure once I had tripped the final trap. Going back to the tunnel, I struggled to swing the stone closed. Once it was in place, I had to realign the locking wheels.

When I touched the sarcophagus holding the ark within, I had another language forced into my mind. It was not the language of any man, not any man in this world. It was the true divine language of the angels, a language man had long forgotten.

I would have to use this forgotten language to set the final trap and then run for my sailboat. Once again, I knelt in the coarse grass of the island. I turned all the locking wheels back to where I had found them. As I returned the wheels to the beginning, I could hear the giant locks rumbling back into place.

Once all the locks had returned to their locked state, I sat looking over the water at the tower again. I wished Josephus was here with me. I wished I could see the merriment in his eyes as we would discover something new, to hear his braying laugh one more time. I looked up to the sky as white clouds floated past the island.

"Joseph, father, if you can hear me, I have her. From this moment on, I will protect her until my death. I will bring the other to her so he can follow our order." I stopped knowing the future was set. I looked at the wheels and smiled. One word would set the trap off. It could only be set by the one who was chosen.

The word was 'Evil.' It had to be spelled out in the language of the angels. It was this language I had received as I was in the grip of the surge of the sarcophagus. As I turned to look at the path back to my sailboat. I touched the chest and then started to turn the wheels of the locks.

As the last symbol of the word clicked into place, it felt like an enormous weight slammed into place. Jumping up, I grabbed the chest and started running for the shore where I had left the sailboat.

I pushed the boat out into the water and used the oars to row away from the falling rocks. Once I was in deeper water, I raised the sail and watched as massive slabs of rock and dirt fell into the sea.

The sound of the island falling into the water was biblical. I wondered if this was what it sounded like when God created our world. Under the great splashes and rumbling, a grating and grinding could be felt through the water. It resonated up through the boat into my bones as I watched the island slowly sink out of site. The island slid under the waves of the boiling foaming water. The only other witness to this cataclysm was the tower.

The wind took me and the chest south, and I knew where I would have to go. I knew who I would have to meet. It was a terrible burden knowing what was to come. To see the level of evil the people of this world were going to have to endure in the future. To know neither my brothers nor I would be able to do anything to stop it. To leave it to another, who I will have to wait for.

Chapter 33

SAILING SOUTH, I WATCHED as islands slid past. I could see small settlements on some while others sat dark and forlorn. The days came with the glory of rebirth, then the night would come to steal the light, the hope. As the stars came to life, one by one, the moon showed what it was to be lost.

A great mist settled over the water I sailed on. To my surprise, I felt my boat come to a gentle halt as it and I pushed into a sandy beach. I decided to wait until daylight to see where I had landed. To my surprise, I was sitting on a beach next to a small settlement. As I looked around, I realized I was on another small island.

A man came to the shore and asked me if I was in need. I found he spoke Gaelic, and he nodded when I asked him if I could buy supplies here. The market was small; it was just what I needed. After I had all the supplies I needed, I returned to my boat. I looked back at the settlement, to the people who busied themselves with trying to live. Then I looked at the chest and pushed my boat onto the water. I looked ahead of my boat as the wind took me away.

Days turned into weeks as I sailed south, and I lost track of the days I had been on the water. One day I came close to a fishing boat, and I asked the men where I was. They smiled then one came to the side of the boat and pointed to land.

"You are by the town of La Rochelle." He waved as I thanked him and sailed towards the harbor. I beached my small sailboat and stood on land for the first time in many fortnights.

Walking through the large town of La Rochelle, I wanted to find a stable where I could buy a horse. The first one I came across had what I was looking for. The man wanted my boat. The owner of the stable and I sat down. Over some tea, we agreed on a price for his horses and what I wanted for my boat. We shook hands, and I was heading east out of town in short order.

I was happy to be back on land; sailing was becoming tedious, to say the least. As I rode towards my final destination, I often thought of Josephus, where he had ended up as the winds took him from the island of Mull?

Riding east, I watched for signs for the town of Nevers. It was here I felt I needed to be; why I needed to be there, I couldn't say at the time. So as the days passed, I rode through the country. Unlike the first time I was alone, Josephus's absents weighed heavily on me.

Reaching the town of Nevers, I couldn't get over how far the church had come. Men stood in the open and preached about Christ and how he had given his life for us. Standing beside my horse, I listened to one of the men.

I had hope in my heart, hope these men were good and, like Christ, loved all people. I knew these men lusted for power when a man and woman walked past, only to be assaulted. The holy men jumped on them for being different. They were from the Languedoc region; the churchmen cursed the man when he fought back. When I asked about this, a young man told me the people from this Languedoc area did not hold to one belief.

"These people believe all have the right to believe as they wish. They also believe all should be able to read what they see fit. This goes against what these men teach, so they attack any they find from that area." The young man told me, then turned and walked down the muddy street.

Looking back at the town of Nevers, I shook my head. The men spreading his word as gospel attacked others because of their freedom and beliefs. Riding south, I headed for the Massif Central; it was here I hoped to find my shelter. A place where I could hide the treasure until I found the others, my brothers, who were also being hunted.

Standing beside my horse one day, I looked out over a valley. Its long grass swayed in the breeze in the middle of the valley, standing against the winds and time. I looked over a large, sharply defined upthrust of black granite, a great mount. Looking at this mount, I smiled. I knew there would be a cave on it somewhere.

It had taken longer to find the path from the top to the bottom of the valley. My horse frolicked when I freed him from his saddle. I laughed as I watched him roll in the long grass, then he would jump, kicking his legs around and playing.

Standing at the foot of the mount, I could feel something; I didn't know what it was. To me, this mount and the valley had a feeling of desperation, angry desperation. This feeling surrounded this place; looking up the side of the mount, I found a game trail and started up. It did not take long before I came across a cave.

I wanted to go into the cave to explore, but my horse had a different idea. It seemed he wanted to go further up the mount. Looking at the cave and then up the trail, I decided to follow him. My horse and I were almost at the top of the mount when we came across another cave.

From this second cave, I could see the valley below. This cave was sheltered from the constant winds. I smiled, knowing I had found my redoubt high on this mount.

Work started the following day; I would have to cut wood along with long grass for my horse. As well as I would have to put food stuff away for myself. Such was my life for many years. I lived from season to season until one day...on this day, I looked out over the valley. A man sat on his horse; he was watching my mount. From where he sat, I knew he couldn't see the top of the mount. As I sat in the shadows of the trees, he sat in the sunshine, looking up the peak. Then to my shock, he started his horse up the faint game trail. I watched as he stopped at the first cave. It was here I stored feed for my horse. He looked into the cave and then turned to look further up the mount.

I was standing at the mouth of my cave as the stranger walked his horse up the trail.

"Why are you here?" I asked the bearded man. At the sound of my voice, his head snapped up, and he looked shocked.

"I am looking for a lost brother." He answered.

"What right do you have to be out looking for anyone lost?" I asked; in my heart, I was jumping for joy.

"My Abbott has sent me here to find our brother. He has been wandering with a treasure for over a hundred years." The monk said as he bowed to me.

"Has it really been such a long time?" I mainly asked myself.

"It has, Rene. It has been one hundred and ten years since you and the cursed one buried Joseph. Your brothers are not far off. They await you." As the monk told me others waited for me to come, I smiled.

"I have to stay here. It is this spot; on this mount, I must build the fortress. This mount will provide all the stone needed for our last bastion." As I told the young monk I was to build a fortress here, he nodded and then dropped his smile.

"You can stay here and build whatever you want. That chest and what it holds will be coming with me." He hissed; I could see the hate, the rage in him now.

"No, son, it will stay with me until the lord himself comes and tells me differently." I returned. I stepped further from the opening of my cave, I watched the young warrior. I watched as the younger man started to swell with anger. I waited for him to either rage at me or attack. I was shocked into stillness as an arrow flew out of the trees.

I was ready for the young monk to attack when an arrow came flying out of the trees. I watched as the arrow hit the young monk above his left ear and burst from the young man's neck. It must have cut one of the great veins. Blood flew from the wound, splashing the trees before he could fall from his injury. I held my sword and shield, waiting for the next arrow. To my surprise, I watched as a tall man holding a bow stepped into view and waved. This tall man held his hands away from his weapons as he walked toward me.

"I have been sent to help you, brother, not to take you or anything you hold anywhere. If you say this is the place we need to build our fortress, then here is where we shall build it," The tall knight said as I watched him.

"How is it you come to know this?" I asked as I slowly circled back towards the cave.

"Forgive me, brother, it has been written. Before Josephus was forced to leave you in the North. He sent word back to us; the king you saved is a good man. Bhaltair sent one of his most trusted to get word to us you were coming back to this land." As the knight explained. To show he was not here to take the chest or to harm me, he stripped off his weapons and chain mail.

"You called my brother by his name, not as the cursed one," I stated as the knight sat down.

"In our order, we do not like to refer to Josephus as the cursed one. It was his father who was to be cursed. The coward found a ritual where he could pass it on to his son. That is exactly what he did to free himself; he placed his curse on his innocent son, a child, our savior weeps because of this." The knight explained why it was his order to never called Josephus the cursed one.

"You keep speaking of your order; I know of an order," I said as I sat opposite the knight.

"Our order, brother, the order of Sionis. We all have sworn on our lives to protect the Holy Mother, her son, and the bloodline.

I am Guillaume; my brothers took me into the order as a charge."
Looking over at this knight, I knew I had been found. The brothers I
had been waiting to meet for over a hundred years had found me.

I looked into the sky, and I wondered again where Josephus had
found himself. If my first brother was alone, if he was tormented still,
or has he found love.

Chapter 34

AS THE YEARS PASSED, the fortress on Mount Bezu took shape. The brotherhood had in our ranks men of great skill working with stone. These men belonged to a hidden order, a hunted order. Like us, they were hunted because the church deemed them heretics. Nothing could be further from the truth; these men were devout.

Sitting on the mount, it was decided we would have to join the crusades. None of our brothers wanted to join, to march south. These crusades had nothing to do with protecting Christians. It was for nothing more than the thirst for wealth.

It seemed as if we marched into the mountains of another land where people were free. Lands, where Josephus and I had traveled and discovered clues to a path laid down so many long centuries before by Joseph. As he sought to protect the love of his life and the grandchildren, he was forced to give up.

Most of the knights were going to kill for no other reason than for what they could pillage from the death of others. From this crusade, our order knew we would need to start another brotherhood. This one would have to be based in the holy land and France. Seeding the church with our brothers took many years. After years we were able to start the Knights Templar.

This order came to be known by us as the sons of Sionis. The men running the church called for more and more knights as they marched into lands that were not Christian. Crusade after crusade came, and the land where the knights fell turned red from the blood.

None were safe; men, women, and children all fell to the knights of the Crusades.

My brothers and I were sitting around our fire one night. After a day of slaughter, we all looked at the stars, then at the sand between our feet.

"I am not for this; this is not what Christ would want. We have fallen far from his teachings." I said as I looked at the stars, I could hear my brothers shifting. When I looked at them, I found they were all smiling.

"So shall we just leave?" I asked, then without another word, we all stood and started north. Months passed as my brothers and I, worn from years of war. Tired of all the senseless killing of others, of mothers and fathers of children. The seasons changed, and time marched on as we made our way back to the mount where now sat our home, our redoubt.

The year is now ten twenty, and I have walked this earth protecting the Holy Mother for over three hundred years. The time I foresaw when my fingers touched the sarcophagus in the tomb of Mary was coming.

I watched as spring turned to summer, and the birds flitted from branch to branch. Always looking for food for their young, bees buzzed past, helping nature along with their hard work, and I waited for the inevitable.

One day I woke and smiled at my brothers; Guillaume had died many years before. Sitting with my brothers, I looked at each one; I knew these good men would soon be dead. All but one, we were going to have to choose one to run with the treasure.

I looked around the room. I know who it was I needed to choose to run with the Holy Mother. It was his great great uncle who loosed an arrow, killing a murderer for the church. I watched my younger brothers, my heart breaking for their lives about to be cut short.

"I believe I will go to the market today for some supplies," I announced. This brought the heads of the others up from their breakfast. It was Guillaume who looked at me with a question on his face.

"Abbot? You know the church is in the village," Guillaume told me.

"Oh yes, this day has been waiting for a very long time, and I would hate to meddle in his plans," I said as I looked at the brother I found as a child and raised. I could never marry and thus never have a son of my own. The day I found Godfroi, I felt I had become a father; I love him as a father loves a son.

Four days before, I had taken Guillaume to the catacombs to show him the secret our order has known for generations. I took a vile of our savior's blood and tricked Guillaume into drinking it.

I watched Guillaume as the first waves of pain crashed over him. When I was purified, the pain and torment lasted four days. For Guillaume, the trial was over in two. I could only assume it was different because he drank the blood.

Now I sat looking at each brother; after our meal, I stood and went to the stable. I was shocked when two brothers came into the stable.

"And where is it you two think you are going?" I asked, knowing the answer.

"Abbott, we need something from the market, so we decided to ride along," Godfroi replied as he climbed into the saddle. It was a beautiful day clouds crossed the blue sky pushed by a light wind.

The market was lively as men and women barked at passers-by. Children ran this way and that, and mothers tried to keep track of which child went what way. I smiled as I strolled through the market. I gathered some things of use to my brothers in the days to come.

The first attack came as we left the market; two men dressed as knights jumped from behind a stall. This first attack was over in mere moments. The two knights lay dead at our feet. The second attack was better planned; they came at us in the valley leading to the mount. This attack killed Jean, the second brother who came with Godfroi.

My arm had been broken in this second fight, and Godfroi had a minor wound to his leg. We threw our horses into a thundering run for the fortress on Mount Bezu. I knew I would not make it back to the mount without a deadly wound.

A wound only felt by the angels before me as I looked behind Godfroi and me. I watched a black arrow sail out of the blue sky.

I felt the arrow pierce my back as Godfroi and I raced for the safety of our brothers. With the arrow, I knew the poison had been delivered. I knew I could never be saved. At that moment, I knew where the church had gotten the pure evil that now wounded me. Josephus and I had left it in the cave, in the cage, the cage of the hidden valley. Where we had discovered the remains of two Nephilim. Somehow the church had found the cave. They realized the feather was infected by the same evil the angels suffered during the first war.

My brothers tried to save me. They removed the arrow and tended to my wound. They sat in earnest as I told them this day had been ordained.

"Though you clean and tend to the wound in my flesh, it is the wound to my soul; it will kill me in short order. I can feel the evil crawling through me at this moment." As I spoke, I could feel my soul turning darker. I worried with this evil in me, would it see me sent to hell.

"Brothers, I have built my own crypt, knowing when my death was to come. You must take me there now; place me in the crypt. There are certain things you must place with me for another to find." As the day turned to night, I explained to the brothers what must be done. I was so proud of them, even though none of them understood what I asked of them. My brothers did as requested, and once everything was as I asked, I called for Guillaume.

"You have been chosen. You know what it is you need to do. Remember, Guillaume, you can not tell a soul where you are going. I will come to you with another, though it will be far into the future. Go, brother, go, run for pity's sake, hide her, keep her." These were the last words I spoke to another as a living being in gods world.

My brothers lowered the lid on my crypt, and the evil raged in me, trying to force me to cry out to stop them. Godfroi whispered he loved me as a father and thanked me for his life. The last face I saw for over three hundred was his.

My soul watched as my brothers kept the church from gaining entrance to our fortress. As the battle raged on, my brothers died, each in his own way. When the last brothers had passed, only then did the Templars gain entrance to the fortress.

The leaders of the church still had no idea. The order they call theirs was actually the sons of the Order Sionis. The men who came into our last home laid their brothers to rest. Then they destroyed any mention of the truth. As ordered by myself, the sons of Sionis destroyed and defaced any mention of the brotherhood. This was done to protect them so they could still be held in high stead in the church.

When the last of the Templars left, the doors were barred, locked against the curious. I so wished to see my father, Joseph, waiting for me when I died. I longed to see the face of my Mother, to feel her hand in mine. To hear her voice as she and Joseph met me at the gates of heaven.

I know my quest is not over yet. In the dark of my crypt, I waited for another, one younger than any before, one not born yet, one I already love as a father loves a son. In the darkness, I wait...in the darkness...I wept for my lost brother Josephus. In the darkness, I prayed for him...in the darkness...of my crypt, I died. The evil raged in me to the very instant I died. Once it had nothing to feed on, the evil faded to nothing.

Chapter 35

Josephus.

STANDING AT THE BOW, Josephus watched the storm race towards him. The rain and wind crashed into him, and the air seemed alive with lighting. Josephus knew he and the treasure would be safe; he would survive. Josephus turned to look at the crew of the ship Bhaltair had sent him west on. Josephus knew none of them would survive. He watched as another in the endless waves of the enraged ocean lifted the ship to the sky, then slammed it back down. As he dared the storm to try and move him, Josephus saw the great gnashing teeth of this terrible new land.

All the men on the ship stopped; they all heard the sound of the surf breaking on rocks. Then another wave lifted the ship to the sky as it came back down on the rocks. Josephus watched the great pointed rocks of the new land rip the hull apart. The sudden destruction of the hull threw men overboard. Their cries were heard for mere seconds, then nothing, as the teeth of the land tore the ship to splinters and ground the sailors' bones to powder.

Josephus used a length of rope to tie the treasure to his waist and jumped into the waves. Now he stood on the shore of new land and looked into the verdant green forest. Turning, Josephus looked back out to the ocean he had fought to cross, a sea he desperately wanted to cross again.

Josephus knew he would never see Rene, his brother, again. He also knew everyone he had ever known and loved would die without him. Josephus felt a tear fall into his beard, his greatest fear realized. He was alone, truly alone.

As Josephus looked back to the forest, he never saw the others watching him. Josephus knew the treasure was safe. It sat at his feet, his weapons hung on his side. Time was something he had never thought about until this moment.

THE END
Todd LeRoux

Don't miss out!

Visit the website below and you can sign up to receive emails whenever Todd LeRoux publishes a new book. There's no charge and no obligation.

https://books2read.com/r/B-A-MMEEB-GPBYC

BOOKS 2 READ

Connecting independent readers to independent writers.

Did you love *The Beginning*? Then you should read *The Quest*[1] by Todd LeRoux!

[2]

Roderique loved growing up on his father's farm; he would dream of far-off lands like most young men. Roderique's older brother Louis was a Catholic priest, making their Mother so proud. Roderique knew that his brother wanted him gone so he could inherit the farm and land. As brothers, they never got along. Louis was always jealous and would go out of his way to cause trouble for his younger brother. Roderique knew what his brother was like and never trusted Louis. So when Louis came to him about going out into the world looking for treasure the Church had lost or stolen, Roderique was skeptical about the offer. Louis was desperate for his brother to leave, and Roderique knew he would take the offer. The year was 1475

---

1. https://books2read.com/u/4E7vX0

2. https://books2read.com/u/4E7vX0

when Roderique, with his old mare, left his father's farm. France was a dangerous land then, and Roderique knew he would have to be careful on this quest. Following clues left in the ruins of the Barberie Cathedral, Roderique finds his way to a dark fortress on top of Mount Bezu. Breaking into the fortress, Roderique makes his camp, knowing he will be in the fortress for days so he can find all he was sent on the quest for. Rene had spent so many centuries waiting for the legend of the young man to come true; when he first heard a horse, Rene thought he was going mad; then he wondered if a spirit could go mad. Rene befriended Roderique, he watched as the young man picked up the golden cross. Rene and his brothers wept as the spike from the cross punctured Roderique's flesh. They knew the pain it would cause. The brothers of the knights of Sionis knew they had a new brother. Their new brother would live for over five hundred years to keep the treasure safe. When Roderique woke up on the third day, he knew the real Quest had started.

Read more at https://www.toddleroux.com/.

About the Author

Todd lives on the banks of the Miramichi river. After years of working away, he now enjoys his time at home with family and friends.

Read more at https://www.toddleroux.com/.